TO

DEAD ENDing

BEST WISHES,

Stephen G. Yanoff

Murder Ink Press
Austin * New York * Boca Raton

DEAD ENDing

An Adam Gold Mystery

STEPHEN G. YANOFF

authorHOUSE®

AuthorHouse™
1663 Liberty Drive
Bloomington, IN 47403
www.authorhouse.com
Phone: 833-262-8899

Published by AuthorHouse   04/05/2023

ISBN: 979-8-8230-0483-1 (sc)
ISBN: 979-8-8230-0484-8 (hc)
ISBN: 979-8-8230-0485-5 (e)

Library of Congress Control Number: 2023906076

Print information available on the last page.

This book is dedicated to

William Arthur Zell

You may all go to Hell,
and I will go to Texas.

— Davy Crockett
August 1835

CHAPTER ONE

Insurance investigators seldom hear the truth, the whole truth, or anything close to the truth. Most of the time they're told half-truths, partial truths, or untruths — which explains why Adam Gold was skeptical about the tale he'd just been told. Irene Kaminski, the president of the Anchor Insurance Company, swore it was the truth, but he was unconvinced, so he took it with *cum grano salis*. Actually, with more than a grain of salt. Something closer to a pillar.

The way his boss had heard the story, a disreputable antiques dealer named Joseph Kemmler had been found guilty of endangering the welfare of a vulnerable elderly person — a class E felony in New York State, punishable by a jail sentence of up to four years. Mr. Kemmler had apparently forced his elderly parents into a nursing home at the height of the COVID-19 outbreak, and since they weren't vaccinated, they contracted the disease and died.

When the trial judge asked Kemmler why he shouldn't receive the maximum penalty allowed, the defendant supposedly replied, "Because I'm an orphan."

Gold offered her a faint smile. "Milton Berle. 1948-49."

"I beg your pardon?"

"That joke's older than dirt."

Sounding a little frustrated, she said, "I heard it from a reliable source. By the way, it was also in the *Daily News*."

"Well, that settles that. How did the judge react?"

"He was not amused."

"Probably not a fan of Texaco Star Theatre."

"Kemmler received a four-year sentence."

"I guess that wiped the smile off his face."

Kaminski shifted uncomfortably in her chair. "You haven't heard the punchline." Her mouth tightened. "The verdict was just tossed out. Kemmler's a free man."

Gold stared at her in amused disbelief. "Tell me you're joking."

"I'm afraid not." Veins stood out on her neck. "The New York Supreme Court overturned his conviction and scolded the prosecution for the way they handled the case."

Gold digested this information. Then he took a deep breath and looked directly at her. "What the hell happened?"

"The supreme court ruled that prosecutors had violated Kemmler's rights by reneging on an apparent promise not to charge him if he cooperated in a nursing home investigation." She paused, acutely aware of how intently he was watching her. "A majority of the justices agreed that the conviction should be thrown out because — and I'm quoting — "due process does not permit the government to engage in this type of coercive bait-and-switch."

"Reminds me of another disgraced comedian."

"Same situation."

"Well, there you go. The wheels of justice fall off again."

Looking solemn, she said simply, "Maybe we can repair some of the damage."

Gold was tempted to ask what she meant, but the last time he'd asked that question he'd ended up in the Florida Everglades, facing a murderous psychopath. She would spill the beans eventually, so why not take a moment to brace himself. God knows he'd been down this road once or twice before, and it was always a treat. A real treat. There was a moment of strained silence, then he said, "I think it's your move."

Kaminski rubbed one hand across her forehead as if she were tired, or getting a headache. "Kemmler's back in the city, and he's causing all sorts of trouble." She swiveled her chair around to face the window. Through the sunlit blinds she could just make out the East River. "A sane person would lie low for a while, but not Kemmler. He's suing the nursing home for negligence, claiming they engaged in medical malpractice."

"Talk about chutzpah."

"The Anchor Insurance Company has been named as a codefendant."

"On what grounds?"

"We insure the nursing home. You know what that means."

"We're the ones with deep pockets."

"He's covering all of his bases."

"Smart move."

"I'm not sure about Kemmler's strategy, but he could come at us from several angles." She reminded him that there were a number of reasons to file a civil lawsuit against a nursing home, convalescent home, rest home, or long-term care facility. She paused for a moment, as if to make certain he was following her chain of thought; then she continued. "Failure to keep the premises reasonably safe, negligent hiring, negligent supervision, failure to maintain health and safety policies, failure to provide adequate medical treatment, and neglect of a resident." With a grim laugh, she added, "Any one of those reasons could spell trouble. Especially with a sympathetic jury."

Gold was reluctant to ask the sixty-four-thousand-dollar question, but he knew he had to. "What's our exposure?"

"Six million."

"Ouch."

"There's a one million primary policy and a five million dollar umbrella."

"Any deductible?"

"Five thousand."

Gold sighed, and his voice grew suddenly somber. "I hope our pricing made sense."

"We got our pound of flesh."

"Well, that's good to know."

She let out a rough laugh. "The premium doesn't come close to the possible payout. FYI, the average nursing home settlement, either in or out of court, is about four hundred six thousand dollars. Even worse, almost twenty percent of nursing home claims include punitive damages."

Gold stared down at his hands, which he had placed on his lap. His long legs were stretched out in front of the chair. He took a deep breath. He pulled himself together with a visible effort, but deep down inside he had a feeling that they were about to take it on the chin.

Nursing home settlements typically awarded compensation for medical bills and other related expenses, and they occasionally included punitive damages for pain and suffering. Generally speaking, punitive damage awards were not meant to compensate injured plaintiffs, but to punish defendants whose conduct was judged to be grossly negligent or intentional. There was no set amount, and contrary to popular myth, punitive damage awards were rare, reasonable, and limited. In fact, only 6 percent of civil cases involved such awards.

Still, as Kaminski knew, the average award from a tort jury was $100,000 — a sum that was sure to catch the eye of the board of directors. She also had to worry about the shareholders. Unfortunately, shareholder lawsuits were *de rigueur*, and individuals were allowed to sue a corporate director, corporate officer, and the corporation itself.

Gold tried not to show too much concern. "If I remember right, the plaintiff would have to prove a degree of personal harm."

"A huge settlement might fit the bill."

"Maybe, but I like our odds."

"Odds are for gamblers — and I hate to gamble with the financial well-being of this company."

Kaminski's gloomy mood was based upon years of experience, and the knowledge that there were several factors beyond her control that could affect the amount of any settlement. In addition to specific evidence and details of the case, she had to worry about jurisdiction, the type of case, and the settlement amounts of similar cases.

Jurisdiction seemed to be her biggest concern, and for good reason. The state and county in which the abuse took place — and the available jury pool — could have a profound effect on the final numbers. The five boroughs were notoriously liberal, and the Bronx and Brooklyn could be downright hostile. In Kaminski's view, all five counties were "hellholes," meaning that they were "plaintiff friendly."

To prove her point, she brought up hedge funds, which had become increasingly involved in tort litigation against companies that made prescription medications and medical devices. Investment firms were lending money to law firms filing product liability lawsuits in return for a portion of any recovery. In essence, hedge funds were turning the civil justice system into a profit center.

Gold shook his head. "There oughta be a law."

Kaminski slumped back in her chair, leaning her head into the leather and swiveling from side to side. "Some of those bastards are offering cash advances to plaintiffs involved in personal injury litigation."

"Sounds like a loan-sharking scheme."

She spun around and faced him, her expression one of grave concern. "I'm worried about a wild card scenario. A partisan judge, a liberal jury, a large punitive damage award. These are the things that keep me up at night."

"You worry too much."

"You think so?"

"I know so."

She locked gazes with him and, in a steely voice, said, "There's always an exception to the rule."

"Well, you know what they say. Rules are made to be broken."

She pulled a newspaper clipping from her suit pocket and handed it to him. "Read it and weep."

Something in her tone made Gold tense. The clipping only increased the tention. According to the *Wall Street Journal*, an eighty-four-year-old nursing home resident in Illinois was severely burned after being placed in a bath that was too hot by nursing home staff members. The resident received a nursing home negligence settlement of $1.5 million.

"Damn," Gold said, "that's one big exception."

"You can say that again."

"Of course, in New York State, Kemmler would have to present clear and convincing evidence of malice."

"Speaking of malice..." Her voice trailed off and she stared at him, chewing on her pale lower lip for a moment, then finally said, "Kemmler's hired a personal injury lawyer. One of the best in Manhattan."

"Who might that be?"

"Marvin Katz."

Gold forced himself to take a deep breath, and then another. The blood had drained from his face, and for a moment he looked like he was going to punch something. He sat quietly for a moment, then spoke. "Well, what do you know. Marvelous Marvin strikes again. My day's complete."

"I knew you'd be thrilled."

"Thrilled doesn't even begin to cover it."

"I thought you boys buried the hatchet."

Gold shook his head. "I wasn't allowed to bury the hatchet where I wanted it."

"Very funny."

"I wonder how a piker like Kemmler landed a big fish like Katz."

"Where there's a will, there's a lawyer. Kemmler inherited a sizeable chunk of change from his parents."

"Blood money," Gold said. Thinking out loud, he added, "In a way, it all makes sense. Piranhas are attracted to the smell of blood."

The remark caused Kaminski's left eyebrow to rise a half inch. "You don't seem very fond of our legal adversary."

"I despise the man."

"Tsk-tsk. The man's a pillar of the legal community."

"The man belongs in a pillory."

"Why the bad blood?"

"Long story. Let's just say I wouldn't cross the street to spit on his hair if it was on fire."

Kaminski leaned back in her chair. Pensive, frowning, she looked around the room, then settled her gaze back on her ace investigator. "I'm not familiar with that saying, but I catch your drift."

"I'm glad we understand each other."

"Do you understand the importance of settling this claim amicably?"

Gold looked at her blankly. *"Amicably?"*

"Out of court."

"Do you think that's really possible?"

"We've got a chance to find out." She put on her brightest smile. "Mr. Katz wants to take you to lunch."

Gold looked as shocked as if she'd slapped him. For a moment words evaded him. Then, "Are you serious?"

"Completely."

"When?"

"Today."

Gold wondered if he should say what he was thinking. Most people didn't go out of their way to antagonize their own bosses. He thought about it for a second, then decided to be a good soldier. He nodded slowly, then asked the million dollar question. "Why?"

"He didn't say."

"No hints?"

"Nope."

Gold looked disconsolate. "The son of a bitch is up to something."

"Maybe he's lonely. Maybe he misses your brilliant repartee. Maybe he wants to settle out of court. Either way, you get a good meal." She tossed a Post-it note across her desk. "You've got a twelve-thirty reservation. Don't be late."

"I wouldn't dream of it."

She leaned closer, as if someone might be listening. "Try not to alienate your host before you hear his proposal."

"I'll give it my best shot."

Kaminski gave him that cool, calculating, skeptical look she had learned from him. "Make sure you do."

CHAPTER TWO

There was a time, prior to the pandemic, when New Yorkers had their choice of fine restaurants. Back then, there were more than twenty-six thousand dining venues, but sadly, half were no longer in business. Fortunately, some of the best had survived, including Sparks Steak House, a venerable establishment on East 46th Street. The midtown mecca had opened its doors in 1966 and was justifiably famous for its tasty slabs of meat. Unfortunately, it was also linked to one of the most notorious mob hits in US history.

Just before 5:30 p.m. on December 16, 1985, Gambino crime family boss Paul Castellano and underboss Thomas Bilotti were gunned down outside the entrance of the restaurant. Four assassins, dressed in trench coats and Russian fur hats, carried out the hit under orders from John Gotti.

Gold wondered if his host had chosen Sparks for a reason. Maybe the clever slug was trying to send him some sort of message. Maybe he was trying to be funny. Whatever the case, Gold was not going to be thrown off his game by a crude prank.

When Gold entered the restaurant, he spotted Katz at a table in the rear of the dining room. Squeezing at his temples, he sighed deeply, dreading the next few hours. Feigning a nonchalance he didn't feel, he sauntered across the room, warily eyeing his host.

Katz, nursing his second martini, broke into a huge grin. He did not, however, stand up or extend his hand. "Well," he said a little too loud, "look what the Katz dragged in."

Gold plastered a fake smile on his face. "You didn't drag me here. It's always a privilege to spend time with a brilliant lawyer."

"Never crap a crapper. You're here because the boss lady told you to come."

"Believe what you will."

"By the way, how is the big blonde? Still got her pretty nose to the grindstone?"

"Better than in a martini glass."

"Touche." He gestured toward an empty chair. "Have a seat. Take a load off."

Gold sat down, and in less than thirty seconds there was a server at his side. "Good afternoon," said a tuxedoed woman. "Welcome to Sparks. May I get you a drink?"

"I'd love a cold beer," Gold said. "Anything on tap."

"A *cold beer*?" Katz said incredulously. Had Gold asked for a glass of milk, he couldn't possibly have been more appalled. "Are you nuts? You're about to have one of the best steaks in Manhattan. Order a real drink."

Gold smiled indulgently. "Cold beer, please."

When the server walked away, Katz leaned forward, resting his elbows on the table. "I thought you were a two-fisted drinker?"

"I used to be."

"What happened?"

"Puberty."

Katz made a face. "Are you trying to tell me something?"

"Nope."

"Maybe you think I have a drinking problem."

"Never gave it much thought."

Katz took a solid belt of his martini and wiped his mouth with the back of his hand. "You need to live a little."

"I need to keep my wits about me."

"Ah, worried about dropping your guard?"

"Wouldn't be the first time."

Katz waved his concern away. "You have nothing to fear. I come in peace."

"I've heard that before."

"Forgive and forget," Katz said. "That's my motto. The longer you hold a grudge, the heavier it gets."

Something about the man's tone — a mixture of arrogance and deceit — struck Gold. He pulled at his ear, amused by what he'd just heard, doubting that a word of it was true. Gold had met Katz three years earlier in a Washington, D.C., courtroom, when he was called as a hostile witness in a civil action. The estate of a psychotic mobster who was recently shot to death was suing the federal agent who fired the fatal shot. Much to his dismay, Gold had been forced to recount the gory details of the shooting, and his testimony was not helpful to the agent's defense.

As fate would have it, the agent was a close, personal friend.

When Gold thought about the trial, he wanted to leap across the table and punch Katz in the face. Of course, fisticuffs were out of the question. Too many witnesses. Still, it was tempting.

The server materialized and placed Gold's beer on the table, then took their orders without writing anything down. Servers with good memories were another sign of a classy joint, Gold told himself.

Katz raised his glass and smiled. *"L'chaim."*

"I'll drink to that."

They each took a sip and put down their glasses. A flicker of concern crossed Katz's face. "Let me ask you something. Are you still mad about that babe?"

"Excuse me?"

"The federal agent. I forget her name." He dabbed his mouth with a napkin. "Sally something."

"Sally Ridge."

"Yeah, that's the name. She was a friend of yours, right?"

"She's still a friend."

"Good-looking woman."

"Yep."

Katz had been about to take a sip of gin, but he paused, the glass a few inches from his mouth. "Mind if I ask another question?"

"Probably."

"Were you schtooping her?"

Gold nearly choked on his second sip of beer. He sputtered and wiped his chin with his sleeve while his host looked on with amusement. Anger spread through him, and he barely stopped himself from saying something he would definitely have regretted. He forced himself to smile politely, then said, "I never kiss and tell."

"Come on, Gold. Be a mensch."

"I'm taking the Fifth."

Katz shrugged. "Your prerogative. I was just curious."

"Remember what killed the cat?"

Another shrug. Gold's glare caught him off guard, and he realized he'd hit a nerve. "Just for the record, your girlfriend only got a reprimand. She still kept her job. She'll still get a pension." He grinned again, flashing a row of porcelain teeth, unnaturally white and regular. "Maybe we should change the subject."

"Maybe so."

They looked around them. The tables were filled with couples and foursomes, some smiling, some serious and intent, their profiles reflected in shiny glass and mirrors. These days, most were business people — very few tourists. Katz took a sip of his drink, smacked his lips, and said, "Have you eaten here before?"

"Several times."

"One of my favorites."

"Mine too."

"There's a new place on Wall Street. A Japanese restaurant. Owned by a law firm. It's called *So-Sue-Me!*"

Gold took a beat deciding whether or not he should laugh; he decided against it. Flashing the smile he used to disarm, he leaned forward and whispered into Katz's face. "Another comedian. Almost as funny as your new client."

Stephen G. Yanoff   16

A little tipsy, Katz folded his arms across his chest and leaned back in his chair. "Ah, my new client," he said softly, then added, "we'll get to him in a minute."

One hour and two filet mignons later, they both ordered coffee and a slice of New York cheesecake. Between bites, Gold became a bit impatient. "Are we going to keep filling our faces or talk business?"

"What's your rush?"

"My rush? That was the longest minute of my life."

Katz faced him squarely. "All work and no play makes Jack a dull boy."

"Jack's done playing. He wants to hear what you have in mind."

Katz tsked. "Gold, please. A little patience." He looked off into space, gathering his thoughts. A small smile began, then faded. "Do you know how dinosaurs became extinct?"

Gold rolled his eyes, irritated. "Here we go."

"Humor me."

"How long is this going to take?"

"Just answer the question."

"No, I have no idea how they became extinct."

"You're not alone." He looked down at his coffee, lifted the cup and took a sip, then put it down carefully. "There are plenty of theories, but nobody knows for sure. Not really. Some say there was a global climatic change, others blame volcanic activity, and a few think that an asteroid collided with the earth. Anything is possible, but like I said, nobody knows for sure." He nodded and folded his hands together, seeming to have forgotten the topic at hand. After a while he raised his index finger and touched the side of his jaw, as if demonstrating the act of thinking. Finally, he said, "I can tell you one thing. The Lord definitely acts in mysterious ways."

Gold looked at him with a puzzled expression. "What the hell are you babbling about?"

"Brace yourself."

"Consider me braced."

"Kemmler doesn't want to settle out of court."

Gold shook his head. "A trial will be long and costly."

"There won't be a trial."

"I don't understand."

"Don't ask me why, but my client is ready to drop his lawsuit."

"I think you've had too much to drink."

"Not nearly enough."

"Are you pulling my leg?"

"Nope. My client is prepared to sign a formal release."

Dumbstruck, Gold shook his head in disbelief. He felt the beginnings of a smile. He fought against it, but he didn't win. He mouthed the word *martini* to the server and she nodded, displaying a sweet smile. "Now I need a drink."

"I figured you might. Did you know that gin was invented in 1689? Most people think it was invented in England, but Holland is the real birthplace of gin. The Dutch used it for medicinal purposes, and after it became popular, they began to give it to soldiers before a battle — to calm their nerves. That's where we get the term *Dutch courage*."

"I hope it will calm my nerves."

"Caught you by surprise, huh?"

"You certainly did."

"Well, it wasn't my decision. I was prepared for a battle royale." He shook his head. "Kemmler is a crazy son of a bitch. Totally unpredictable. I don't even know why I agreed to represent him."

"Because there was *mucho dinero* on the table."

"Man does not live by bread alone."

"So I've heard."

"I'm not in this racket for the money."

Gold leaned forward and with a suave smile said, "Just the free lunches?"

Katz's eyes flashed with annoyance. "Don't be a wise guy. There are other things in life besides money. Other reasons to practice law. Did you ever hear of truth, justice, and the American way?"

Doing a slight double take, Gold said, "I should have ordered a double."

"I'm being serious. I took Kemmler's case because the nursing home mistreated his parents. They mistreated a lot of patients. They deserve to be punished."

"What about your client? The one who forced his parents into the nursing home. Does he deserve punishment?"

"He was just following orders."

Gold sat and stared, his jaw dropping open. "Excuse me?"

"The family doctor. He advised Kemmler to put his parents in a nursing home facility. What was he supposed to do, ignore the medical experts?" His eyes widened in surprised indignation.

He wasn't used to having his judgement challenged by a layman. "What the fuck did our politicians do?"

Gold dropped his gaze, embarrassed.

Checkmate.

CHAPTER THREE

While it was too early to take a victory lap, Gold sensed that he was close to the finish line. If Katz was on the level, he was going to save Gold a lot of time and trouble — and save the Anchor Insurance Company a bundle of money. Suing a nursing home — and its insurance carrier — was an expensive proposition for all of the parties involved. The devil, as they say, was in the details. Basically, there were five steps, all of them costly.

Step one meant hiring a lawyer and filing a lawsuit in the proper jurisdiction. Step two involved a pretrial investigation, commonly known as discovery. The third step was the issuance of a demand letter, followed by two other steps: mediation and a settlement offer.

Legal expenses varied, but a decent tort attorney would make at least one hundred dollars per hour. In most cases, clients also incurred litigation costs, including postage, document copying, database management, court filing fees, and expert witness fees.

A shrewd attorney would often entice a client to sign a contingency agreement, which stipulated that a hefty fee would be paid for legal services if — and only if — the plaintiff received compensation from the at-fault party.

Katz had made a great deal of money by working on a contingency fee basis, and by charging a contingency fee of 40 percent — double the percentage of most personal injury cases. If Katz had played hardball and won in court, Kemmler could have pocketed a tidy sum, most of it courtesy of the Anchor Insurance Company.

Gold smiled, knowing his employer had dodged a bullet. Time to celebrate. He took a sip of his martini, then nodded approvingly. "Damn good bartender."

Katz muttered something under his breath, then said, "You got lucky, Gold. I could have won this case with my eyes closed."

Gold was having trouble keeping a straight face. "You think so?"

"I know so." Frowning in concentration, he pulled at his collar and tie. "Let me tell you something about your insured. Those bums ran the worst nursing home in the state. The absolute worst."

"You don't say."

"I did a little digging before I agreed to represent Kemmler. Did you know that your insured had been cited by the Department of Health and Human Services?"

"No, I wasn't aware of that."

"Not once, but three times." He shook his head disdainfully. "They were also in violation of regulation 42."

"Sounds serious."

"You bet your ass it's serious. Your insured accepted Medicare patients, which meant that they were supposed to follow federal guidelines."

Gold let out a bored sigh, then said, "Those can be confusing."

Katz snorted derisively. "The law is perfectly clear. If you accept Medicare, you must provide adequate supervision to prevent accidents. Your nursing home failed to comply with the law. Seniors were injured. Grandma and grandpa. How do you think a jury would have felt about that?"

"I guess we'll never know."

"No, I guess not."

Gold had spent the better part of his career reading faces, but Katz was a tough nut to crack. The lawyer was clearly agitated, but what was the cause of his pique? One of two reasons, Gold thought. Either he was pissed about not taking on Goliath or he was pissed about taking a financial hit. Maybe both. On average, nursing home cases took about eighteen to twenty-four months, or longer, from trial to judgment. So now, as things stood, Katz would have to find something else to do for the next two years.

Katz looked contemptuously at him. "Some days it just doesn't pay to get out of bed."

Gold leaned back, savoring the moment. After a while, he said, "Are you all right?"

"Yeah, I'm fine. Why do you ask?"

"You seem a little depressed."

"I hate to walk away from a sure thing."

"There are no sure things in a courtroom. You should know that by now."

"Trust me, this one was a cakewalk."

"Which begs the question, why is Kemmler willing to drop his lawsuit?"

"He's doing it out of the goodness of his heart."

A slow grin spread over Gold's face. "From what I've read, he doesn't have a heart."

"Don't believe everything you read."

"Thanks for the warning."

Katz scowled at him for perhaps ten seconds, then said, "You'd be wise to remember the words of Mark Twain. 'If you don't read the newspaper, you're uninformed. If you do, you're misinformed'"

The mocking grin faded from Gold's face. "So what's the deal? Kemmler woke up one morning and decided to turn a new leaf? Is that what you're telling me?"

Katz gave him a blank stare for a long moment and then said, "Let he who is without sin cast the first stone."

"My goodness, you're a regular *Bartlett's Familiar Quotations*."

"Well, since you enjoy my quotes, try this one on for size: Never count your chickens before they hatch."

"You've lost me there, amigo."

"Kemmler's willing to drop his suit, but he wants something in return."

Gold frowned slightly and looked around the room. "What would that be?"

"Insurance coverage."

"Come again?"

"Kemmler owns an antiques shop, and from time to time he needs to ship merchandise. State to state, not overseas. He needs a trip transit policy. One million limit. To show good faith, he's willing to accept a high deductible."

Gold studied the lawyer's face for a long moment with a keen, assessing look. After a time he said carefully, "Let me get this straight. You want my company to insure a convicted felon?"

"Maybe you didn't notice, but the verdict was overturned."

"On a legal technicality."

"Hardly a technicality, but that's beside the point. My client is a free man, and he should be allowed to make a living."

"He needs a trip transit policy to make a living?"

"Would you ship an antique without insurance?"

"No, I wouldn't. Nor would I buy one from a crook."

"Must you be unpleasant?"

"Part of my charm."

Katz cleared his throat and shifted his weight just a bit. "There's nothing charming about your insults."

"Or your client."

"Judge not, lest ye be judged."

Gold tilted his head, a pained expression on his face. "Tell me something. Have you actually read the Bible?"

"Cover to cover. Old and New Testaments. I can quote biblical verses all day long. Juries love that sort of thing."

"Well, you know what they say. Even the devil can cite Scripture for his purpose."

Katz let that one pass. "So what do you think? Do we have a deal?"

"No coverage, no deal?"

"You're a fast learner."

Gold drew a breath and let it out slowly. All in all, it was a reasonable offer, but as he knew, there were certain risks that had to be considered. A trip transit policy covered personal property for theft, disappearance, or fire, and any one of those perils could result in a major loss. After some deliberation, he said, "We would need a policy cap. Our reinsurers would insist upon it."

"What sort of cap?"

"One million per occurence, two million aggregate. Would Kemmler accept those limits?"

"No harm in asking. What about the deductible?"

"Fifty thousand minimum."

"Steep."

"Yep."

"I'm almost afraid to ask about the premium."

"Our hands are tied on that score. We can only use the rates we've filed."

"Give me a ballpark."

"Somewhere between one and three percent of the total insured value."

"Sounds reasonable."

"We aim to please."

Katz didn't say anything for a full minute, then he let out a deep breath and looked directly at Gold. "Say your terms are acceptable. Do we have a deal?"

Gold gave him a droll look. "You know how this game works. I don't have the authority to accept or decline."

"I see. You're just on a fact-finding mission."

"More or less."

"I was hoping for a prompt resolution."

"The boss lady, as you call her, never acts rashly. Slow and steady, that's her motto."

"I've got a motto, too. Never look a gift horse in the mouth."

"Look, if it was up to me, I'd probably accept the offer and move on with my life, but I'm not calling the shots. That's Irene's job, and remember, she has people looking over her shoulder."

"The board of directors."

"Tough bunch to please. They're all afraid of the shareholders."

"Don't they have insurance?"

Gold explained that a D&O policy — covering directors and officers — protected the personal assets of board members for actual or alleged wrongful acts in managing a company, but it did not cover a host of other perils. For instance, it did not cover dishonesty, fraud, or malicious acts committed deliberately. A disgruntled shareholder, represented by a tenacious lawyer, could easily focus on the coverage gaps and become a royal pain in the ass.

Katz raised his hands to his forehead and massaged it, pressing his fingertips hard against his scalp. "I'm getting a headache."

Gold smiled grimly. "Keep in mind that a director and officer can be sued individually for acts or errors they commit while serving on the board. In other words, they can be held *personally liable*, and their personal assets may be used to pay damages."

Katz gazed at him in helpless frustration. Dammit, he realized that Gold was right. "Thanks for the legal seminar. So when can I expect an answer?"

"I'll run it by Kaminski when I get back to the office. I'll call you as soon as she makes a decision."

Katz smiled condescendingly. "What more could I ask for?"

"The check."

CHAPTER FOUR

Irene Kaminski became the president of the Anchor Insurance Company at the ripe old age of forty-nine, a remarkable achievement for a woman who grew up in Vienna, Austria, at the height of the Cold War. Both of her grandparents had been killed during World War II, and her parents imprisoned by the Communists, so by the time she graduated from the University of Vienna, she was sick of totalitarian regimes. After thirty years in America, she still retained a slight Austrian accent, which, combined with her brains and beauty, made her the stuff of dreams in certain quarters of the insurance industry.

Now in her mid-fifties, twice divorced, she was all work and mostly no play, except for an occasional Tae Kwon Do class. Her punching and kicking skills were quite good, which explained why her employees were seldom late for a meeting.

When Gold walked into the 92nd Street Y, Kaminski greeted him with a slight bow. She was still wearing her *dabok*, the Tae Kwon Do uniform, which consisted of a plain white v-neck top with heavy cotton pants. There was something awfully sexy about a sweaty blonde in a robe, Gold thought. He kept that thought to himself, but he couldn't keep his eyes off her ample cleavage, protruding beneath the robe.

A small grin formed on Gold's lips. "How was class?"

"Exhausting."

"So was lunch."

"Do you come bearing good news?"

"More or less. Where can we talk?"

They found a vacant conference room and sat at a long, oak table, facing each other. Kaminski pulled a pad from her pocket and scribbled a few notes, then wiped away a drop of sweat that coursed down the side of her face from her headband. "Okay," she said softly. "Speak the speech, I pray you."

So Gold told her all about Katz hitting the booze, defending his client's honor, theorizing about the extinction of dinosaurs, and of course, dropping the lawsuit against the nursing home — and by extention the Anchor Insurance Company. The last part intrigued her the most, and she asked him to repeat it one more time.

When he finished, Kaminski leaned back in her padded leather chair and heaved a great sigh. "All right, what's the catch?"

"You won't believe it."

"Try me."

"Insurance coverage."

"I beg your pardon?"

Gold suppressed a smile that would be inappropriate given the gravity of the situation. "Kemmler wants to purchase a trip transit policy."

"From *us*?"

"I guess nobody else will deal with him."

"There's a surprise."

Gold paused a beat before saying, "He's willing to drop the suit, but only if we provide coverage. No coverage, no deal."

Kaminski slammed the table top with her right hand, then let out a lengthy string of expletives in German. Gold was a little startled by the force of her response. In all the years he'd known her, he'd never heard her curse so much. "Blackmail," she said angrily. "Out-and-out blackmail."

Gold smiled a little, sighed, put a hand on her forearm. "He's holding all the cards."

"For the moment."

"Would you like to break a few boards?"

"I'd like to break a few bones."

"Take it easy, Irene. We've dealt with clowns like this before."

"I'm sorry about the outburst, but Kemmler makes my blood boil."

"Yeah, I can tell."

"I don't trust the son of a bitch."

"Neither do I, but we don't have much choice."

Kaminski's and Gold's eyes locked in some kind of shared understanding across the small space between them. Not for long, though. Both of them, realizing it, looked away. "Did you discuss policy limits?"

"I told Katz that our reinsurers would insist upon a cap. I mentioned one million per occurence, two million aggregate. He didn't flinch."

"What about the deductible?"

"I threw out fifty thousand."

"Nice round number."

"I thought so, too."

"Too round, if you ask me."

"What do you mean?"

"Most insureds would freak out over such a high deductible, but if I hear you right, Kemmler didn't bat an eye. He's awfully anxious to obtain coverage."

"Well, according to Katz, Kemmler needs to ship antiques, but he can't make a move until he gets a policy."

She went silent while she considered this. "We're missing something," she said finally. "I can feel it in my bones. Kemmler's up to no good."

Gold slouched back in his chair and looked at the ceiling. He closed his eyes and nodded ever so slightly, sighed, then shrugged his shoulders. "You're probably right, but it's still our move. What do you want to do?"

Kaminski fixed him with a cold eye, then smiled slyly. "Like you say, we don't have much choice. If we go to the mat, we have legal costs and the possibility of a large jury award."

"Agreed."

She went on to admit that Kemmler was holding the best hand. All jury trials were risky, but a trial that involved elder abuse was particularly dangerous. If the truth be told, the public was fed up with the daily stories of elder abuse and the shocking statistics related to such crimes. An estimated five million seniors were abused each year in nursing homes, and sadly, one in ten Americans over the age of sixty had experienced some form of abuse.

To make matters worse, the public perception of the insurance industry was generally unfavorable, and many jurors believed that insurance companies had "deep pockets," meaning extensive financial wealth or resources.

Even the legal system was somewhat tilted in favor of plaintiffs. In criminal cases, the prosecution had to prove every element of the crime with which the defendant had been charged, but in a civil case, the plaintiff only had to prove their case by a "preponderance of the evidence," meaning "more likely than not."

The more Kaminski thought about it, the more annoyed she became. She closed her eyes for a minute. Told herself to relax.

Breathe through the mouth. Deep, steady breaths.

She opened her eyes and gave a cheerless grin. "Our insured has a less than stellar track record. I reviewed their file and found several violations, all of them serious."

"Yeah, Katz mentioned that."

She raked her long fingers through her hair. "He's done his homework."

"That's why he makes the big bucks."

"How do you think he would present that information to a jury?"

"I'm not sure, but he'd probably be nominated for an Academy Award."

"Undoubtedly. But my concern is a jury award. If things go badly, we could be hit with punitive damages, and God only knows what those might be."

Gold rubbed the back of his neck, the muscles tight with tension — tension brought on by thoughts of Katz and Kemmler celebrating. "So what's the verdict? Damn the torpedoes, full speed ahead?"

Kaminski stared blankly at him for a long minute, then brought her hand up and chewed at the knuckle of her index finger. The color had drained from her face. "First we talk to Kemmler. Tomorrow morning. Surprise visit. Try to squeeze him a little. Maybe he'll drop his guard and reveal something."

"Katz won't like that."

"I don't care what that ambulance chaser likes — and neither should you. Did you forget about your friend? The federal agent. What was her name?"

"Sally Ridge."

"He almost ruined her career."

"Yeah, we touched on that subject at lunch."

"Did he apologize?"

"No, not exactly. He wants to forgive and forget."

"There are things you don't forget." Her face grew taut. "Let me tell you about that snake, so you understand who we're dealing with. Before he became a tort specialist, he made a name for himself in medical malpractice. Fifteen years ago he was involved in one of the largest settlements in history. A Florida jury awarded a plaintiff one hundred and sixteen million dollars, after he was left brain-damaged and confined to a wheelchair. I don't recall the exact details of the case, but I remember that doctors misdiagnosed the plaintiff's stroke symptoms. After prescribing painkillers, they operated on him, and he spent the next three months in a coma. As a result, he had limited cognitive abilities and was at risk of suffocating every time he swallowed food." She shook her head pityingly. "I didn't think the award was unfair, but then Katz demanded punitive damages."

"How much?"

"One hundred and sixteen million."

"Jesus, that is punitive."

"The jury didn't see it that way. They were happy to award the money, and of course, Katz got a healthy cut."

Gold gave a bleak smile. "I assume the doctors filed for bankruptcy?"

"Before you could say Jack Robinson."

"I can guess what happened next."

"You guessed right. The plaintiff's attorneys sued the physician's insurer, believing they had deep pockets. Then the damn defendants sued their own carrier, claiming they never conducted a reasonable investigation and accusing the company of having a policy of refusing to settle even valid claims."

Gold winced. "There is no honor among thieves."

"The company wasn't to blame. They were only trying to protect their shareholders. In order to prevent bankruptcy, they declined to reimburse their insureds, claiming they violated their professional liability policy. That led to a new round of lawsuits."

"God, what a nightmare."

"Several of our reinsurers took a hit, and a lot of good underwriters lost their jobs. I blame Katz. He's the one that opened Pandora's box."

Gold was digesting this, but not comfortably. "You don't care for lawyers, do you?"

She looked at him, irritated. She was in no mood to worry about professional courtesy. "Do you know what they call a group of lawyers that are drowning?"

Gold broke into a grin. "Nope."

"A good start!"

CHAPTER FIVE

Gold arrived at his office bright and early the next morning, anxious to prepare himself for the surprise visit to Kemmler's place of business. Preparation meant reading — lots of reading. The company had a thick file on Kemmler, and Gold spent three full hours studying educational transcripts, employment records, claim files, investigative reports, and third party interviews. From what he gathered, Kemmler had a lot of annoying habits, but the one that irritated people the most was the way he chewed bubble gum — incessantly smacking his lips and blowing bubbles. It was an odd habit for a fifty-year-old man who'd graduated from Heidelberg University in Germany and then received a master's degree from the Sorbonne in Paris.

Oddly enough, some interviewees were amused by his masticating, but his detractors, who were more numerous, found it appalling. Several neighbors, noting the black eyepatch he wore, referred to him as "Bazooka Joe," the comic strip character associated with Bazooka bubble gum. Surprisingly, Kemmler wore the nickname as a badge of honor, adding the sobriquet to his business card and plastering it across the front window of his shop.

One crazy cat, Gold thought. He opened a folder and read a report generated by the FBI's central database. His eyebrows went up as he read, eventually accompanied by a smile and a slow shaking of his head. Joseph Kemmler also had a foot fetish. He studied the photograph attached to the folder, comparing the actual person to the image he had formed. He had pictured a disheveled, unshaven brute, but in reality, Kemmler was rather ordinary. In fact, he looked like a goddamn insurance salesman — expect for the stupid eyepatch.

Gold poured a cup of coffee and blew across it gently, then took an experimental sip. The more he studied the photograph, the more unsettled he became. Troubled souls like Kemmler, he knew, could sometimes be the most dangerous adversaries. He made a mental note to pack a weapon and reminded himself he could not afford to be anything less than focused.

Kemmler's shop was on East 69th Street, smack dab in the heart of the Upper East Side Historic District, an area bounded by 96th Street to the north, the East River to the east, 59th Street to the south, and Fifth Avenue to the west. Once known as the Silk Stocking District, it was still one of the most affluent neighborhoods in Manhattan.

Gold strode up to the front window and peered inside — with some difficulty since the glass hadn't been cleaned in a while. When he rang the door bell, a buzzer sounded and the door unlocked. An attractive brunette wearing too much makeup was talking on the phone when he entered. She glanced at Gold, told the caller that she would get back to him, and hung up.

"I'm here to see Mr. Kemmler," Gold said when he had the woman's attention.

"What does this concern?"

Gold gave the woman a business card. She glanced at the card, then disappeared behind a beaded curtain. A moment later, she emerged and held the curtain open. "Mr. Kemmler will see you now."

When Gold stepped into the room, Kemmler got up and came around from behind his desk to formally shake his hand. Some people had trouble looking at Gold squarely during an investigation even if they had nothing to hide; Joseph Kemmler, he thought, was the sort of man who would look him straight in the eye no matter how innocent or guilty he might be.

Gold looked around the room. The furniture was unremarkable — two end tables, a bookshelf, one armoire, a small desk. No windows or overhead lighting. A single Tiffany lamp - or rather, a good reproduction - provided just enough light to read.

"What can I do for you?" Kemmler asked. His voice had an impatient edge.

Gold hesitated just a fraction of a second before saying, "You could turn up the lights."

Kemmler didn't respond at first, but then his words came out with a tone of self-pity. "I suffer from photophobia. Increased sensitivity and aversion to light. A drunk driver ran me off the road, and I was left with a corneal abrasion."

"I'm sorry to hear that. Is that how you lost your other eye?"

"My other eye is not lost. Just damaged." He returned to his chair and crossed his legs, displaying an expensive pair of alligator loafers. "Did you come here to inquire about my health?"

"Not exactly. I'd like to discuss your lawsuit — your pending lawsuit."

"Talk to my lawyer."

"I've spoken to Mr. Katz. He outlined your proposal."

"Did he send you here?"

"No, but I'm sure he wouldn't mind if we had a friendly chat."

"Don't be so sure. The man is anal retentive."

"I'll take your word for it."

"Maybe I should get his permission."

Gold smiled. "You need Marvin's permission to have a chat?"

Kemmler raised his hand and fit his chin into his fist, studying him across the desk, making a determination, Gold assumed, about how much he should tell him and what he should keep to himself. After a while, he reached for his heavy desk lighter and made a ritual of firing up a cigar, inspecting the smoldering tip, and blowing the smoke on and on for several minutes. He then looked directly at Gold and said, "What's on your mind?"

Gold cocked his head to one side, surprised by Kemmler's pronounced German accent. He wondered if it was genuine, or part of a silly act, meant to compliment the black eyepatch. He gave a weak facsimile of a smile, then said, "You're not from these parts, are you stranger?"

"What's that supposed to mean?"

"I detect a slight accent."

Kemmler smiled to be polite. "I was born and raised in Germany, but I've lived in New York City for many years."

Gold's sharp eyes had swept the shop while the brunette was on the phone, and he'd been quite surprised by the inventory. Almost everything on display was Western Americana: paintings, sculptures, photographs, and furnishings. Totally unexpected, much like Kemmler. Looking at the armoire, Gold noticed that it was actually a well-secured gun cabinet. "Is that where you keep the six-shooters?"

Kemmler made a dismissive gesture with his hand. "No handguns for me. Too much paperwork."

"I'm surprised by your inventory. I was expecting to find the Palace of Versailles, not the O.K. Corral."

"What can I say? I have eclectic tastes." He set the cigar aside and popped a piece of bubble gum in his mouth. Then, suddenly, he found himself chuckling. "European antiques are so yesterday."

"I'll take your word for that, too."

Kemmler just stared at him, this conversation already far beyond his tolerance level. He was a difficult man to read, but he seemed to be a precise and deliberate man whose stoic expression and one dark eye shielded even a hint of emotion. He stared at Gold without blinking, deep in thought. Finally he said, "What brand of socks do you wear?"

Gold made a face. "What does that have to do with the price of tea in China?"

"I'm just curious." Kemmler's voice was flat and emotionless. "Be a good sport, and I'll answer all of your questions."

"Well, let's see," Gold said, giving it some thought. "I think I'm wearing Gold Toe socks."

"Boring, but functional."

"Much like me." Not having a clue where Kemmler was going with this, Gold gave him a half smile and said, "Question one. About your offer. Why the change of heart?"

"I'm a businessman. In order to conduct business, I need to ship merchandise, and in order to do that, I need trip transit insurance. Is that so difficult to understand?"

Gold kept his expression polite and as casual as possible. "Not many people would be willing to drop a lawsuit just to obtain insurance coverage."

"I've always been contrary to ordinary."

"No offense, but I don't see customers beating down your door. How much shipping do you actually do?"

Kemmler was silent for a moment, hoping the hesitation would send a message to Gold that he was seeking information that was none of his business. He restrained an urge to make a rude comeback and said, "Quantity and quality are two different things."

"Meaning?"

"Meaning I don't ship a lot, but when I do ship, I ship valuable items — antiques and artifacts that are quite expensive."

"It would be helpful if I could see a sample bill of lading. Maybe two or three bills. I'd like to get a feel for what we might be insuring."

Kemmler chomped on his gum, obviously agitated. "Maybe you'd like to see my tax returns, too?"

"No, that won't be necessary."

"Are you sure?" he asked sarcastically. "I'd be happy to make some copies."

"Some other time."

Kemmler stared at him in icy silence, and Gold could feel his resentment, his pent-up anger at being pestered by a lowly insurance investigator. To his credit, he managed to keep his voice calm and even. "I've got a surprise for you, Mr. Gold."

"I love surprises."

"I no longer need an annual policy. I only intend to ship two items. Two rare artifacts."

Gold scrunched his face in concentration for a second. "Just two?"

"You look disappointed. I thought you'd be happy."

"Why would I be happy?"

"Two measly shipments. A lot less exposure for your company."

Gold crossed his arms, gave him a flat look. "You're willing to drop your lawsuit to cover two shipments? Is that what you're saying?"

"That's the deal." He nonchalantly reached for a stack of papers on the corner of his desk. "Katz was kind enough to draw up a letter of intent. Shall we sign it?"

Gold showed no reaction — not the faintest hint of emotion. This ability was his strength, had won him the respect of many adversaries, and had helped him climb to the top of his profession. A good poker face was worth its weight in gold. He glanced at the letter of intent, then gave Kemmler a small smile that said *no can do*. "Not so fast. Tell me about these two shipments."

Kemmler gave him a cunning smile. "Alamo memorabilia."

"Well, that narrows it down."

"A rifle and a sword."

Gold rolled his eyes at him, wondering if he was just baiting him now. "You want to insure a rifle and a sword?"

"To be precise, a flintlock and a saber."

"They must be pretty damn rare."

"Rare and priceless."

"But you're willing to settle for a modest amount of coverage."

Kemmler showed Gold most of his teeth in a broad smile. "What choice do I have? A half of a loaf is better than none."

Gold hated it, this game of cat and mouse, but he supposed it had to be done. "Are these artifacts in your possession?"

He gestured toward the armoire. "Safely under lock and key."

"Where do you want to ship them?"

"Austin, Texas."

"Who's your buyer?"

"I'm not selling the artifacts, I'm donating them."

Gold stared at him wide-eyed, mildly startled. "You're donating them?"

"Out of the goodness of my heart."

Gold allowed himself a thin smile. "Who's the lucky recipient?"

"The state of Texas. I'm gifting both items to the Texas General Land Office, the guardians of the Alamo. I've been assured that

both artifacts will be prominently displayed in their new museum
— pending authentication."

"So, you're turning over a new leaf, eh?"

"Better late than never."

Gold peered at him for a few moments, thinking. "How did
you obtain these artifacts?"

"Through a middleman."

"Does the middleman have a name?"

"Yes, but that information is strictly confidential."

"Naturally."

Kemmler almost groaned out loud. "Nobody wants their name
bandied about, especially on big-ticket items. Too many crooks
and con men around."

"I don't doubt that for a minute."

"You know what they say. Discretion is the better part of
valor."

Gold smiled. A fake smile. Like he had a pain in his side but
was trying not to let on. His voice remained unruffled, placid. "I
must say, I'm overwhelmed by your generosity."

"You don't know the half of it."

"Enlighten me."

Kemmler adjusted his eyepatch and gave Gold one of his
patented scowls. He was thinking. He folded his arms across his
chest and snapped his gum. He could see where this was going,
and he pretended not to like it. "Very well," he said with a sigh.
"I suppose I'd have to divulge the truth sooner or later." His lips
twisted into a lopsided smile. "The flintlock was owned by a

very famous person. So was the saber, or the sword, whatever it's called. I'll tell you their names, but you must promise to keep them in-house."

"You have my word."

Kemmler paused for effect, then said, "The flintlock was owned by Davy Crockett. The saber belonged to Colonel William B. Travis."

Gold was rendered momentarily speechless. He could hardly believe his ears. He gave Kemmler a long, measured look, which the antique dealer avoided by staring at his fancy loafers. He remained silent for a full minute, then threw back his head and guffawed. "Davy Crockett and William Travis." He became instantly serious. "You're a piece of work, Kemmler."

For a long time Kemmler said nothing at all. The tense silence stretched. Reviewing his announcement, Kemmler was pretty sure he'd revealed too much too soon, though he could be wrong — he might have revealed too little. In any event, he knew he hadn't convinced Gold. If he had, he'd have asked to see the artifacts by now. He sighed, impatiently. "I suppose you think I'm full of shit."

"Let's just say I'm highly skeptical."

"I understand your skepticism. I still can't believe my luck." He looked at him uncertainly for a moment, then broke into a sunny grin. "I just remembered something. An old German saying. *Sehen ist glauben.*"

Gold unleashed a long sigh, exhaling like a spent balloon. "What does that mean?"

"Seeing is believing."

CHAPTER SIX

Kemmler found the key to the armoire and unlocked the door, glancing over his shoulder to make sure he had Gold's full attention, which of course he did. Very gingerly, he reached into the armoire and took out a rifle and a sword, then placed them on his desk. He had an iron grin on his face, not a look of amusement or pleasure, but of power. "Feast your eyes on these, *mein freund*."

Gold fished a mini-Maglite flashlight out of his sports coat pocket and swept it along the desk in front of him. "Your artifacts need to be cleaned."

Kemmler let irritation show. He looked at Gold, then gently blew on the weapons, removing a fine layer of dust. "There you go," he muttered. "Clean as a whistle."

Gold took his time, then said, "They're not in very good condition."

Kemmler didn't respond immediately. He glared at Gold for several moments, then said haltingly, "You've got a keen eye for detail."

"Just saying."

"Good Lord, they're two hundred years old. What do you expect them to look like?"

"Priceless artifacts."

"Excuse me?"

"Clean and polished. A lot more TLC."

Kemmler made a sour face. "You've got a lot to learn about antiques. If you mess with the finish, you devalue the item." He spit his gum into a trash basket and relit his cigar. He blew a stream of smoke toward the ceiling, then said, "Antiques are like virgins. Once you mess with them, they lose their appeal."

Gold's face showed he did not entirely agree with that statement, but he let it slide. He cleared his throat, then said, "Should you be smoking in here?"

"I always smoke when I'm tense."

"Bad habit."

"Smoking or getting tense?"

"Both."

Kemmler pouted, his bottom lip fuller, his eye narrowing. "You missed your calling, Gold. You should have been a priest."

"No can do. I'm Jewish."

"I thought so."

Gold turned his head this way and that, trying to figure out what that remark was meant to convey. He decided that this was not the time or the place to dwell on it. He looked at Kemmler, all trace of amusement lost from his face. "Mind if I take a closer look at your precious artifacts?"

"Knock yourself out."

Gold leaned over the weapons but didn't touch either one. He could scarcely believe his eyes. The flintlock bore the name "D.

Crockett," and the sword was engraved with the initials "W.B.T."
He felt goosebumps run down his arms. Then he came back down
to earth. How could two priceless artifacts have fallen into the lap
of a creep like Kemmler?

What were the chances?

He drew a breath, collected himself, let the breath out. It
was possible, he supposed, though doubtful, that they could be
authentic. Thinking out loud, he said, "What do you suppose
they're worth?"

"Impossible to say."

"Take a wild guess."

"Seven figures each."

Gold whistled softly. "I can't believe you're willing to part with
them. Seriously, I'm astonished by your generosity."

Kemmler filled his lungs with smoke and exhaled. "I'm not
the first person to contribute to the betterment of mankind. I'm
not even the first to donate Alamo artifacts." He studied the tip
of his cigar for a moment, then said, "I assume you've heard of
Phil Collins?"

Gold nodded. "What about him?"

According to Kemmler, the British rock star once owned one
of the most valuable collections of Alamo memorabilia in the
world. In 2014, he donated his entire collection — worth about
fifteen million dollars — to the state of Texas.

A smile tickled the corners of Kemmler's mouth, and then
slowly he shook his head from side to side. "The man's generosity
knows no bounds."

For a moment, Gold thought he'd misheard him. "Wait a minute. Are you trying to tell me that Phil Collins — the front man of Genesis — collected Alamo memorabilia?"

"From an early age. He owned artifacts, weapons, relics, and original documents. The man was obsessed with the Alamo." A dry chuckle caught in his throat. "He spent decades building his collection, and then he gave it all away." He flashed a quick grin. "They'll probably name the museum after him."

Gold smiled without a hint of humor. "Did you expect that honor?"

"I'd settle for a wing."

"That's big of you."

"Vanity is the fruit of ignorance."

Gold was looking at him with overt disbelief. "I've been a Phil Collins fan for a long time, and to be perfectly honest, I never heard or read a word about his Alamo collection."

"Perhaps you were too busy denying claims." He crushed out the remains of his cigar, lit a fresh one, blew smoke. They looked at each other through the gray haze. "I'm starting to get the feeling that you don't trust me."

"Whatever gave you that idea?"

"Your general attitude. Suspicious, distrusting, condescending."

"Just doing my job."

"Not very well, I'm afraid." His mouth tightened, the lips conveying a mild distaste. "I'm tempted to withdraw my offer."

Fat chance, Gold thought. He smiled and said in a pleasant voice, "When it comes to insurance, I'm from Missouri. You know, the 'Show-Me' state. Maybe you could show me the provenance of your artifacts. I'd love to see the history of ownership."

"I'm sure you would."

Art and artifacts were commonly accompanied by documentation, known as provenance, from the French word *provenir*, meaning "to come from." Good provenance provided a clear record of ownership history and left no doubt that the item in question was genuine. As they both knew, provenance took many forms, including a signed certificate or statement of authenticity from a recognized authority or expert, an exhibition or gallery sticker, a signed receipt from the original owner, a photograph of the owner holding the artifact, verifiable names of previous owners, letters or papers from recognized experts, and newspaper or magazine articles mentioning the artifact.

Kemmler had none of the above.

Not a single shred of evidence.

Gold tilted his head and looked vaguely skeptical. "How do you explain the lack of provenance?"

Kemmler gave him a forced smile. He spoke slowly, as if he felt that Gold would otherwise have difficulty understanding. "Some items are so exceptional that they become exceptions to the rule. For instance, would you expect to find the provenance of King Arthur's sword or the Holy Grail?"

"I wouldn't expect to find those items at all."

Kemmler patted Gold's shoulder solicitously and raised an eyebrow. "Great expectations are the essence of being a collector. Never knowing what wonderful treasures you'll stumble across."

"Well, you've certainly done your share of stumbling. So, tell me, when would you like to ship your artifacts?"

"As soon as possible."

"Do you understand which perils are covered?"

"Katz mentioned fire, disappearance, and theft."

"Those are the common perils."

"Those are the ones that concern me."

"Just for the record, wear and tear and breakage are excluded."

"Not a problem."

Gold cleared his throat, a nervous habit indicating that he was about to let the other shoe drop. "The policy would have to be issued with a high deductible — somewhere between fifty and one hundred thousand dollars."

Kemmler gave him a frosty look. "Sounds like you're expecting a claim."

"*Semper paratus.*"

"You speak Latin?"

"Just a smidgen."

He set his mouth, drew a determined breath. "You should have said *caveat emptor* — buyer beware. After all, I'm the one taking most of the risk. Wouldn't you agree?"

Gold sat on the edge of the desk with his arms folded nonchalantly against his chest. It was hard taking his eyes off the rifle and sword, but he had business to conduct. "Would you like to discuss the premium?"

"Didn't you discuss all these details with Katz?"

"Yeah, but I want you to hear them from the horse's mouth. I wouldn't want you to be blindsided."

"How considerate."

Gold went on. "The going rate is 1 to 3 percent of the declared value, but since we're unsure of the value — and only covering two shipments that are well beyond the policy limits — we'll have to get creative."

A dry chuckle caught in Kemmler's throat. "By creative you mean expensive?"

"If there's a claim, it will pierce the policy limits. We have to underwrite around that fact. Nothing personal. Simply a business decision."

Kemmler made no attempt to conceal his displeasure. "No offense, but you sound like the mafia."

Gold ignored the comment, forging ahead. "I don't make the rules. Neither does my boss. We're sort of boxed in by regulation, if you know what I mean."

"I know exactly what you mean. You follow the rules as long as they benefit you — and the bottom line."

"Don't take it personally."

Kemmler's face transformed into something between a frown and a wince. Another one of his painful expressions. "Let's finish this dance so I can get back to business." He signed the letter of intent, then handed it to Gold. "Your signature, s'il vous plait."

Gold let him dangle for a moment, then said, "I can sign the letter, but it won't be valid."

Kemmler's face grew a shade darker. "Why not?"

"It has to be signed by a corporate officer. My boss, for example."

"Tell me you're joking."

"I'm afraid not."

Kemmler let out a long, exasperated breath. "Jesus Christ," he said angrily, "you people are intolerable."

"Like I said before, I don't make the rules."

He shot a bewildered look at Gold, then said, "Very well, I'll play along." He folded the letter, stuffed it into an envelope, then handed it to Gold. "I'll expect a prompt reply, so tell your boss to get her act together."

"Will do."

Kemmler thought of something else when he returned to his chair. Leaning across the desk, he spoke in a low, conspiratorial tone. "I'm an impatient man. You might have noticed that minor flaw."

Gold scratched his face, thinking. "Actually, I noticed serveral flaws."

Kemmler looked contemptuously at him. "Don't push your luck."

"I was referring to smoking and chewing gum."

"Just deliver my message, and tell your boss that I want a policy issued ASAP."

"I'll tell her."

"Remember something. I have my limits, too."

CHAPTER SEVEN

By the time Gold got back to the office, John Street was buzzing with worker bees in pursuit of a midday meal. During the summer, they were joined by throngs of tourists, many of them seeking directions to the local points of interest, such as the National 9/11 Memorial, the New York Stock Exchange, or Fraunces Tavern. Navigating the streets of Lower Manhattan during lunchtime was not for the feint of heart — or anyone in a hurry.

Much to his dismay, Gold discovered that Irene Kaminski had left for the day, bound for her summer rental on Long Island. She had left a note inviting him to join her for an early dinner at Gino's Restaurant in Long Beach.

It was an offer he couldn't refuse.

The plan was to make a few calls, straighten up his desk, and then head for the subway, catching the number 2 or 3 train to Penn Station. From there he would hop aboard the Long Island Railroad and take a train directly to Long Beach, a distance of roughly twenty-one miles.

That was the plan. But as they say, life is what happens while people make plans.

Halfway up John Street, at the corner of Gold Street, a black Chevy Tahoe pulled in front of Gold, blocking his path. In a perfect world, he thought, a cop would be around to ticket the driver. He was half right. There was a cop around — a federal agent to be more precise — and he was driving the vehicle.

When the passenger window came down, Gold stuck his head inside, surprised to see his life-long friend Kevin McVey. He shook his head, smiling, as if McVey had said something funny. "Where the hell did you learn to drive?"

"Freeport High School."

"Figures."

McVey glanced in the rearview mirror to make sure that he wasn't blocking traffic. "I think I'm lost."

"I've known that for a long time."

"How do you get to Carnegie Hall?"

Right on cue, Gold said, "Practice, my boy. Practice."

McVey gave him a warm smile. "Climb in. We need to talk."

Gold climbed inside and buckled his seat belt. After they shook hands, McVey hit the gas, driving rapidly toward the Brooklyn Bridge. When they reached the Manhattan ramp, he swerved off to the right and parked in front of the Bridge Cafe, a former restaurant permanently closed by Hurricane Sandy.

After a half-second pause, McVey said, "Lucky we found a spot."

Gold glared at him. "I feel lucky to be alive."

"Concerned about my driving?"

"Nah, we all gotta go sometime."

"Let's grab a beer."

"I could certainly use one."

The bar McVey chose was an odd one — dark, smoky, and reeking of stale beer. Most of the patrons were laborers from the fish markets that dotted the South Street Seaport. Almost everyone wore jeans and T-shirts, and as Gold noticed, some of the T-shirts had clever sayings such as "divers do it deeper."

They sat at the end of the bar, apart from the regulars who didn't seem to notice them. The bartender eyed them for a moment, making a professional evaluation that the newcomers posed no potential threat to his thriving business. Finally, he walked over and said, "What can I get you, gents?"

"Two beers," McVey said.

"And two shots of bourbon," Gold added.

When the bartender walked away, McVey said, "What do you think of this place?"

"Hard to say. The smoke is clouding my vision."

"Count your blessings."

"Why'd you pick this dump?"

"I like the crowd."

"They look fishy to me."

McVey felt the impulse to smile and resisted it. "To tell you the truth, I'm on assignment. I'm trying to keep a low profile."

"You can't get much lower than this place."

"They happen to have great pretzels."

"They must be expensive. I don't see any."

"Give the man a chance. We just sat down."

"The pretzels should be on the bar."

"They'd get stale. Like your jokes."

"They better be worth the wait."

McVey let out a humorless laugh. "How are Patty and the girls?"

"Fine and dandy. Rachel and Rebecca are engaged."

"To each other?"

"Very funny. They met their fiances online. On one of those dating sites."

"I should try that."

"Still looking for Mrs. Right?"

"Right, wrong, or halfway in-between."

"You should give Irene a call."

"Maybe I will." He flushed slightly and said, "When did the girls get engaged?"

"Last month. I tried to contact you, but your office said that you were unreachable."

"Imbedded would be a better word."

"Where?"

"None of your business."

"Ah, the intriguing world of espionage."

"Shitholes are seldom intriguing."

"I don't know. I'm starting to like this place."

"You're a riot, Alice."

The bartender delivered their beers and a bowl of pretzels, mumbling about assholes who refuse to use coasters. When he left, they clinked their mugs and toasted to old times. Gold popped a handful of pretzels into his mouth, smiling as he chewed. "So what brings you to my neck of the woods? Or is that confidential, too?"

McVey laughed nervously and, not knowing exactly where to begin, did a little drumroll on the bar. Lowering his voice, he said, "I'm after one of the bad guys."

"How bad?"

"One of the worst. A murderer, drug smuggler, and human trafficker."

"Damn, that's quite a resume."

"I forgot to mention something. He's also a con artist. A big-time swindler."

Gold studied the serious look on McVey's face and said, "What's wrong? You look worried."

McVey lowered his voice to an all-but-inaudible whisper. "I recently left the Department of Energy. I'm now working with HHS — the Department of Health and Human Services. I'm in charge of a task force assigned to rescue and restore victims of human trafficking. We coordinate with the FBI and ICE."

"Those are some heavy hitters." He took a long sip of his beer, studying McVey over the rim of his mug. "I hear those traffickers are nasty bastards."

McVey nodded in agreement, then spent the next thirty minutes explaining just how nasty they were. Nothing could have prepared Gold for the awful details, which landed on him like a ton of bricks. Each year almost twenty thousand men, women, and children were trafficked into the United States, with the highest numbers in California. Texas, Florida, and New York also had horribly high numbers.

In general, women were used for sexual exploitation while men were used for forced labor. One in five human trafficking victims were children, exploited for begging, child pornography, or child labor.

Human trafficking was considered a "hidden crime" because victims did not frequently seek help — due to language barriers, fear of traffickers, and fear of law enforcement. Nevertheless, statistics showed that the majority of sex trafficking victims were white or black, while most labor trafficking victims tended to be Hispanic or Asian.

McVey had only been with the task force a short time, but he had already seen a 20 percent increase from the year before, and the future looked bleak. One of the reasons for McVey's pessimism was the fact that the American city with the highest number of reported human trafficking cases was Washington, D.C. — the "Capital of America."

Incredibly, human trafficking wasn't illegal until 2000, when the federal government finally passed the Trafficking Victims Protection Act, which made it a federal crime.

"I don't blame Washington," McVey said softly. "When we go outside, look across the East River. The borough of Queens is the epicenter of trafficking on the eastern corridor." He took a sizeable gulp of beer, then wiped his mouth with the back of his hand. "Every other business of Main Street in Flushing seems to be an Asian massage parlor. The women who work there are forced to see more than twenty customers a day — with little or no pay. I know this sounds like bullshit, but there are four times as many illegal massage parlors in Queens as there are Starbucks in the whole damn city of New York."

Gold shook his head. "You got your work cut out for you."

"I'm not complaining. I've been busting my ass for the last few months, but when the bad guys get convicted, they're looking at a ten-year sentence." He grabbed a handful of pretzels, then added, "Unless, of course, they get nabbed in the Philippines. Those crazy bastards have reintroduced the death penalty."

"Sounds like a good idea to me."

"I wouldn't lose any sleep over it either."

"You don't lose sleep over anything."

"That's what you think."

Gold frowned thoughtfully. "How do you like working at HHS?"

"I don't have any complaints. I've got a corner office in the Hubert Humphrey Building on Independence Avenue. Nice view of Barthold Park. Not too far from the Air and Space Museum."

"Still living in Georgetown?"

"No, I moved across the river. I rent an apartment in Arlington. Close to the Pentagon."

"Nice area."

"If you like living near the biggest office building in the world. Six and a half million square feet of space. Over twenty-five thousand employees. If you don't make reservations for lunch, you're screwed. Dinner can also be a problem."

"Don't you have any pull?"

"Everybody's got pull in Washington."

Gold nodded, smiling, as if McVey had said something funny. "Where are you staying?"

"Manhattan."

"Where?"

"Here and there."

"Top secret, huh?"

McVey turned around, looked at him, and then grinned. "I don't want you popping over in the middle of the night."

"I go to bed at ten o'clock."

"Since when?"

"Since I received my first solicitation from AARP."

"I feel your pain."

"Yeah, I can tell."

"What's that supposed to mean?"

Gold said what he was thinking. "You look tired, amigo. Tired and worried."

McVey sat back, leveled his gaze at him. He put his hand on Gold's shoulder and squeezed it gently, then spoke in his mildest tone. "I'm a little of both. I didn't think you'd notice."

"You notice a lot after thirty years of friendship."

"Has it been that long?"

"Maybe longer. I forget when we first met."

"How could you forget such an important date?"

"I don't know, but I keep trying."

McVey looked at him like maybe he didn't believe him. "You really know how to hurt a guy."

"Look who's talking."

"Let's not go down that road."

Sometimes, Gold realized, you just had to put yourself out there. You didn't necessarily need a plan. You just had to wing it. He forced his game face back into place, then said, "Let me help."

"What?"

"The bad guy you're after. Let me help you find him."

"We already found him."

"You did?"

"He became entangled with a nursing home under our jurisdiction."

"Has he been arrested?"

"Not enough evidence."

"Too bad."

McVey started to say something, then changed his mind. "I'll nail his ass. It's only a matter of time."

"Is he under surveillance?"

"Twenty-four hours a day."

"Smart move."

"I usually take the morning shift."

"Nice way to start the day."

McVey formulated his next sentence carefully. "Oddly enough, it can be quite interesting. Almost unbelievable. For instance, earlier today I was uptown, parked outside my suspect's place of business. All of a sudden I see a familiar face come into view, and lo and behold, he walks into the suspect's store. I didn't know what to think. I was completely baffled. A hundred questions ran through my mind, but I kept coming back to the same damn one." After a long moment, he turned and looked at Gold again. He didn't look angry. Maybe a little defeated. "Why the hell is Adam Gold visiting a scumbag like Joseph Kemmler?"

CHAPTER EIGHT

Whenever McVey showed up, it was a signal to batten down the hatches and prepare for rough seas. He was that type of person. Always on the move. Always involved in something surreptitious. Never a dull moment. Funny thing was, Gold shared the same DNA, sans the targeted assassinations.

Gold leaned back slowly on his bar stool as he absorbed what McVey was telling him. If anyone else had said it, he'd have been laughing by now. But McVey didn't joke about such matters. Jesus, talk about a punch in the gut. He breathed quietly for a moment, marshalling his thoughts. "Damn," he said under his breath. "Bazooka Joe really gets around."

McVey's voice was calm, calculating. "Time to burst his bubble."

"How can I help?"

"You can start by explaining your visit."

There was a lot to explain, but Gold took his time, remembering that it was often the little things — the so-called minor details — that mattered the most. McVey knew about the nursing home lawsuit, but he was surprised to learn about Kemmler's offer, and he almost fell off his stool when he heard about the Alamo artifacts.

McVey pretty much knew the answer to his question but decided to ask anyway. "Are we talking about *the* Davy Crockett? The King of the Wild Frontier?"

"The old bear hunter himself."

"Talk about tall tales."

"I saw the rifle myself. The lighting was bad, but I could tell it was a flintlock. A .40-caliber model."

"Probably a reproduction."

"Possibly."

"What about the sword?"

"I saw that, too. Kemmler claims it was owned by Colonel Travis. If that's true, it could have been used at the Alamo — to draw the line in the sand."

McVey's reaction was delayed a bit. He grunted as if to laugh, but there was no humor in it. "Just for the record, I've studied the history of the Alamo, and that story about Travis drawing a line in the sand is questionable at best. The first mention of it wasn't made until decades after the battle, and it was made by a man who may not have been at the Alamo during the siege."

Gold smiled at him. "You should be on a game show."

McVey went on, telling him that the story of the line in the sand was first published in 1873, by a journalist who had heard the claim from Moses Rose, a soldier of fortune who had supposedly escaped from the Alamo.

"I don't know if it's true," McVey said, "but it's a great story."

Gold nodded slowly, seemingly thinking about what he'd just heard. "Let me ask you something. What's the difference between a saber and a sword?"

McVey gave it some thought, then said, "From what I recall, a saber is a light weapon, whereas a sword is a long-bladed weapon with a hilt, and usually a pommel and cross-guard. One is used strictly for stabbing, and the other is designed to stab, slash, or hack."

"God, you're a fountain of knowledge."

"Why do you ask?"

The little things, Gold said to himself. He stayed quiet for a moment, then said, "Kemmler referred to Travis's weapon as a saber, but from what you just told me, it was actually a sword."

"So?"

"A legitimate collector should know the difference. I think he's full of shit."

McVey put his hand on Gold's shoulder and looked him in the eye. "Did you ever think otherwise?"

"There's something else. Did you ever hear the saying, 'You're not from these parts, are you, stranger?'"

"Every time I watched a John Wayne movie."

"Kemmler had no idea what that meant. How could a collector of western artifacts be so clueless?"

"I don't think they have cowboys in Germany."

"They have movies."

"Good point."

"If Kemmler's a fraud, then his artifacts are probably fake, too."

"That would be my guess."

"Of course, that does raise an interesting question. If they're fake, he wouldn't dare turn in a claim, so why insure them in the first place?"

"Good question. What does Irene think?"

"I haven't briefed her yet."

"What are you waiting for?"

"She left work early. I'm meeting her for dinner."

"Better bring some Alka-Seltzer. She's gonna have indigestion after you tell her about the artifacts."

"You know her well."

"Well enough."

Gold glanced at him, squirming with uneasiness. "I'm not sure why, but Kemmler's gotten under her skin. She's determined to nail his hide to the wall. I could be wrong, but it seems to be something personal."

After nearly a minute of silence during which both men simply stared into their beer, McVey said, "We know a lot about Kemmler, but I could dig deeper. I could contact my friends in Germany. Maybe the BND knows something we don't."

"The BND?"

"The German equivalent of the FBI."

"Nice to have friends in spy places."

"Yep."

Gold hesitated, thinking. "I guess it couldn't hurt." Then in a lower voice, he said, "Let's keep this German thing just between us girls."

"Roger that. I've seen Irene's roundhouse kick."

"I may see it tonight. She's gonna hit the roof when she hears about my meeting with Kemmler."

"Not if you play your cards right."

"What do you mean?"

"You just told me that she's chomping at the bit to nail Kemmler's hide to the wall. Well, now he's given her a hammer and nails."

"You've lost me."

"Look, you and I know that his artifacts are fake, and sooner or later he's gonna try to pawn them off on some poor sucker. When that happens, we pounce."

"*We?*"

McVey held up his hand, signaling him not to interrupt. "Try to follow me. If Kemmler donates the artifacts, which is questionable, he'll most likely claim a tax deduction. In my world, that's known as tax fraud. A federal crime. When we get done with him, you can charge him with two counts of insurance fraud."

Gold broke the hint of a smile. "What's the penalty on your end?"

"He could be ordered to pay a fine of up to $250,000, sentenced to a maximum of three years in prison, or both."

"The wages of sin are steep."

McVey scratched his face, thinking. "We could probably convince Irene to refer the matter to the New York Attorney General."

"It wouldn't take much convincing."

"Insurance fraud is a serious crime."

A typically astute suggestion, Gold thought. With any luck, Kemmler could be charged with insurance fraud in the first degree, a class B felony equal to grand larceny. In order for prosecutors to raise the degree of insurance fraud to a felony offense, they would have to prove beyond a reasonable doubt that Kemmler wrongfully took or obtained property or money worth more than one million dollars. Since fraud was rarely a stand alone crime, he could also be charged with enterprise corruption, forgery, and falsifying business records. If convicted of any of those "white collar crimes," he could be sentenced to as much as twenty-five years in prison.

After sharing his thoughts, Gold slapped McVey on the back. "I like the way you think."

"You don't say."

"Kevin, my boy, I think this is the beginning of a beautiful friendship."

"Thanks, Rick, but we've been friends since high school."

"So we have." He gulped down the remainder of his beer. "Time flies when you're having fun."

"You call this fun?"

"Fun and games. I think we both enjoy the games."

"Speak for yourself. I can't wait to retire."

Gold let out an aborted chuckle. "I can't picture you on a golf course."

"I don't play golf, but I do play softball. I also love to fish."

"Where would you retire?"

"Florida."

"Florida?"

"A nice, warm state. A little south of here."

"I'm familiar with the place. My mother lives in Boca Raton."

McVey looked a little sheepish. "I've been looking at a place called The Villages. It's a retirement community in the central part of the state. Forty-five miles from Orlando. They've got everything a body could want. Homes, villas, bike trails, pools, golf, tennis, shopping, and a softball league for seniors."

Still smiling, Gold said, "They've also got something else. Sinkholes."

"Sinkholes?"

"Central Florida is full of them, and The Villages is smack dab in the middle of Sinkhole Alley."

McVey sighed heavily. "What the hell are you talking about?"

"We insure some of the homes in Sumter County. I happen to know that three huge sinkholes recently opened up in The Villages, draining the water from a pond and shutting down a recreation center and swimming pool." He grinned mischievously. "If you plan to stay above ground, stay out of Central Florida."

McVey would have burst out laughing if someone hadn't tapped him on the shoulder. When he turned around, he came face to face with a giant of a man, wide-necked and barrel-chested. He was wearing a Bass Pro gimme cap, but most of his shaggy brown hair hung over his ears and curled around the collar of his work shirt. McVey thought he looked like he was wearing a bullet-proof vest under his shirt, only there was no vest, just solid muscle.

Almost instinctively, McVey reached for his beer mug and braced himself for trouble.

Unsmiling, the man said, "You're sitting on my stool."

McVey smiled at him. "I didn't know we had assigned seats."

"Find another stool."

"I'm comfortable here."

He poked McVey in the chest with his index finger. "You won't be too comfortable if I break your nose."

Still smiling, McVey said, "I don't like to be poked."

"Tough shit."

"Do you know that it takes two to eight weeks for a broken finger to heal?"

The man acted like that was the funniest thing he'd ever heard and covered his mouth while he leaned back and laughed. Suddenly, he stopped laughing and said, "Are you threatening me?" He looked directly at Gold. "I think your date is threatening me."

Gold shrugged. "The man's incorrigible. Do you know what that means?"

"Fuck you, pal."

"I'm not your pal."

"You guys make a sweet couple."

McVey bristled, his back straightening. He let out a sigh, more frustration than anger. "We're not looking for trouble. Would you walk away if I bought you a drink?"

"You trying to bribe me?"

"More or less."

Another poke. "Don't bust my balls, mister."

"I'd rather bust your balls than your head," McVey said.

"You've got a bad fucking attitude."

"A bad temper, too."

Gold cleared his throat. "I think you should leave."

The man gave Gold a withering look. "Why don't you mind your own fucking business?"

"Just trying to help."

He laughed derisively. "I don't need your help."

"Whatever you say."

The man glared at McVey, and his voice grew more strident. "I'm through playing games." He put his face close to McVey's and said in a slow, angry tone, "Get off my stool, or I'll pull you off it."

McVey's smile wavered, and for a brief moment there was a crack in his facade, allowing a quick peek at the harsh intention beyond the smile. "Do you know why football players wear shoulder pads?"

"Who gives a shit?"

"Because it only takes seven pounds of pressure to break a collarbone."

"All right, asshole, I'm done talking."

What happened next happened quickly — and brought the confrontation to an abrupt end. The man stepped closer and made two mistakes, both of them costly. First he came within striking distance, and then he put his hands on a federal agent. The wrong federal agent. In the blink of an eye, McVey swung his beer mug up and over his head, slamming it on the man's clavicle and breaking the bone in half. The man fell to his knees, clutching his worthless arm and cursing up a storm.

McVey shook his head. "There's always one in every crowd."

Gold glanced at the bartender, who was staring at them with his mouth open. He tossed a fifty dollar bill on the bar, then said, "I think we've worn out our welcome."

McVey nodded. "We should leave."

"I'll lead the way."

"If you insist."

"Don't forget to keep a low profile."

"Shut up."

CHAPTER NINE

McVey insisted driving Gold to Long Beach, which gave them plenty of time to formulate a plan and decide on their next move. They even had enough time to reminisce about their glory days in high school, bragging about cheerleader conquests and wrestling victories that might have been imaginary. Under normal circumstances, McVey would have joined them for dinner, but as he explained, he was on his way to Freeport to celebrate his parents' anniversary.

Gino's, as usual, was packed. Finding a long line and a crowded foyer, Gold was glad that Irene had made a reservation. Walk-ins were welcome, but during the warm weather months the wait could be interminable. There were many good restaurants in Nassau County, but Gino's Restaurant and Pizzeria was in a league of its own. In Gold's opinion, it was not only the best Italian eatery in Long Beach, but on all of Long Island.

Gino's had opened its doors in 1962, founded by Gino Branchinelli, the culinary genius who created the famous Italian ices that bore his name. There was no other restaurant that could match its menu, and despite the crowd, Gold couldn't wait to dive into a plate of linguine di mare.

Irene Kaminski had arrived early, and she had taken the liberty of ordering a bottle of Chianti. When Gold sat down, she poured him a glass of wine, then said, "You're late."

"Actually, you're early."

She glanced at her watch. "Never contradict your boss."

"I do it all the time."

"Don't remind me." She poured herself some wine. "If you're hungry, we can order."

"I can wait."

She sat brooding for a half minute and finally said, "How did it go with Kemmler?"

"*"Comme ci, comme ca."*

"Should I order another bottle?"

"The news isn't bad, just a little weird."

"I'm listening."

Gold drained his glass, but before he began his tale of woe, he asked her about something that had been on his mind all day long. Something about the file they had on Kemmler. Anchor Insurance kept files on a lot of bad actors, but Kemmler's file was unusually thick, and most of the pages had been added by Irene Kaminski. Gold knew that because her initials — I.K. — were on the bottom of the pages. He smiled disarmingly, then said, "Am I missing something?"

"What do you mean?"

"You seem to have taken an unusual interest in Kemmler."

She fiddled with her silverware, avoiding eye contact. "He doesn't interest me in the least."

"Why the thick file?"

"Just doing my job. Keeping tabs on the enemy." She looked up and gave him a weak smile. "You know the old saying. Better safe than sorry."

Gold thought he knew what she meant, so he forged ahead, giving her a description of Kemmler's shop and its inventory of Western Americana. She found it puzzling but not worth dwelling upon. Then he told her about the request to amend the trip transit policy, and that startled her. She found it hard to believe that anybody would drop a lawsuit in order to insure two shipments of merchandise. It just didn't make any sense.

Kaminski leaned in close and murmured, "He's up to something."

"Definitely."

"What the hell does he want to ship?"

Gold started to explain, then stopped, then started again when he realized there was no good way to spin the bad news. He braced himself for the third-degree that was sure to follow, then said, "Alamo artifacts."

"Alamo artifacts?"

"A rifle and a sword."

"That's it?"

"That's it."

She thought swiftly. "They must be pretty damn valuable."

"According to Kemmler, they're priceless."

"Priceless?"

"Because of who owned them."

"Who might that be?"

"Are you familiar with the story of the Alamo?"

She nodded. "I took two years of American history."

"According to Bazooka Joe, they belonged to Davy Crockett and Colonel Travis."

Kaminski looked at him to see if he was serious. He appeared to be. She lapsed into a brooding silence for a minute or two, then a smirk thinned her lips. "The man's crazy."

"Crazy as a fox. He plans to donate the artifacts to the state of Texas. I don't know the real reason, but he claims to be concerned with the betterment of mankind."

"We both know what he could do to make things better."

"Uh-huh."

"How did our generous benefactor obtain the artifacts?"

"Through a middleman. He refused to divulge the man's identity — for security reasons."

She thought about that for a bit, then said, "Did you actually see the weapons?"

Gold nodded, cleared his throat, and said in near disbelief, "The rifle bore the name 'D. Crockett,' and the sword was engraved with the initials 'W.B.T.' Both were in poor condition, so I couldn't really tell how old they were."

She folded her arms across her chest and appeared sullen, saying nothing for a moment. "Most people wouldn't part with a reproduction, much less a genuine artifact. There's something rotten in the state of Denmark."

"You don't buy the 'betterment of mankind' routine?"

She swallowed the obscenity that was on her tongue and shook her head. "Not for a second."

"Neither do I, but Kemmler's donation wouldn't be the first. Ever hear of Phil Collins?"

"How old do you think I am? Of course I've heard of him."

"Well, believe it or not, he once owned a major collection of Alamo memorabilia. According to Kemmler, he donated the entire collection to the state of Texas."

"When?"

"About eight years ago."

"Interesting."

Gold stared at her, struck by another thought. "Kemmler might be trying to capitalize on the publicity."

"I wouldn't put it past him."

"There's one big difference, though. The Collins collection was supported by provenance. Kemmler couldn't produce a single shred of evidence."

"Nothing?"

"Nada."

"Well, there you go. Another bad sign."

"We spent some time going over the terms and conditions of a trip transit policy, and he didn't have a problem with the coverage, deductible, or limits. He was even prepared to sign a letter of intent." He reached into his sport coat pocket and handed her an envelope. "I told him that it had to be signed by a corporate officer."

She opened the envelope and read the letter. After a while, she looked up, her head cocked, wearing a slight frown. "Why do I feel like I'm walking into quicksand?"

"Allow me to throw you a lifeline."

Before Gold could finish his thought, a perky waitress appeared at his side, asking if they were ready to order. Kaminski ordered cavatelli Bolognese and Gold went with his favorite dish, linguine di mare. When the waitress left, Kaminski leaned over the table and stared at Gold with an unsettling intensity. "What were you saying about a lifeline?"

"You'll never guess who I ran into today. Come to think of it, he almost ran into me."

"Who?"

"Kevin McVey."

She smiled indulgently. "What's that rascal been up to?"

"He's no longer with the Department of Energy. He now works for HHS. As a matter of fact, he's leading a task force against human trafficking."

"Good for him."

"Good for us, too." He beckoned her closer. "He's after a creep named Joseph Kemmler."

She stared at him, caught by surprise, as if she were unsure how to react to the news. Finally, she took a sip of wine, then said, "What a lovely coincidence."

"Our generous benefactor is up to his neck in trafficking, and the feds are determined to throw his ass in a cell. McVey's in charge, and he's willing to do whatever it takes — which is where we come in. He thinks we should work together, and maybe, if we're lucky, we can nail Kemmler on state and federal charges. Insurance fraud and tax fraud. Two felonies, two long prison sentences. How does that sound?"

Kaminski nodded in a noncommittal way, but other than that did not respond. Sensing her uncertainty, Gold told her about the plan that he and McVey had hatched on the way to Long Beach. If Irene agreed to issue a policy, then Kemmler would have to notify the Anchor Insurance Company about his shipments, providing the name of the transit carrier and the exact dates of transit. Once they had that information, the task force could monitor the shipment and keep a watchful eye on the artifacts. Sooner or later, they were bound to be the catalyst for a crime, and if all went well, the bad guys could be rounded up in one fell swoop.

The plan wasn't perfect, but Gold thought it could work.

Kaminski was almost convinced. *Not half bad,* she told herself. *Well thought out.* She digested the idea for a minute and then said, "McVey's a smart cookie. A good strategist. He understands that in unity there is strength."

"Kemmler's a tricky bastard. We could use all the help we can get."

"Well, that's true, but..." Her words trailed off, and she began to fiddle with her silverware again.

Gold frowned. "But what?"

"I'm not in the habit of working with a federal agency."

"You don't have to worry about McVey. He's what you call a straight shooter."

"I wish you'd invited him to join us."

"I did. He had a previous engagement."

She seemed genuinely disappointed. "A date?"

"Parents' anniversary."

"Sweet."

Gold was confused by her reaction. He had expected her to enthusiastically embrace their plan; instead, there was an undeniable hesitancy in her voice. "We thought you might need further convincing." He handed her a newspaper clipping from *USA Today* and asked her to read it. "McVey gave me the clipping on the way here. Take your time."

Kaminski read the article slowly, her face taking on almost a pained expression. The article described the recent arrest of a Mexican art dealer who had tried to sell a vase and paintings purportedly created by Keith Haring, the artist who became famous for his subway drawings before his death in 1990. The art dealer had created his own provenance documents and then contacted a number of New York auction houses, hoping they would sell the artwork to an unsuspecting buyer. The FBI's art crime unit had assisted with the investigation, which was now being handled by the US attorney for the Southern District of New York.

A long, uncomfortable silence ensued. Finally, Gold spoke. "The art dealer is facing a maximum of twenty years in prison."

Kaminski looked at him, a smile playing across her lips. "Two decades behind bars. What a wonderful thought." Her voice dropped to a near whisper. "I have one suggestion. I think we should assign the transit company. Once we agree on a carrier, we can plant a person on the inside to keep an eye on the insured property."

"Do you think that's really necessary?"

"The feds will be focused on Kemmler. I'd like to nail the bastard, but I'd also like to prevent a loss."

"Makes sense. Who do you have in mind for the job?"

Kaminski took a deep breath, as if what she had to say was going to be physically painful. "Someone who understands claims. Someone who's not afraid of Kemmler. Someone I can trust." She bit the corner of her lip, lowered her head demurely and looked out the tops of her eyes at him — her little girl look. "Let's get another bottle." Allowing a full grin, she added, "I think you'll need more wine."

CHAPTER TEN

While Gold waited for news about the transit company that would ship Kemmler's artifacts, he decided to educate himself about antique firearms, which were clearly defined in the National Firearms Act. Legally speaking, an antique was "any firearm not intended or redesigned for using rim fire or conventional center fire ignition with fixed ammunition and manufactured in or before 1898." By definition, this included matchlock, flintlock, and percussion cap weapons.

As Gold discovered, detecting a fake antique rifle was difficult at best, mainly because they were so rare and there was little to compare them to. Realizing that he was a neophyte, he turned to Victor Wong, a trusted friend, for help. Wong was the owner of Jade Electronics, a Chinatown establishment that specialized in surveillance equipment and all sorts of gadgets used for legal — and mostly illegal — snooping.

Wong was also a world-class gun collector and an acknowledged expert on firearms. "The Mensch of Mott Street," as Gold liked to call him, would hopefully agree to a short tutorial, but that would depend on how well he'd slept the night before.

When Gold entered the store, he nearly tripped over a fat, Siamese cat, and that set the stage for another memorable visit. The commotion startled Wong, who was reading something on his laptop, but he smiled when he saw who was there. He closed the computer, then waved Gold forward. "Careful, my friend. Bad luck to step on cat."

"Bad luck for me or him?"

"Her."

Gold pulled himself together with a visible effort. "Do you have a parking permit for that animal?"

"She parks wherever she pleases."

"Like my wife. Ever hear of a trip-and-fall claim?"

"You'd be wise to remember a Chinese proverb." Wong hid his grin by looking down at the floor. "A man who cannot tolerate small misfortunes can never accomplish great things."

Gold let out a halfhearted chuckle. "I can tolerate cats. Your proverbs are a different story." He pulled a chair around and straddled it backward. "Did I interrupt your mah-jongg game?"

"I wasn't playing mah-jongg. For your information, I was scouring the Internet on your behalf."

"You don't say."

"I was searching for articles about antique weapons."

"Find anything interesting?"

Wong smiled. "Patience is a bitter plant, but its fruit is sweet."

"I'm not interested in fruit, only flintlocks."

"When you called, you mentioned a .40-caliber longrifle. A weapon of that sort would be quite old. Quite rare, too. The longrifle has many names, but most people refer to the weapon as a Kentucky rifle or a Pennsylvania rifle. Both were first produced in southeastern Pennsylvania, at the beginning of the eighteenth century. An original weapon in good condition could be worth a lot of money. Did you find one?"

Gold didn't answer. Instead, he brought his feet up on a box in front of him, resting his elbows on the top of the chair. After what seemed like a long time, he said, "What makes them so valuable?"

"Age and artwork. The older the better, assuming the rifle is still in working order. Artistically, the longrifle is famous for its maple stock and ornate decoration. Some rifles are truly works of art."

Wong poured himself a cup of green tea, took a tentative sip, and then gave Gold a brief seminar on the history of the weapon. From what he'd learned, the original longrifles were rather plain, but by the start of the nineteenth century, ornate decoration had become popular and gunsmiths began to add custom stocks, silver inlays, wood carving, and decorative engraving. He popped a piece of an almond cookie into his mouth and chewed thoughtfully. "If I remember correctly, the flintlock has a range of eighty to one hundred yards, but a skilled shooter can often hit a target at two to three hundred yards. Not bad for a hand-built rifle."

Gold nodded. "Not bad at all." He chewed his lip a moment in thought. "How much are they worth?"

"Depends on the age, condition, and how much a person is willing to pay. Do you watch the *Antiques Roadshow?*"

"I try to avoid television."

"The wise man knows that learning is a weightless treasure that can easily be carried."

Gold opened his mouth and then closed it again. He muttered something, shifted position, then said, "What were you going to say about the show?"

"A few years ago they featured an 1810 Kentucky rifle. In good condition. It was appraised at twenty thousand dollars."

Gold looked at him, expressionless. "How would a person build a reproduction?"

Frowning in concentration, Wong told him that building a reproduction would be relatively simple. Over the past fifty years, hobbyists had gained a new interest in custom-made longrifles, and nowadays there were organizations like the CLA — Contemporary Longrifle Association — that offered all sorts of advice and guidance. Parts and supplies were readily available from a number of manufacturers, including Dixie Gun Works, Track of the Wolf, and Stonewall Creek Outfitters.

Gold's expression grew serious. "How would someone like me know the difference between the genuine article and a reproduction?"

"Well, you'd start by checking the provenance — if there was one."

"What if there wasn't one?"

Wong made a skeptical face. "I would be worried."

"Worry is a useless emotion."

"Chinese proverb?"

Gold smiled. *"Psychology Today."*

Wong stood up, put his bony hands on the small of his back, and twisted his torso. His spine cracked. "Step two would be weapon dating," he said at last. "You'd need to find a specialist, someone with in-depth knowledge of authentic materials and craftsmanship."

"Where would I find such a person?"

"You're looking at one. I have my own test lab in the basement."

"Seriously?"

"Guessing is cheap, but guessing wrong can be expensive."

Gold sighed. "What sort of tests do you conduct?"

"Visual examination under light and magnification. Metallurgic analysis, X-ray, and, on special occasions, magnetic resonance imaging."

"*Special occasions?*"

"When my son-in-law can sneak me into his medical clinic."

Gold assumed he was joking, but it didn't make much of a difference, because the services he provided required an actual "sample," and there was no way he was going to get his hands on Kemmler's flintlock, or the sword.

After listening to Chinese proverbs, Gold had another thought. *If the mountain will not come to Muhammad, then Muhammad must go to the mountain.* Maybe it was time to think outside the box. He waited until Wong was done stretching, then said, "How's your back, Victor?"

Wong shrugged. "Touch of arthritis. My son-in-law prescribed hydroxychloroquine. Works pretty good."

"Would you be able to do some fieldwork?"

"I haven't worked in a field since I left China."

"Not that kind of fieldwork. I'm talking about research, exploration, breaking and entering."

Wong snorted a gruff little chuckle, half amused, half indignant. Time for another proverb. "The more acquaintances you have, the less you know them."

"I'm not sure what that means, but I'll take your word for it."

Wong rubbed one hand across his forehead as if he were tired, or getting a headache. "Do I look like a burglar to you? Do I?"

"No, but I thought you might be up for a caper."

"I'm too old for capers."

Gold looked at him with a stricken expression. "Where's your sense of adventure?"

"In the medicine cabinet." He looked at Gold and shook his head. "Aren't you a little old for that sort of thing?"

"What sort of thing?"

"Breaking and entering."

"You're never too old to break into a warehouse protected with barbed wire, armed guards, and vicious dogs."

Wong smiled, showing most of his tea-stained teeth. "If I didn't know you better, I'd think you had a death wish."

"Not hardly. I just need to find a partner in crime. Someone I can trust."

"Well, don't look at me. I'm already in trouble with the authorities."

Gold's mouth tightened. "Which authorities?"

"DHS."

"Department of Homeland Security?"

"Unfortunately."

"What's the problem?"

Wong chuckled darkly. "The problem? The problem is that when China snaps its fingers, people jump. Those bastards in Beijing have never forgiven me for protesting in Tiananmen Square in 1989. For over thirty years, I've been forbidden to visit or conduct business on the Chinese mainland. I can't even show my face in Hong Kong." He removed his small silver-rimmed glasses and began to clean the lenses with a tissue. "The People's Republic of China has a long memory, and they have tried to make my life miserable. From time to time they spread false rumors and whisper lies about me, trying to convince our government that I'm some sort of security threat."

Gold rose and started pacing. Several moments passed, and then he said, "How long have the feds been busting your chops?"

"Too long. I've been audited three times in the last seven years."

"Jesus, that's terrible."

"No, that's harassment."

"You're right."

Wong steadied himself against the desk. "I'm on the verge of taking legal action."

"Maybe I can help you out. I've got a friend at HHS. He's high up on the food chain. I'll put in a good word for you as soon as I get back to the office."

Wong was pleasantly surprised, as this was all news to him. "You're very kind. Perhaps I can repay your kindness."

"I sense another proverb."

"Well, I could say that a friend in need is a friend indeed, but I've got a better idea." He rummaged through a desk drawer and pulled out a rumpled business card. "Do you remember Christine Penny?"

"No, but the name sounds familiar."

"She used to work for the Anchor Insurance Company." He gave Gold the card. "She was an inland marine underwriter. She retired four years ago. Moved to the Pocono Mountains and became an appraiser of antique weapons. Very smart woman." A small, contented smile settled on his face. "She also has a wild streak."

Gold studied the card, thinking. "Where is Bangor, Pennsylvania?"

"Eastern part of the state. Close to Stroudsburg."

"Near the Delaware Water Gap?"

"Twenty miles south."

"Scenic country."

"Edge of the Lehigh Valley. Very remote."

Gold's mind clicked into high gear. "Did she have red hair?"

"Red hair and freckles."

"Attractive woman? Always smiling?"

"Yes, that's Christine."

"I remember her. We used to chat on the elevator. I think she lived in Brooklyn. In Bensonhurst. Maybe Sheepshead Bay."

"I'm not sure where she lived, but she was a character."

"How do you know she has a wild streak?"

Wong found the question amusing, but he gave a serious answer. "If you were a single woman, would you live in bear country by yourself?"

CHAPTER ELEVEN

Three days later, Irene Kaminski convened a meeting in her office, attended by an in-house attorney, Adam Gold, and Marvin Katz. The purpose of the meeting was to finalize the agreement between the Anchor Insurance Company and Joseph Kemmler. As previously agreed, Kemmler would drop his lawsuit against the company — and the nursing home they insured — in exchange for the issuance of a trip transit policy.

After going over the terms and conditions one last time, the in-house attorney, whose name was Jarrett Musumeci, asked both parties to sign and date two copies of the agreement. Each party got a copy, and then Musumeci, a wunderkind from Miami School of Law, informed them that they were now subject to a binding contract.

The whole process stuck in Kaminski's craw, but she politely dismissed her legal representative and waited until he was gone before turning her ire on Katz. "You realize this is blackmail."

Katz shook his head and steeled himself for a lecture. Truth was, it didn't matter. He was holding a signed contract. "You win some, you lose some," he said with a smile. "Don't be a sore loser. It doesn't become you."

She resisted the temptation to deliver a swift kick to Katz's head, but it wasn't easy. "I'm glad you're pissed, but I don't see what you've won."

"All in good time my dear."

"Please don't call me dear. It grates on my nerves."

Gold cleared his throat. "I have a question for Clarence Darrow." He looked directly at Katz. "When we met for lunch, did you know that your client only wanted to cover two shipments?"

"No, I was surprised by that, too."

"Do you know what he's shipping?"

"A couple of artifacts."

"Alamo artifacts."

Katz gave a bored yawn. "I couldn't care less."

"You don't care?"

"Not in the least."

"That's odd."

"To be perfectly honest, I feel that I was retained under false pretenses. I thought there'd be a trial, a favorable verdict, a huge judgment. All of sudden my client decides to play *Let's Make A Deal*. Boom! No win, no windfall. I'm working for peanuts."

Gold glanced at Kaminski, wondering if she was thinking the same thing he was — that Katz had no earthly idea what his client was up to. Maybe the street-smart lawyer wasn't so smart after all. Maybe Kemmler had kept him in the dark all along, playing him for a sucker until he got what he wanted. Jesus, could Marvelous Marvin be that dumb?

Only one way to find out, Gold thought. "Your client is shipping a rifle and a sword."

"Good for him."

"Two priceless artifacts."

"Priceless?"

"If they're genuine."

"What do you mean, if they're genuine?"

"There's no provenance. Nothing to prove who owned them."

Kaminski broke in, hoping to stir the pot. "Kemmler made a bold claim. He told us that the rifle belonged to Davy Crockett and the sword to Colonel Travis. He intends to donate both items."

Katz almost fell off his chair when he heard about the artifacts, but like any good lawyer, he recovered quickly, barely acknowledging his shock. His mind began to race. The wheels turning rapidly. Deep down he knew he'd been taken for a ride, but he would deal with that later. Right now he had to focus on recouping his losses. "Have you seen the artifacts?"

Kaminski shook her head. "Gold saw them."

"When?"

Gold answered. "When we met."

Katz raised an eyebrow. "You met Kemmler?"

"A few days ago. I stopped by his store to have a little chat."

"You had no right to do that."

"All's fair in love and war."

"I'll have to remember that."

"I'm sure you will."

"So tell me something, now that you've seen the artifacts. Do you think they're real?"

"They're real all right. I just don't know who they belonged to. If they were actually owned by Crockett and Travis, they'd be worth a fortune." He sighed theatrically. "Too bad you don't have a piece of the action."

Katz hid his anger. "Haven't you heard that money is the root of all evil?"

"Sure, but I'd still be pleased."

"Que será, será."

"Yeah, what can you do. Some guys have all the luck."

Katz was fuming, but he kept calm and stayed on point. Years of courtroom haggling had taught him how to stay cool and elicit information, which was precisely what he was attempting to do. "What do you think those artifacts are worth?"

"God only knows. A number with a lot of zeros."

Kaminski began to file one of her fingernails, pretending to be absorbed in the task. "How does it feel to be out of the loop?"

Katz glared at her. "I'm sure my client has a reasonable explanation."

"If you say so."

Gold chuckled, loud enough to attract Katz's attention. "Would you be good enough to deliver a message? Kemmler's waiting for the name of the transit company we want to use. We have two recommendations. One at LaGuardia, the other at JFK. Both reliable firms."

Katz frowned. "You're not using consolidated freight?"

"They won't accept such valuable items."

"Kemmler would choose LaGuardia. It's closer."

"Fine with us." He gave Katz the name and address of the air freight company. "The company will pick up the artifacts tomorrow and ship them to Texas the following day. They handle all the paperwork, packing, and transfers, so all Kemmler has to do is point them in the right direction."

"Easy enough."

"Any questions?"

Katz showed his teeth in what was definitely not a friendly smile. "No, I think I understand the situation."

Kaminski stood up, a signal that the meeting was over. Nobody shook hands, but Katz did thank them for their time. After he left the office, she turned toward Gold. "Well, that was fun."

Gold flashed a wicked smile. "I think we put a bee in his bonnet."

"I hope so. He deserves to feel the sting of defeat."

Later that evening, as storm clouds gathered over the city, Katz left his Park Avenue law office and took a cab up to East 69th Street, hoping to squeeze some money out of Kemmler. He'd spent a good deal of time preparing for a legal battle, and now that his client had thrown in the towel, he felt cheated. Cheated out of a courtroom victory. Cheated out of praise. Cheated out of money.

Nobody was going to make a fool out of Marvin Katz.

Kemmler had left the door unlocked, so Katz was able to enter the store and lock the door behind him. The ditzy brunette secretary was on the phone again, but this time she didn't bother to look up. In his gut, Katz knew that confronting Kemmler was risky, but he figured he could talk his way out of trouble, and besides, he'd only be asking for a fair share of the loot. Little did he know that fairness would be the last thing on Kemmler's mind.

Katz marched through the store in a huff, building up steam. When he burst into Kemmler's office, he found him in repose on a divan, sipping a cognac from a "tulip" glass. The sight of his client sprawled out, seemingly without a care in the world, was infuriating. He walked across the room and planted himself in front of the divan, fists clenched. Sucking in a deep breath, he said, "What the fuck is wrong with you, Kemmler?"

Kemmler didn't move a muscle, and he took his time responding. "Tsk-tsk. Such awful language."

"You haven't heard anything yet."

"Have a seat, Mr. Katz. Pour yourself some cognac."

"I don't want to sit down, and I don't want a goddamn drink. I want to know why you met with Adam Gold behind my back."

"You're my lawyer, Mr. Katz. Not my babysitter. I'll meet whomever I please, whenever I please."

"You went behind my back!"

"You're wrong about that. Gold showed up unannounced. Uninvited. What was I supposed to do? Throw him out?"

"You didn't have to talk to him."

"What's done is done."

Katz looked at him with contempt. "You didn't tell me about the policy change. If I'd known there were just two shipments, I could have negotiated a better deal."

"I'm not complaining."

"Well, I'm complaining. You made me look like a schmuck. You should have consulted with me."

"Next time."

"There won't be a next time."

Kemmler exhaled sharply and gave Katz a look that said his patience was gone. "Look, to be perfectly honest, the policy change occurred to me at the last moment. I thought it might lower my premium. No such luck."

Katz scoffed and shook his head. "So you sold your soul to cover two lousy shipments. What a moron."

Kemmler stared coldly at him, the sudden anger narrowing his eyes. "I don't care for your name-calling, Mr. Katz."

"Get used to it, pal. You're on my shit list."

"How unfortunate."

Katz got a little better control of his anger and said, "Let's get down to brass tacks. Those artifacts can generate some big bucks. How the hell did you get your grubby hands on Daniel Boone's rifle?"

Inwardly, Kemmel sighed. "Davy Crockett, Mr. Katz. The rifle belonged to Davy Crockett."

"Whatever. You never mentioned a word about him or that other guy, the one that owned the sword."

"Colonel Travis."

"Why all the secrecy? Don't you trust me?"

Kemmler answered with mounting irritation. "Frankly, it was none of your business."

"None of my business?" He swore under his breath and then said very slowly, "Let me tell you something, my kraut friend. I busted my ass for you, and I'm entitled to something more than a handshake. Do you understand what I'm saying?"

Kemmler stood, leaned forward, and said with a suave smile, "Not exactly."

"You owe me, Kemmler. I want a cut of the action."

"You can't be serious."

"You bet your Prussian ass I'm serious. Either you cough up some dough, or I start making trouble. Which is it gonna be?"

Kemmler said nothing, but his physical demeanor changed. His face, already hard, turned to stone. His eyes narrowed again, the lips went tight, the jaw muscles by his ears quivered. He stood motionless for a while, then said, "Maybe you're right. Maybe you deserve a cut."

Regaining his composure, Katz feigned a smile. "I thought you'd see it my way."

Without another word, Kemmler walked over to the armoire, pulled out the antique sword, turned, and stabbed Katz in the chest. Chuckling under his breath, he said, "Here's your goddamn cut!"

Katz tried to speak, but a knotting sensation gripped his chest. He stumbled backward, staring at Kemmler in disbelief. He forced himself to take a breath, but then he began to cough up blood. Looking down, he saw a large red spot near his heart. A moment later, his knees buckled and he fell to the floor, gasping for air.

Kemmler stood over him for a moment, then said, *"Auf wiedersehen, mein Jüdischer freund."*

CHAPTER TWELVE

The next day, after a hearty breakfast at the Valbrook Diner, Gold and McVey drove to Pennsylvania, hoping to convince Christine Penny to join them on a caper. The plan, so to speak, was to sneak into the warehouse at LaGuardia Airport and conduct a basic metallurgical test on Kemmler's artifacts. Hopefully she would be able to work her magic without attracting too much attention and, in the process, provide an educated guess about the age of the artifacts.

McVey was uncomfortable with the breaking and entering part, but there was no other way to enter the premises without being seen. He kept his thoughts to himself while they were driving in New York, but as soon as they crossed the George Washington Bridge, he spoke up. "Tell me about this woman. Christine Penny. How'd she come into the picture?"

"She was highly recommended for the job."

"Who recommended her?"

"Victor Wong."

McVey gave him a bleak smile, then said, "How is that old rascal?"

"Limping along."

"Still quoting proverbs?"

"Every chance he gets."

"He'll never change."

"I hope not." Gold glanced sidelong at McVey, sensing the time was right to ask a favor. "Do you have any friends at DHS?"

"A few. Why do you ask?"

Gold told him that the feds were hassling Wong on behalf of the Chi-coms. He also explained why they were giving him a hard time. "They're making life hard for the poor guy. Maybe you could put in a good word for him?"

"I'll see what I can do." He looked out the window, thinking. "How does Wong know Christine Penny?"

"She used to work for Anchor Insurance. Inland marine underwriter. They're both gun lovers. He didn't say how they met."

"When was the last time you saw her?"

"Four years ago."

"Does she know we're coming?"

"I tried to reach her by phone, but nobody answered."

"So she may not be home?"

"Keep your fingers crossed."

McVey didn't like the sound of that, but he let it pass. How, he wondered, did he let himself be talked into such a harebrained scheme? Knowing Gold, something was bound to go wrong. So much for experience being the best teacher.

They spent the next hour and a half reminiscing about the joys of growing up on Long Island, and as usual, they covered a lot of ground: Jones Beach, pizza parlors, Nathan's, wrestling matches, and the New York Yankees. They reached the outskirts of Bangor before they had a chance to discuss the opposite sex, but that was no big loss, since they'd both be telling lies.

The town of Bangor was located in eastern Pennsylvania, in an area known as the Slate Belt — despite the fact that there were only a handful of quarries still in operation. The population was around six thousand, and most of the residents were of German, Welsh, and Pennsylvania Dutch descent.

Driving down Main Street it became clear that Bangor had seen its better days, if it had any. McVey joked that it looked like the type of town where minimum wage was a great salary. A town so small the local phone book had only one yellow page.

Gold let him vent, more concerned with finding Oak Street, which was supposed to be near South Main. After several wrong turns, they asked for directions and were directed to a two-story frame house adjacent to St. Johns Cemetery. The house was old and sorely in need of a fresh coat of paint, but the front yard was in decent shape, the lawn recently mowed and edged. The beds were filled with colorful flowers, mostly columbine, asters, and coreopsis. A tall hemlock and two red maples provided shade.

All in all, just what Gold had pictured.

McVey looked the place over and sighed. "Nobody's home."

"How can you tell?"

"There are two newspapers on the lawn."

"Maybe she's a slow reader."

"Maybe you should ring the doorbell."

Gold was halfway up the front walk when the garage door opened and a man dressed in bib overalls greeted him. He looked vaguely familiar, but Gold couldn't place him. He introduced himself as Steve Penny, the brother of the homeowner.

Gold handed him a business card, then said, "Have we met before?"

Penny studied the card, then smiled. "Five years ago. We met on John Street — or rather, under it. I was doing some cable work for Con-Ed and you were escorting my sister to the subway station. You've got a good memory."

"How's my sense of timing?"

"What do you mean?"

"I came to see Christine. Is she home?"

"No, I'm afraid not. She flew to Nashville yesterday. She's attending a longrifle convention. She'll be gone about a week."

Gold was crestfallen, but he tried not to overreact. "A whole week?"

"I'm afraid so."

"Too bad. I was hoping to talk to her."

"Anything wrong?"

"No, not at all. The Anchor Insurance Company is having a reunion, and I'm on the contact committee."

"Would you like her cell phone number?"

"Sure, that would be great."

He wrote his sister's number on a slip of paper, then handed it to Gold. "She'll be happy you called."

"Well, it's been a while. I hope she remembers me."

"I wouldn't worry about that. She talks about you from time to time. She always admired your investigative skills."

Gold smiled. "Do you know where she's staying in Nashville?"

"The Hermitage Hotel. I think it's downtown."

"Yeah, close to Music Row."

"I wanted to join her, but my back flared up."

"Arthritis?"

"No, I got injured on the job. I had to take early retirement."

"Tough break."

"I don't mind. The job was killing me."

"I know how you feel."

Steve glanced over Gold's shoulder, then waved at McVey, who was still sitting in the car. "Would you and your friend like a beer or something?"

"Thanks, but we've got a few other stops to make."

"Maybe next time."

"Definitely." They shook hands, then Gold turned to leave. He took a couple of steps, then stopped in his tracks and turned around. "By the way, you might want to pick up those newspapers. No sense advertising your sister's absence."

"Christine was right. You don't miss a trick."

McVey took one look at Gold's face and knew that the trip had been a complete waste of time. He didn't know why, but he was sure of it, and he couldn't contain himself. "Well," he said, crossing his arms, "this is another fine mess you've gotten me into."

"She went to Nashville."

"Figures."

Gold managed a brief smile. "All is not lost."

"The eternal optimist."

"We should take advantage of this opportunity."

"What did you have in mind?"

"First we grab lunch, then we drive up to Columcille Megalith Park."

McVey stared at him, faintly annoyed. "What the hell is Columbine Megadeath Park?"

"Pennsylvania's version of Stonehenge."

"Never heard of the place."

"You need to get out more often."

"I need to get out of this car."

"Relax, pardner. You're in for a treat." He turned his wrist a little so he could see his watch. Twelve on the nose. "By the way, I'm paying for lunch."

Scowling, McVey sat back, unable — or unwilling — to put his thoughts into words. There were times when Florida, even with sinkholes, seemed so inviting. "Find a lunch place that serves beer."

"Want to drown your sorrows?"

"I'd rather drown you, but I'm so close to retirement."

Lunch was a quick affair at Renee's Cafe on South Main, and then it was off to the park, which was located five miles north of town. Gold had done his homework, so while they were driving, he explained what they were about to see. The park billed itself as a Celtic-inspired outdoor sanctuary providing space for quiet meditation, inspired by the Isle of Iona, off the coast of Scotland. The tiny island of Iona had been a source of spiritual guidance dating back to the seventh century, but it was best known for its monastic community established by St. Columba and a group of twelve companions who sailed to Ireland in 563 AD.

The present day park also had a unique history. It was supposedly inspired by a vision received by William H. Cohea, an American Presbyterian minister. The reverend claimed to have received his vision during a visit to Iona, and when he returned to America in 1975, he purchased twenty acres of land and began to recreate a smaller version of Stonehenge.

The name of the park, a mouthful by any standard, came from two places: St. Columcille, the sixth-century monk, and the word *megalith*, which was a large, prehistoric stone.

Gold paid the ten-dollar admissions and pointed out that there were nearly one hundred stone monuments in the park, the largest being twenty feet high and weighing roughly forty-five tons. He smiled, cocked his head, and gave the grounds the once-over. "Pretty impressive, eh?"

McVey was almost at a loss for words. "Give me a moment," he said at last. "I'm trying to contain my excitement."

"You have to admit it's different."

"Different is a good word."

"You don't think it looks like Stonehenge?"

"No offense, Fred, but it reminds me of Bedrock."

"Very funny." He walked under an arch, admiring its massive stones. "There's something magical about this place."

McVey found a bench and sat down, then asked Gold to sit beside him. "Since we're on the subject of magic, are you familiar with the term misdirection? It's a form of deception in which the magician draws attention to one thing to distract it from another. Sometimes it works, sometimes it doesn't. Depends on the audience. Do you get my drift, Houdini?"

"I think so."

"Stop being tricky, and tell me what's on your mind."

Gold stood up and began to pace, an old habit that helped him think. He didn't have an earth-shattering confession to make, but he did have something on his mind. "Irene's concerned about a loss, so she asked me to keep an eye on the artifacts."

"A man on the inside?"

"Exactly. She arranged for me to pose as a risk manager, which, strangely enough, is what I'd be."

McVey closed his eyes and sighed, leaning his forearms on his thighs and letting his hands dangle between his knees. He looked tired and maybe a little worried. "The shipment will be closely monitored, but it's fine with me if you want to keep an eye on the merchandise."

"Just so you know, some of my best men will be aboard the plane when it leaves for Texas," Gold continued.

"I figured they might be."

Gold looked a bit sheepish. "One other thing. I was wondering if you could arrange a quick stop in Nashville. I'd like to meet with Christine Penny at the airport."

"You don't give up."

"Family trait."

"What's she doing in Nashville?"

"Attending a longrifle convention."

"Good timing."

"So what do you think? Can you make it happen?"

McVey gave it some thought. "One condition. No more tourist attractions."

"You drive a hard bargain."

"Excuse the humor, but it looks like you're stuck between a rock and a hard place."

CHAPTER THIRTEEN

Diverting the flight to Nashville International Airport required several phone calls to the FAA, but after some gentle coaxing, they agreed to an unscheduled stop. The airport code was BNA, a slightly confusing code that stood for Berry Field Nashville, in honor of Colonel Harry S. Berry, the administrator of the original airport project.

Gold had hoped to meet Christine Penny at the air cargo terminal, but her convention schedule did not permit a trip to the airport. Despite the risk, he agreed to bring the artifacts to The Music City Convention Center, which was located in the heart of downtown.

The two million square foot facility was hosting a regional meeting of the Contemporary Longrifle Association, a three-day event attended by gun enthusiasts from across the nation. The CLA had more than two thousand members and their annual meeting, held in Lexington, Kentucky, often featured three hundred to four hundred exhibitor tables. The Nashville event was considerably smaller, but still crowded with colorful characters, some dressed in frontier garb and coonskin caps.

Gold had no trouble finding Christine Penny, who was wearing an Annie Oakley costume and holding court behind a display table covered with muzzle-loading weapons. Even in costume, she looked the same. She was a sturdy woman, buxom and curvaceous at 5' 6" or so and around 150 pounds. She wore her long, red hair pulled back over her ears and gathered at the back of her head with an elastic band. When their eyes met, she waved him off to the side, and they exchanged pleasantries. Nudging him behind a small curtain, she said, "How do you like my outfit?"

"You're the prettiest cowgirl I've ever seen."

"I bet you say that to all the sharpshooters you meet."

"Well, I do aim to please."

She got the joke and laughed. "Sorry I missed you in Bangor."

"No problem. I'm glad you're keeping busy."

"I spoke to my brother this morning. He mentioned a company reunion."

"Well, that was actually a cover story. I'm really working on an insurance matter."

"Must be important if you flew down to Nashville."

"To tell you the truth, I'm on my way to Austin, Texas. But you're right, it's something important." He placed a long duffel bag at her feet, unzipped the bag, and took out Kemmler's artifacts. "Would you take a look at these weapons? I'm wondering how old they are."

She looked at the rifle and the sword with a startled expression. "When did you become a collector?"

"These aren't mine. I'm just trying to verify their age and authenticity."

"Should I ask why?"

"Probably not."

"One of those matters, eh?"

"You got it."

She fell silent a moment, her lips pressed tightly together. "I don't mean to be a nag, but the TSA requires that all weapons be packed in a hard-sided container with a proper lock. You should also be aware that black powder and percussion caps are banned."

"I flew down on a cargo plane."

"How did you manage that?"

Gold glanced around furtively. "Top secret."

She laughed again, and Gold thought it brought a whole new dimension to her face. It also made her look much younger. When she stopped laughing, she put on a pair of cotton gloves and picked up the rifle. Looking through a magnifying glass, she scanned the stock and barrel, then murmured, "Interesting."

Gold pulled his chair closer and lowered his voice. "Why the gloves?"

"Antiques should never be handled with bare hands. Skin oils can cause permanent damage."

Gold shook his head admiringly. "I should have guessed."

"The rifle's in decent condition, but it was stored incorrectly." She pointed to some small cracks, barely visible on the wooden stock. "Older rifles need to be stored at 70 degrees Fahrenheit, otherwise the wood will expand and begin to crack." Her eyes now focused on the barrel, and she did not look pleased. "Longrifles are rather finicky. They require fifty percent humidity in storage, otherwise the metal will corrode and crack. As you can see, this rifle has some permanent scars."

Gold gently touched the barrel with his index finger. "What's this gooey substance?"

"Microcrystalline wax."

"Sounds illegal."

"If it was illegal, I'd be in big trouble. The wax is used to protect metal from the elements, but it's also found in cosmetics, creams, lotions, mascara, lipstick, and eyeliner."

Gold shook his head in wonderment. "Wong was right. You're a veritable genius."

"I wouldn't go that far."

Gold stared at her, struck by another thought. "How did you and Victor meet?"

"We met at a gun show at the Javits Center. I was trying to decide whether to buy a dueling pistol or a musket, and Victor was kind enough to offer some advice — in the form of a Chinese proverb. After that he bought me a drink, and we became fast friends. He's such a dear man."

"Yeah, Victor's a good egg. I get most of my surveillance equipment from him."

"Have you seen his basement?"

"No, but I've heard he's got a full-blown lab."

"Everything a gun lover would need." She looked up from the rifle that was on her lap and lifted an eyebrow. "I'm surprised he referred you to me."

"He knew what he was doing."

"Well, let's see if I can live up to my billing." She found a plastic bottle that was filled with water and a mild detergent and proceeded to spray the stock of the rifle. Then she took a clean, dry cloth and wiped off all of the moisture. She did the same thing with the metal parts, spritzing the hammer, trigger, pan, frizzen, and barrel. When the rifle was dry, she examined her work using the magnifying glass. "I can tell you one thing. If this is a reproduction, it's a damn good one. The stock is cherry, the wood most commonly used in the nineteenth century." She told him that cherry, despite being a hardwood, was easy to shape and carve. There were at least fifteen different types of cherrywood, but black cherry was the most popular among early American gunsmiths. "Some longrifles were signed, but I don't see a signature on this one."

Gold felt something in his gut tighten. "What does that mean?"

"If I had to guess, I'd say this was a basic hunting rifle. The stock is simply adorned, without a butt plate or a patch box. The rifle would be more valuable if it was signed, but it's still got some nice features. For instance, it's American made, and it's a flintlock, which is worth more than a cap and ball rifle. It also has a full stock, which is more valuable than a half stock."

Gold rubbed his chin, thinking. "So regardless of its provenance, it's worth some money."

"Somewhere between twenty and forty thousand."

Gold smiled humorlessly. "Not too shabby."

Her next comment surprised him. "It could be worth more. A lot more."

"What do you mean?"

"Age isn't the only determining price factor. The condition of the rifle is also important, and there's even a rating system, ranging from excellent to poor. The most valuable weapons have something else in common: they're linked to a famous person or a major historical event. Sometimes both. If you get your hands on one of those bad boys, the sky's the limit. Speaking of bad boys, you might be wondering which gun is the most valuable in history." She gave him a moment to think, but when he couldn't come up with an answer, she said, "The single-shot .44 caliber derringer used by John Wilkes Booth to assassinate President Lincoln. Needless to say, it's priceless."

"I've seen that gun. It's on display at Ford's Theatre in Washington."

"The second most valuable firearm is the Mannlicher-Carcano rifle owned by Lee Harvey Oswald — the one he allegedly used to kill President Kennedy."

"I've seen that one, too. It's on display at the Sixth Floor Museum in Dallas."

"That's right, but what you saw is a replica. The actual rifle is kept in a secure location in the National Archives Building."

Gold looked a cross between perplexed and amused. "Is there anything you don't know about guns?"

"Several things. I don't know the exact age of your rifle, who built it, or where it was built. I can't even say for certain that it's the genuine article, although it feels authentic to me." She sounded frustrated. "If I were you, I'd bring it to an actual gunsmith. Somebody who could tap out the straight pins and examine the barrel. Many rifles were inscribed with the owner's initials, and you might discover his identity. Imagine how cool that would be."

"Sounds like wishful thinking."

"You think so?" She waved him closer, then lowered her voice to a near whisper. "Seven years ago, a gunmaker in Columbia, Tennessee, tapped out the pins of a two-hundred-year-old muzzle loading longrifle. When he examined the barrel, he discovered that it was inscribed with the initials 'S. & A. C.' Those were the initials of the gunmakers who operated a business at Forge Seat, the family home south of Nashville. Their full names were Samuel and Andrew Crockett. Father and son." She made no effort to disguise the fact that she was now enjoying herself. "Now for the best part. When the guy in Columbia examined the muzzle, he discovered that the number nineteen was engraved into the metal. At the breech was the number eleven, and in between was the letter 'C.' The number probably meant that the gun was number nineteen in a run of guns made in 1811, and the letter 'C' was for Crockett."

Gold tried his level best to remain calm, but her story had hit close to home. Too close. Reeling from this latest revelation, he struggled to control his voice. "Are you saying that the rifle belonged to Davy Crockett?"

"It was brought to the guy in Columbia by Crockett's descendants, and they had documents proving its authenticity."

Gold shifted uneasily in his chair. "How many Crockett rifles are out there?"

"Nobody knows for sure, but at least four or five."

"Four or five?"

"Those are the ones with provenance. There are others that are more questionable."

Gold looked incredulous and exasperated at the same time. His mind was racing. He'd been counting on Christine Penny to help him, but now she'd opened a wide range of possibilities. One of them would require a simple effort. He scrutinized the rifle a bit longer, then said, "Why don't we tap out the pins?"

She looked at him skeptically and he looked back, forcing his face to be blank. She held his eyes trying to determine if he was serious. "You want me to remove the pins?"

"How else can we examine the barrel?"

She shook her head. "I can't do that."

"Why not?"

"Well, for starters, I don't have a workbench."

"We could use your table."

"I would also have to borrow a hammer and a drift punch, and that would raise a few eyebrows."

"I don't need the attention."

"Do you have the time to drive down to Columbia?" Christine asked.

"How far is that from here?"

"About fifty miles."

"I-65 South?"

"I believe so."

He gave it some thought, but decided against it. Too far. Too much exposure. Better to keep a low profile. "What were those tools you needed?"

"A hammer and a drift punch."

"Are they available online?"

"Most likely. Why?"

"Maybe I could remove the pins when I get to Austin."

She pasted on a tolerant smile, keeping any anger out of her voice. She wanted to stay calm, but her friend was not making it easy for her. After she took a deep, steadying breath, she said, "I hope you're joking."

"How hard could it be?"

"If you don't do it right — exactly right — you could damage the rifle. Are you willing to risk forty thousand dollars?"

"Do you have a better idea?"

"As a matter of fact, I do. Tomorrow is the last day of our convention. Why don't I fly down to Austin and we can find a reliable gunsmith together? She gave him a sweet smile. "You know what they say. Two heads are better than one."

Gold took a moment to consider her offer, as if asking for help had never occurred to him. He was rather surprised that she would be willing to stick her neck out without knowing what was at stake. Or who they would be dealing with. After a while, he said, "You'd be willing to do that for me?"

"What are friends for?"

"You'd be a long way from home."

"As our Chinese friend might say, the journey of a thousand miles begins with a single step."

Gold did a double-take. "Are longrifles hard to load?"

"Just takes practice. Why do you ask?"

"If I hear another proverb, I'm might have to shoot myself."

CHAPTER FOURTEEN

The flight time from Nashville to Austin was relatively short, two hours and ten minutes door to door - or more accurately, cargo terminal to cargo terminal. The first task on the agenda was securing Kemmler's artifacts, which was a fairly simple procedure. Since 9/11, air cargo facilities had implemented all sorts of security, making it much more difficult to tamper with shipments. As Gold soon learned, the new measures included access control, site surveillance, physical security, mandatory background checks, and security threat assessments of all air cargo workers.

In-flight measures had also improved, with new protocols designed to prevent the hijacking or bombing of an aircraft using an explosive device carried in a cargo shipment. During the flight to Austin, Gold noticed that the plane had reinforced cockpit doors and that both of the pilots were armed. He later learned that the Homeland Security Act allowed pilots to fly armed, even though most carriers were hesitant to arm their pilots because of liability concerns.

Once they were off the tarmac, the freight forwarders took over, and their main job was to unload the cargo and make arrangements for distribution. Gold spoke to the man in charge and told him that the artifacts would remain in the terminal until someone claimed them in person. At that point, Gold was to be contacted, and hopefully make it back to the airport in time to question the recipient. In the meantime, he'd play a hunch and drop by the Texas General Land Office, the oldest state agency in Texas, often referred to as the GLO. If he got lucky, he might meet a talkative bureaucrat — if there was such a thing.

The lady at the rental car counter assured him that he'd have no trouble getting out of the airport, but after that, it was the luck of the draw. Reaching downtown should have been easy, as it was only ten miles away from the airport as the crow flies. A flying crow could have made the trip in a half hour, but any poor soul heading north had to contend with Interstate 35, aka "The Parking Lot." Nowadays, the parking lot was filled with a bunch of new arrivals from the blue states, and none of them gave a hoot about road etiquette.

Embassy Suites was right across the street from the Land Office, so Gold made a quick stop and reserved two adjacent rooms — one for himself and one for Christine Penny. He had just enough time to play his hunch. Dashing across the street, he was greeted at the entrance and given a handful of brochures to read. They were actually quite informative and provided a clear overview of the agency.

The GLO had been formed in 1836, ostensibly to determine who owned what and where after the Texas Revolution. Over the years it had morphed into something much bigger and was now responsible for the management of state lands, funding for public education, veterans benefits, and the operation of the Alamo. The importance of the agency could be seen in its premier location, 1700 Congress Avenue, the heart of downtown Austin.

Finding someone to talk to was easy, but finding someone who was willing to talk about artifacts was not. After shuttling between floors, Gold was directed to the Archives and Records Division, which was home to more than 35 million documents and 45,000 maps dating back to the year 1561. The records were housed in a state-of-the-art archival vault, and safety features included all the bells and whistles; continuously monitored temperature and humidity, UV filtered lighting, dedicated HVAC and air cleaning systems, and a fire control system that was second to none.

A young Hispanic woman agreed to meet with Gold, but she was clearly annoyed that he'd interrupted her scanning project. She gave him a weak facsimile of a smile, then introduced herself as Maria Mendez. *Ms.* Maria Mendez. "How can I help you, sir?"

Gold gave her a card. "I'm curious about your Alamo collection. The most recent additions."

A troubled expression clouded her face. She peeled off her eyeglasses with a slow, measured motion and looked at him. "You're an investigator."

"Insurance investigation."

She let the silence extend for a moment. Finally, she asked quietly, "What are you investigating, Mr. Gold?"

"I'm afraid that's confidential."

She watched him closely, wariness gathering inside her. What the hell was this about? Did he really work for the Anchor Insurance Company? "You're a long way from home."

"One thousand seven hundred and forty-two miles." He smiled at her. "I'm a UT graduate. I lived in Austin for six years."

"It took you six years to graduate?"

"I was ahead of the other students."

She was not amused. "I might have to check with your employer."

"Be my guest. The number's on the card."

For a long moment, she just glared, as if weighing her words, and then she glanced at her watch. "They're probably closed for the day."

Gold exhaled heavily and shook his head. The happy-go-lucky facade disintegrated. He rubbed his face in a weary gesture. "Do I detect a note of hostility in your voice?"

"Well, that would depend upon your motive. If you're one of those loony revisionists looking for a way to diminish our shared history, you can just turn around and leave." Gold opened his mouth to respond, but she cut him off before he could say a word. "You'll note that I said our *shared* history. For your information, Texians *and* Tejanos fought and died at the Alamo, and they did the same for Texas Independence. I'm one of those proud Latinas who don't want to rewrite history to appease a bunch of politically correct morons. Do I make myself clear?"

"Loud and clear."

"I hope so."

Gold's face showed something like sympathy. "No need to worry. You and I are on the same side."

"Are we?"

"Most definitely."

She looked out the window a while, examined her fingernails and finally directed her gaze back to Gold. She seemed to be wrestling with something. Finally, she came out with it. "Forgive me for being rude. My ancestors fought and died for Texas independence, and sometimes I get sick and tired of all the liberal nonsense in this city. I apologize for my behavior."

"No need to apologize."

She tried to smile, but it came out crooked. "I'm surrounded by people who want to erase our history, so I'm a little defensive. Maybe too defensive. I, er, thought you might be trying to dig up dirt on the Collins collection. The leftists have been targeting his donation."

"What's their beef?"

Simply put, critics felt that the Collins collection was not everything it was cracked up to be. They were particularly concerned about three artifacts, arguably the most valuable: Jim Bowie's famous knife, Davy Crockett's shot pouch, and a knife belonging to William B. Travis. Items owned by the three most famous defenders of the Alamo. She went on to explain that it was not unusual for an organization to accept a donation of historical artifacts without checking their authenticity. However, in this case, the donation was tied to the construction of a new museum, and there was the rub.

She laughed harshly. "Money is the root of all upheaval."

"What do you mean?"

"Everyone and their mother has an opinion about how the museum should look and who it should honor. Some folks think there should be two museums. One for Texas and one for Mexico. There's no end to the foolishness."

Gold listened politely, but he was much more interested in the Crockett and Travis artifacts she'd mentioned. When she was finished venting, he said, "Are those artifacts in Austin?"

"No, I'm afraid not. If you want to see them, you'll have to go to San Antonio. They're part of the Alamo Museum collection, and I think they're displayed near Crockett's favorite rifle, *Old Betsy*."

Gold let this register a moment before asking the next question. "What about the Bowie knife?"

"Well, that's a different story. The so-called experts are still arguing about the knife, so nobody can say if it actually belonged to Bowie." Without providing too much detail, she stressed that every item in the Collins collection had been thoroughly examined. "The GLO is confident about the authenticity of the knife, but the battle rages on."

An uneasy silence lingered between them for a minute. The conversation seemed to be stalled, so Gold, against his better judgment, prompted, "What's the issue with the Bowie knife?"

"No provenance."

"That could be a problem."

"Well, there were other clues. For instance, the initials "J.B." were scratched into the metal blade."

Gold's ears perked up. "Was that a common practice back then?"

"For certain people. Mainly the rich or famous. Of course, anyone could have scratched those letters into the metal, including

James Black, an Arkansas blacksmith who might have made the very first Bowie knife. I suppose that's why the knife was examined metallurgically."

Gold stood still for a moment, composing himself and listening intently. "What did the test reveal?"

She told him that the steel dated back to the 1830s and was made in a relatively primitive charcoal furnace. A second examination revealed that the brass portion was consistent with alloys made in small workshops during that era, and more importantly, the brass contained trace elements matching those found in a green sand, derived from marine sandstone. "The sand was an important clue."

Gold looked puzzled. "What's so important about green sand?"

"Well, for one thing, it's quite rare. Secondly, a group of archaeologists found a large mound two hundred and fifty yards from James Black's workshop."

"Fascinating."

"Phil Collins thought so. He paid one and a half million for the knife — and then donated it to the Alamo Museum."

"I'd sure like to see it."

She cleared her throat loudly, slightly startling him. "I don't mean to be rude again, but I thought you were interested in our recent additions."

Gold gave her a blank stare for a long moment and then said, "That's correct. Last several months, actually."

"Well, that's easy to address. There haven't been any."

Gold recoiled slightly. *"None?"*

"Not a single item."

"Are you sure?"

The smile fell from her face and her entire bearing changed. "I know what I'm talking about, Mr. Gold. All donations are entered and catalogued in this office prior to examination." She opened a thick ledger and showed him several blank pages. "As you can see, we have not received any donations this year." She peered at Gold for a few moments, thinking. "I realize your investigation is confidential, but can you tell me the name of the donor you're looking for, or a brief description of the artifacts?"

Gold was thinking as fast as he could, trying to find a way to give as little information as possible and still accomplish his goal. After giving it some thought, he realized that he had to spill the beans, or at least a portion of them. Hopefully he wouldn't create a hot mess. "The donor's name is Kemmler. Joseph Kemmler. He's an antiques dealer. Lives in New York." He spelled the name for her. "He was supposedly donating a couple of Alamo artifacts. A rifle and a sword."

In a couple of seconds, her face went through a range of expressions, and then she let out a burst of fake-sounding laughter and clapped her hands together. "Oh my goodness," she said, "who wouldn't remember that kind of donation?" She did not avert her gaze. "Those are one in a million gifts."

"Yeah, I suppose so."

"Trust me, that would be the talk of the town."

Gold searched for some encouragement in her face, found none, but continued anyway. "Maybe they were sent directly to the Alamo Museum."

She shook her head forcefully. "That's not the way it works. All donations come through the Land Office, and there are no exceptions to the rule."

"If I had a nickel for every time I heard that..."

She cut him off mid-sentence. "You're wasting your time. Mine, too. I'm sorry, but there were no donations from the mysterious Mr. Kemmler." It was late in the day, and they were both tired and stressed. In another moment she might have said something else she would have regretted. She closed the ledger and sank into her chair. "I have your card. If something arrives I'll give you a call. Fair enough?"

Gold thanked her for her time, and as he was leaving, he noticed a small flag hanging on the wall. It bore the historic slogan, "Come and take it," a phrase that had become synonymous with Texas defiance during the Revolution against Mexico.

Come and take it.

Exactly how he felt about Kemmler's artifacts.

CHAPTER FIFTEEN

Friday was usually one of the busiest days of the week at the Austin airport, but on this particular Friday the arrival concourse was almost empty. The pace had slowed because school was back in session, and summer vacations were winding down. Without passengers, the concourse was rather quiet, and the ubiquitous announcements could almost be understood. First they came in English, then Spanish, but they were on some kind of loop, so nobody paid much attention to them.

Gold found a seat near the baggage claim area and waited for Christine Penny to arrive, hoping that her flight from Nashville wouldn't be delayed by the band of thunderstorms moving across the Hill Country. Gold hated waiting. Yes, it was part and parcel of being an investigator, but it was still annoying. This kind of waiting — hanging around an airport — was torture to him. Rather than sulk, he used the time to weigh the information he'd gotten from Maria Mendez, and after careful consideration, he came to the conclusion that none of it made much sense.

If Kemmler wasn't donating artifacts to the Land Office, who the hell was he giving them to? Maybe nobody. Maybe he was planning to sell the rifle and the sword.

Suddenly Gold had another thought. What if Kemmler had purchased insurance coverage as a ruse in order to legitimize his artifacts? An unsuspecting buyer might be fooled by an actual policy issued by a well-known company from New York. After all, a policy was a legally binding contract in which the insurer agreed to indemnify an insured in case of a loss, and that also implied legitimacy.

Maybe legitimacy had been the goal all along.

Of course, Gold still didn't know if the items in question were fake or genuine, but that would soon be determined by a gunsmith and a metallurgical examination.

Fortunately, Christine Penny arrived on schedule, looking fresh as a daisy as she rode down the escalator wearing snug-fitting jeans and a pink cowgirl shirt. When she saw Gold, she waved, and when they were face to face, she gave him a big hug. The embrace was longer than expected, but Gold enjoyed the greeting. In fact, it felt pretty damn good.

"Welcome to Texas," Gold said. He gave her a long-stemmed yellow rose. "Bluebonnets are the state flower, but roses smell better."

She sniffed the rose, then blushed. "Y'all know how to treat a lady."

"Yes ma'am, we sure do. How was your flight?"

"Smooth as silk. Which reminds me, your text mentioned a swanky hotel. Where are we staying?"

"Well, since we'll be acting as goodwill ambassadors, I thought we should stay at some sort of embassy."

She placed her hands on her hips and gave him a look. "Let me guess. Embassy Suites?"

"We get a free buffet breakfast."

"Do you know why it's free? Because it's not worth anything!"

"That might be true, but it's all you can eat."

"What a deal."

After a quick stop at the hotel, they grabbed lunch at Terry Black's Barbeque on Barton Springs Road, and then it was time to get down to business. Gold had picked up Kemmler's longrifle and he was hoping to have it disassembled in Austin, but Christine had something else in mind. She had an Internet friend who lived in Fredericksburg, a small city west of Austin, who was supposed to be a firearms expert. The guy was someone she trusted, and she insisted that he was the right man for the job. An eighty-mile jaunt was not what Gold had in mind, but he grudgingly agreed to make the trip.

Two hours later, they pulled into Fredericksburg and found a parking spot on Main Street, a tourist-laden thoroughfare lined with over one hundred and fifty shops, boutiques, art galleries, and restaurants. Gold had been to Fredericksburg once or twice before — during his college days at the University of Texas — but back then it was just a sleepy Hill Country town. Now it looked like Rodeo Drive, with the emphasis on the word *rodeo*.

Despite the influx of retailers, the city was best known for its German heritage, its wineries, and the National Museum of the Pacific War. At first blush, the placement of a Pacific War museum in the Texas Hill Country, three hundred miles from the nearest salt water, seemed a little odd, but there was actually method to the madness. In addition to being a tourist mecca, Fredericksburg was also the birthplace of Chester Nimitz, who had served as commander in chief of the Pacific Fleet during World War II.

Nimitz, a German Texan, had a storied career that could have easily filled a second museum. During his tenure as fleet admiral, he participated in the Battle of the Coral Sea, the Battle of Midway, the Solomon Islands Campaign, the Battle of Leyte Gulf, the Battle of Iwo Jima, and the Battle of Okinawa.

By strange coincidence, Lane Dietrich, the gunsmith they had come to see, claimed to be a distant relative of Admiral Nimitz. He did bear a resemblance to the famous naval hero, and as they soon discovered, he also had a distinguished military background. After they exchanged pleasantries, Gold asked about a pair of gold medals displayed in a shadow box. Dietrich explained that they were Navy medals, awarded for qualifying as an expert marksman with a 9mm Beretta pistol and an M4 rifle. In order to become an expert marksman, a shooter had to master several firing positions and, as one might expect, know his weapon like the back of his hand.

"I haven't lost my touch," Dietrich said proudly. "I can still take down and strip a M4 in under thirty seconds — while blindfolded."

Gold whistled between his teeth. "I don't think I could aim that fast."

"Takes some practice."

"Takes skill, too."

"Never hurts to have a steady hand."

"Or a sharp eye."

"Yes sir, that helps."

"How fast can you disassemble a longrifle?"

"Say what?"

Gold placed a duffel bag on the counter, unzipped the top, and took out Kemmler's longrifle. "I'd like you to take this apart. You don't have to do it in thirty seconds, but we are in a hurry."

Dietrich stared at the rifle for a moment, then smiled. "Damn, that's a good lookin' weapon."

"Belongs to one of my associates."

"Is it for sale?"

"I'm afraid not."

"Too bad. Those bad boys are getting hard to find."

"Harder to service," Christine said. "Have you ever worked on one?"

"I repaired a musket last week. Took a while to find parts, but I got 'er done."

"We don't need any parts, just information."

"What do you mean?"

Gold answered, "Anything that might reveal age or ownership."

"We'd also like to know where it was made," Christine said. "And who made it."

Dietrich thought it over, then nodded. "Well, it's a tall order, but I'm willing to give it a try. I'd normally charge two hundred dollars, but since Christine's a friend, I'll do it for a hundred. What do you say?"

Gold smiled at him. "Let's get to work."

"By the way, I'd prefer cash."

"Not a problem."

Dietrich took the rifle over to his work bench and secured it in a barrel vise fitted with soft jaws. Moving carefully, he slipped on a headband magnifier, adjusted the fit, and then took a close look at the barrel. He mumbled something to himself, then dipped a cotton patch into a bowl of solvent, squeezing out the excess fluid. After he cleaned the barrel and the working parts of the rifle, he carefully examined the surface, but he found nothing of great interest.

"No marks?" Christine asked.

"Just dirt, but that's to be expected." He picked up a ball peen hammer and a slender punch and began to gently tap the tension pins that held the barrel to the forestock. The pins were very small, about the diameter of pencil lead, and rusty, too. Dislodging them took some time, but after several firm taps, they began to move. Once they protruded, he pulled them out with a pair of needle nose pliers, and then he removed the tang screw, taking great effort not to damage the cherrywood stock. "Success," he said softly. "The hard part is over."

Christine glanced at Gold. "The moment of truth."

Gold crossed his fingers. "Let's hope so."

Dietrich placed the barrel under a bright lamp and inspected it closely. He kept his head down, so it was impossible to tell what he was thinking. He rotated the barrel three or four times before looking up and speaking. "Sweet," he said, smiling. "I haven't seen one of these in ten years."

Christine bit her bottom lip. "So it's not a reproduction?"

"No ma'am, it's a nineteenth century musket. A rare one, too."

She smiled at Gold. "Jackpot!"

Gold stepped closer, biting his thumbnail. "Any lettering?"

"The letters 'H.F.A.' are stamped near the breech."

Gold seemed puzzled. "Are those somebody's initials?"

"No, that's the name of the manufacturer. Harpers Ferry Armory. They produced thousands of rifles during the mid-nineteenth century. You've got one of their most popular rifles: the Springfield Model 1840." He weighed and measured the barrel. "The barrel weighs nine point eight pounds, and it's forty-two inches in length. The overall length is fifty-eight inches."

"It's the right length," Christine said. "What caliber?"

"Appears to be a sixty-nine caliber model."

"That matches, too."

Dietrich straightened and wiped the sweat off his forehead with the back of his hand. He peered through the barrel, then nodded. "Definitely a Model 1840."

Christine noticed how Gold flinched when he heard the verdict. Gold's reaction made her wonder if she was missing something, but now was not the time to head down that road. "I concur," she said at last.

Gold was the only holdout. He sighed, rubbed his eyes with his knuckles and said, "How can you be sure of the model? Is there a stamp or something?"

Dietrich shook his head. "No stamp, but the barrel's been rifled, which was common with the Model 1840. It's also heavier than its predecessor, the Model 1835." For a brief moment they locked eyes. It was Dietrich who looked away, turning his attention back to the rifle. "The Model 1840 was the last flintlock musket produced at the Springfield and Harpers Ferry armories. Most of them were converted to percussion lock before they were used in the field, and the ones that weren't are few and far between. That's what makes this one so rare."

Christine felt excitement coursing through her. To engage in a conversation like this was enthralling; there were so few people who understood the joy of owning a rare firearm. "I haven't seen one in years."

"Nobody had one in Nashville?"

"Not a flintlock."

"Percussion locks are pretty cool, but they're easy to find."

"Too easy."

Gold listened quietly, thinking, *Nothing's ever easy.* But he didn't say it.

Christine lowered her voice artificially. "What's an 1840 flintlock worth?"

"I couldn't say for sure, but they don't come cheap."

"Give us a guesstimate."

There was a beat before Dietrich cleared his throat and said, "I'd be more than happy to pay ten thousand, and I'd even buy the first few rounds." He thought that through for a second, then added, "The first few rounds of alcohol, not ammunition."

Christine smiled at him again. "We knew what you meant." She glanced at Gold, who was frowning thoughtfully. "What do you think?"

Gold shrugged. "Nice round number."

"Less than you expected?"

A shadow passed over Gold's face and it turned into a mask. "I wasn't thinking about money." He continued, an edge to his voice. "I was hoping it might be an Alamo artifact."

"How do you know it's not?"

"It's a Model 1840."

She cocked her head slightly to the side, puzzled. "So?"

"The Battle of the Alamo took place in 1836."

Dietrich interceded, "March 6, 1836. After a thirteen-day siege."

"We're off by four years," Gold said glumly. "So close, yet so far away."

CHAPTER SIXTEEN

Gold didn't speak much on the way back to Austin, and Christine thought she knew the reason. Back in Nashville, when she'd told him about the gunsmith who found the initials "S. & A. C." on a long rifle, his eyes had lit up and he'd made no effort to conceal his excitement. He probably thought that lightning had struck twice, and that his rifle also had a connection to Davy Crockett. In retrospect, it would have been wise to tell him that the chances of that were slim to none.

Crockett had undoubtedly possessed numerous rifles during his life, but only four were well documented and widely acknowledged by gun collectors and historians. The first was a .48-caliber flintlock that he acquired at the ripe old age of eight — the weapon he used for hunting. The second, and arguably the most famous, was a .40-caliber flintlock, a rifle awarded for service in the Tennessee State Assembly in 1822. This was the rifle that Crockett affectionately named *Old Betsy*, after his oldest sister.

In 1834, Crockett was awarded with another rifle from the Whig Society of Philadelphia, and this weapon was called *Pretty Betsy*. A Tennessee newspaper described the rifle as a .40-caliber flintlock, 40.5 inches in length, adorned with gold and silver wildlife images and an inscription that read, "Go ahead." (A reference to Crockett's famous admonition to "Be sure you are right, then go ahead.")

None of these rifles played a role in the Battle of the Alamo, which meant that there was a fourth rifle that was unaccounted for — and therein lay the problem. Every now and then some shady collector would pop out of the woodwork and claim to have found the fourth and final rifle used by the famous backwoodsman, and naturally, all hell would break loose.

Christine regarded Gold with a quizzical look, wondering if she had hit the nail on the head. Did he really think he had a priceless artifact? *A Davy Crockett rifle?* If so, he had a lot to learn, because the odds of finding such a treasure were one in a million. Maybe more. Finally, after thirty minutes that felt like ninety, she spoke up. "Cat got your tongue?"

The question took Gold off guard, and the fact that she'd noticed he was unusually quiet startled him. "Excuse me?"

"You haven't said much since we left Fredericksburg."

"I've been thinking about that rifle."

"I thought so."

"I didn't mean to give you the silent treatment."

"No problem." She tried a comforting smile on him. "A penny for your thoughts."

Unable to fake even a stab at levity, Gold simply said, "You might be overpaying."

"I can afford it."

"Be careful what you wish for."

She leaned over and gently patted his knee. "Stop feeling sorry for yourself. It won't change anything."

"Uh-oh, I sense a therapy session."

"I know what's bothering you. Or at least I think I do. You were hoping that your rifle was a genuine Alamo artifact. I'm not sure how, but it has something to do with your investigation. Am I right?"

Gold felt his poker face fall into place. "Don't be so nosy."

"Yeah, that has to be it."

"If you say so."

"Surely you knew it was a long shot."

"A long shot?"

"No pun intended."

"Look, kiddo, I wasn't born yesterday. I don't take anything for granted."

Christine smiled, then rested her hands on her lap. "Since we're friends," she said, "I know you'll take this reminder in good humor. A wise man once said that there's a broken heart for every light on Broadway." Something passed in her eyes, as if maybe she'd said something she shouldn't have. "Do you understand what I mean?"

Gold grew uncomfortable and cleared his throat. "Do I look brokenhearted to you?"

"No, just disappointed."

"Disappointment comes with the job. I'll get over it."

"I blame myself."

"For what?"

"I should have explained about Crockett's rifles."

"Who said anything about Davy Crockett?"

"Isn't that who we're talking about?"

"Don't be ridiculous."

She gave him a look that said *really?* "I think you were under the impression that you had one of his rifles. The one he used at the Alamo."

"You've got a vivid imagination."

"Nobody knows if the rifle is still in existence. It might have been taken back to Mexico by one of Santa Anna's men."

"C'est la vie."

"I think we should turn our attention elsewhere."

"We?"

"The visiting team."

Gold cocked his head. He wasn't sure where she was going with this. "Are you offering to stick around?"

"Why not? We still have work to do."

"What do you mean? What kind of work?"

"Did you forget about the sword?"

Gold pretended he didn't hear the question. "You're too much."

"Yeah, I know."

"You don't miss a trick, do you?"

"How could I miss a sword?" She gave him a coy smile and wagged her finger at him playfully. "Never carry a sharp weapon in a duffel bag."

"Thanks for the tip."

"Don't mention it."

"I won't if you won't."

"So tell me, are you planning to test the metal?"

"Maybe."

She searched for some encouragement in Gold's face and found none but continued anyway. "I think that would be a good idea. A metallurgist might be able to date the mineral elements. I could be useful, too. I know the right questions to ask and what tests we need." Gold's cheeks reddened. She thought he wanted to say something, but the words never came. "What do you think? Can I tag along?"

"Don't you have anything better to do?"

"What's more exciting than working on a claim?"

"I can think of a million things. Besides, I'm not working on a claim. Not yet, anyway."

"Well, whatever you're working on, I'm game."

"Jesus, you're a glutton for punishment."

Gold was only half kidding. Investigating claims, be they actual or potential, was a mild form of punishment marked by long hours of legwork. Christine might have heard stories about daring deeds, but the images in her head didn't match the reality of the job. Few, if any, cases involved misplaced treasures, damsels in distress, or kidnapped celebrities. Most investigations were rather dull, and most led to nothing more exciting than an out-of-court settlement.

There were, of course, exceptions to the rule, but those investigations were few and far between. In all likelihood, Kemmler's case would end with a simple arrest, so Gold was inclined to let Christine accompany him. In addition to being smart, she was also good company — and easy on the eyes, too. Why not enjoy himself while traipsing around the Lone Star State?

"All right," Gold said at last. "You're welcome to stay." He pointed through the windshield. "The Austin Airport is straight ahead."

"Why are we going there?"

"I need to return the rifle and pick up the sword."

She stared at him in disbelief. "You left it in a locker?"

"No, of course not. The sword is under lock and key at the cargo terminal."

"That's a relief."

"The artifacts were shipped to Austin, but they haven't been claimed yet. I have no idea who the recipient is or when he'll show up."

"It might be a woman."

"Anything's possible."

She bit one of her nails. "What if the person shows up and both artifacts aren't there?"

"The cargo manager was instructed to say that one of the items was delayed in shipment."

"Smart thinking."

"I'm glad you approve."

She threw a quick glance toward him. "You seem tense."

"I'm past tense."

That made her giggle. "What do you mean?"

"I'm used to working alone."

"Am I throwing your game off?"

"We're not playing games, Christine."

She smiled at him with affection. "Are you worried about my safety?"

Gold waved the thought away. "You won't be in danger, but you might die of boredom."

"I doubt it. I've heard about your exploits."

"Water cooler gossip?"

"You had a big fan club."

Gold felt himself blush, and it made him uncomfortable. "I don't suppose you know a local metallurgist?"

"No, but I took the liberty of looking one up in case you wanted to test the sword." She rummaged through her purse and found an envelope with writing on the front. "Lone Star Labs. 1600 West Stassney Lane. Somewhere in South Austin."

"Just west of I-35."

"They've been in business for over thirty years."

"Do you have their number?"

"In my iPhone."

"You called them?"

"To check on their hours." She looked at her watch. "If you put the pedal to the metal we can get there before they close."

"Aye aye, captain."

Now in a race against time, they hightailed it to the cargo facility and exchanged the rifle for the sword. On the way to the metallurgist, Christine explained their testing options, which included microstructure examination, corrosion analysis, and microhardness testing. Most importantly, Lone Star Labs employed a scanning electron microscope, capable of providing magnification of 300,000x for microanalysis.

"They can also identify alloys," she added excitedly. "And that might provide some great clues."

Gold nodded pensively, trying to remember his high school chemistry, but to no avail. "What the heck is an alloy?"

"A metal made by combining two or more metallic elements."

"Like steel?"

"Exactly."

"Chemistry wasn't my strong suit."

"Some alloys can only be found in certain places and were only used during certain periods of history."

Gold thought about this for a while, then remembered that he'd heard something similar from Maria Mendez at the Texas Land Office. She'd told him about a Bowie knife that might have been made by an Arkansas blacksmith named James Black. The brass portion of the knife contained trace elements found in a rare green sand, derived from marine sandstone. "I don't remember why the sand is green."

She gave him a sunny smile. "Glauconite."

"Excuse me?"

"The sand owes its color to a mineral called glauconite."

"What the hell is that?"

"An iron potassium silicate. Silicate minerals make up ninety percent of the Earth's crust."

"Tell me something I don't know."

Another smile. "Chemistry was my strong suit."

"Obviously."

"I didn't mean to show off."

"You're one smart cookie, my dear. I'm glad you decided to stay."

"Well, I appreciate the compliment, but I'm not a sword expert — just a history buff." She fell silent, but her active mind continued to race. "What do you know about swords?"

"Not very much."

"I've seen the most famous sword in the world. Three years ago, when I was visiting my relatives in Scotland. It was a sight to behold."

"Excaliber?"

"No, that was part of the King Arthur myth. I saw the sword of William Wallace, the knight who fought for Scottish independence. Wallace used a massive claymore sword. The darn thing was over five feet long and weighed about six and a half pounds." She went on to tell him that the famous sword had disappeared for a few centuries but then resurfaced around 1825 for repairs to the hilt. It was now in the Wallace Museum in Stirling, and it was considered one of the most prized artifacts from Scottish history. "What's the deal with your sword?"

Gold had no intention of telling her the whole sordid story, so he simply told her that it might be an Alamo artifact. After the rifle bust, he figured the sword was a fake, but he had to know for sure. He was probably spinning his wheels, but even so, he might churn up something of value.

Hope springs eternal.

Unless the spring dries up.

When they pulled into the parking lot of Lone Star Labs, they were surprised to find only one vehicle in the lot: a gray minivan with the company logo painted on the side. A bad omen, Gold thought. He was right. The front door was locked, and the lights were out in the lobby. He muttered something under his breath, then looked at Christine in bewilderment. "I thought you checked their hours."

"I did. They're open from nine to five, six days a week."

"They don't look open to me."

"They must have closed early." Her face was expressionless, but inside a sinking feeling had taken the bottom out of her stomach. "I don't understand what's going on."

Gold pointed toward the minivan. "Maybe she knows."

Christine looked back over her shoulder, relieved to see a woman fiddling with her car keys. She had stepped out of a side entrance and was standing beside the minivan. "Excuse me," she shouted. "Do you work here?"

The woman seemed startled, but she recovered quickly and took a few steps toward them. "Y'all with FedEx?"

"No ma'am, we're customers."

"Hopefully," Gold said to himself. "Are you still open?"

"No, sir, we closed early. Trouble with the power grid. No AC. Did y'all need something?"

"We were hoping you could test some metal."

"What kind of test did you need?"

Christine answered, "Alloy identification. We're trying to determine where and when our sample was made."

"Well, I'm sure we could help, but we no longer offer same-day or next-day service. Too shorthanded. Nobody wants to work anymore."

Gold chewed pensively on his lip. "What's our time frame?"

"Two weeks."

The blood drained from Christine's face. "No sooner?"

"I'm afraid not. We just can't handle the workload."

"Can you recommend a competitor?"

"I could give you a couple of names, but you'd just be wasting your time. We're all in the same boat."

"The *Titanic*," Gold said sarcastically. He gave a little snort-half of impatience, half amusement. "I think we just hit an iceberg."

Christine put an arm around him clumsily, unpracticed at consolation. "When life gives you ice, make iced tea."

"What the hell does that mean?"

"Time for Plan B."

CHAPTER SEVENTEEN

Back in Washington, as the workday was ending, McVey drove to the embassy of the Federal Republic of Germany, which was located in the northwest section of the city. He'd arranged to meet an old friend, a fellow intelligence officer, who he hoped would be able to shed some light on the mysterious Mr. Kemmler. After flashing his badge, he was waved through a sturdy gate and told where to park. A few yards away stood an original piece of the Berlin Wall, a troubling reminder of the Cold War era. He took a moment to study the artifact and another few moments to admire the modern architecture of the embassy, which evoked the Bauhaus school of design.

When he entered the lobby, a second ring of security checked his credentials and politely relieved him of his sidearm. He was subsequently instructed to walk through a large metal detector, and then, as a final precaution, he was patted down by a beefy security guard.

The admittance process was annoying and time consuming, but after 9/11, nobody was taking any chances.

Least of all the OCD Germans.

"Guten abend," said a familiar voice. *"Willkommen in der deutschen Botschaft.* Please come in."

For the briefest moment there was no response. Then, almost as if the words had finally registered, McVey's eyes sharpened, his shoulders came back, and he stood upright, smiling. The voice belonged to an old friend, Ernst Mueller, a high-ranking official in the *Bundesnachrichtendienst*, Germany's foreign intelligence service. The BND, as it was commonly known, was located in central Berlin, and my most accounts, its seven thousand employees occupied the largest intelligence headquarters in the world. Founded in 1956 during the Cold War, the elite organization currently had over three hundred offices in Germany and other countries.

The BND spent a great deal of time collecting, processing, and analyzing information gathered through wiretapping and electronic surveillance of international communications. In order to prevent internal strife — and duplication of effort — the organization was divided into directorates, each responsible for a specific area of intelligence gathering.

Mueller was a member of Directorate TE, the group that kept an eye on international terrorism, organized crime, drug trafficking routes, and money laundering. Like many BND agents, he worked closely with the CIA, and he was exceedingly knowledgeable about the workings of the American government.

They regarded each other for a moment without speaking, then McVey said, "Nice to see you again."

"And you."

"How are things on your side of the Atlantic?"

"These are precarious times."

"What else is new."

Mueller, a tall, thin bald man with a crooked nose, who tended to look like a prizefighter, said, "You've lost weight."

"A few pounds."

"You look good, *mein freund*."

McVey continued to look steadily at Mueller. "You look fit as a fiddle."

"Danke schön."

"What's your secret?"

"Plenty of exercise." He patted his stomach, which was flat as a board. "Have you ever seen the embassy gym?"

"No, I don't believe I have."

"You might find it interesting."

"I'm sure I would."

"Follow me. I'll give you a brief tour."

They walked downstairs to the basement gym, where Mueller opened one of the lockers and pulled out a leatherbound dossier, marked "Top Secret." He placed the dossier on the bench, then sat down. With a strange, set expression on his face, he opened the front cover and took out a photograph of a German soldier — a high-ranking officer dressed in a Nazi SS uniform. He pulled in a deep breath, then said, "Colonel Otto Kemmler."

McVey looked at him solemnly. "Did you say *Kemmler?*"

"Joseph Kemmler's grandfather. Do you recognize the insignia on his uniform?"

"Unfortunately, I do."

Not a big believer in sugarcoating, Mueller explained that the colonel was wearing the uniform of the Schutzstaffel, or SS, the most powerful and feared organization in all of Nazi Germany. By the start of World War II, the SS had more than 250,000 members and multiple divisions which engaged in activities ranging from undertaking intelligence operations to running Nazi concentration camps. During the Nuremberg trials, the SS was deemed a criminal organization, but many of its members escaped prosecution.

Including Otto Kemmler.

McVey was looking at Mueller with a frown. "How did the bastard slip through the cracks?"

"He switched sides."

"What do you mean?"

"He went to work for the Soviets. From all accounts, he became a valuable source of information."

"Well, that's one way to avoid a firing squad."

"The record shows that he willingly provided the names of his fellow officers and assisted in their capture and interrogation. Needless to say, many were executed. Those that survived ended up in Siberia. To show their gratitude, the Soviets nominated Kemmler for the Order of Lenin, the highest civil decoration they ever gave out. The medal is awarded for outstanding service to the motherland. We're not sure if he actually received the medal, but his nomination speaks volumes."

McVey made a sour face. "Don't tell me he lived happily ever after."

"Not quite. The Mossad began to look for him in the early fifties and either they or the CIA caught up with him in Cyprus and put a bullet through his eye. Unfortunately, the family saga did not end there." He looked up at McVey with a sad little smile. "Colonel Kemmler had two sons. Karl and Walter. Karl hanged himself during his teens, but Walter followed in his father's footsteps and became an intelligence officer. He was a brutal young man, but his brutality served him well. He rose through the ranks rather quickly and gained a good deal of power and authority."

"How long did he work for the KGB?"

"He didn't work the the KGB. He worked for Stasi, the East German security service. They were headquartered in East Berlin, and Walter Kemmler was at the top of the food chain."

"I've heard about Stasi. Those guys were worse than the KGB."

"Many Germans thought they were worse than the Gestapo."

"What do you think?"

"Well, that was before my time, but I think they were just as evil — and a lot more sophisticated." Something changed behind Mueller's eyes. He'd been asked a tough question, and it triggered an emotion that looked a lot like fear. A frown settled on his face. He looked down, looked up, looked down again. He told McVey that Stasi's main task was spying on the population through a vast network of informants. During its reign of terror, over 250,000 people were arrested, and many were imprisoned and tortured. At the height of its power, Stasi had 90,000 full-time employees and 170,000 full-time collaborators who kept files on about 5.6

million people. "By the time I was nine years old, almost two-point five percent of East Germany's population between ages eighteen and sixty were Stasi informants."

McVey muttered, "Jesus Christ."

Mueller went on to tell him that Stasi had spies in every major industrial plant, every apartment building, and every school, university, and hospital in East Germany. They even encouraged spouses to spy on each other. "Walter Kemmler was in charge of Division Fourteen, the group that handled criminal prosecutions and ran the Stasi prisons. He was also one of the creators of a psychological harassment program called *Zersetzung*, which means "biodegradation." Have you heard this word before?"

"Not that I recall."

Mueller's voice dropped a notch. "Unlike his colleagues, Kemmler felt that arrest and torture were too crude, so he helped to devise a program that could secretly destroy the self-confidence of people by damaging their reputations, organizing failures in their work, and destroying their personal relationships. The program was used against perceived enemies of the state. Anyone who displayed an "incorrect attitude" about politics, culture, or religion. Their diabolic tactics included home break-ins, property damage, travel bans, career sabotage, smear campaigns, wiretapping, and bugging. The harassment continued until a person had a mental breakdown or committed suicide."

"Was the program successful?"

"Stasi files were published after the Berlin wall fell, and if I remember right, about ten thousand victims were identified. Half of them sustained irreversible mental damage. In my view, that's hardly a rip-roaring success."

McVey nodded in agreement. "So what happened after unification? How did Kemmler avoid prosecution?"

"You'll have to ask your other friends."

"What other friends?"

"The CIA. They whisked him out of East Germany and brought him to Langley, Virginia. I'm sure he went through a lengthy interrogation, and it seems that he was quite cooperative. What's the saying? A fountain of information?"

McVey frowned. "What makes you think he spilled his guts?"

"They gave him blanket immunity. He was never charged with a crime. Never incarcerated. Never deported. In fact, he became an American citizen. A model citizen. I believe he settled somewhere in New York."

"Queens."

"I beg your pardon?"

"He lived in the borough of Queens. Across the East River from Manhattan." He cracked a smile, then added, "He died a couple of months ago. So did his wife. You might want to make a note of that."

Mueller remained silent. But his eyes said quite a bit. After a while, he said, "Good riddance. How did they die?"

"The official cause of death was COVID-19, but there's more to the story. Do you remember the old saying about the apple not falling far from the tree? Well, old Walter had a son, and as you might expect, he was rotten to the core."

Mueller glanced at the dossier. "Are you referring to Joseph?"

"That's right."

"I'm afraid we don't have much information about him."

"He wasn't your problem."

"But he became a problem. Is that what you're saying?"

McVey nodded glumly. "In addition to forcing his elderly parents into a COVID-infested nursing home, he led a life of crime and became involved in some serious shit."

Mueller stared hard at him. "What's he done?"

"Nothing good. He buys and sells antiques as a cover, but his real passions are drug smuggling and human trafficking. He's been on our radar for some time, but now he's a top priority, and HHS is determined to take him down."

"I understand your desire, but that might prove tricky."

"What do you mean?"

"How long has Kemmler been on your radar?"

"Eight or nine years."

"A long time."

"Too long."

"Has he ever been arrested?"

"Only once. He was tried and convicted of endangering the welfare of a senior citizen, but his conviction was overturned on appeal."

Mueller lifted his brows, surprised. "How do you suppose he led a life of crime without being charged with anything else?"

McVey smiled ruefully. "I've wondered about that myself. Maybe it was skill. Maybe luck. Who the hell knows?" He grunted in disgust. "You think it's something else?"

"When I first came to America, I was introduced to *Monopoly*. Are you familiar with the game?"

"Of course."

"Well, it seems possible that Kemmler received one of those "get out of jail free cards." Maybe you should find out who gave it to him. Maybe they'd be willing to tell you why he received special treatment."

"Sounds like a daunting task."

"I'm sure you can handle it."

"You think so?"

Mueller placed the dossier back in the locker, spun the combination lock, then said, "As the song goes, you just need a little help from your friends."

CHAPTER EIGHTEEN

Washingtonians awoke the next morning to thunderstorms that dumped a torrential amount of rain on the nation's capital. For most, it was a welcomed event that temporarily ended the intense heat wave that had made life miserable for the past week. While the rain lowered the temperature, it also raised the level of humidity and reminded the city's residents that the official end of summer was still four weeks away. September 22, to be exact.

McVey's alarm clock went off at six in the morning, giving him plenty of time to shower, shave, and get dressed before grabbing a cup of coffee at Starbucks and heading to the office. He spent most of the day playing catch-up, but his thoughts were not on office matters. After meeting with Ernst Mueller, he'd decided to drive down to Langley, Virginia, and ruffle a few feathers at the CIA. On that score, he knew exactly where to begin.

Prior to joing HHS, he'd been interviewed by a woman named Molly Walker, a top recruiter of personnel for "The Company." Walker had offered him a position in the Directorate of Operations, one of the five main divisions of the CIA. The Directorate of Operations was responsible for collecting foreign intelligence and implementing covert action. The division was created after 9/11 to eliminate the rivalry between the CIA and the Department of Defense. So far, the results were mixed. More information was being shared, but despite increased cooperation, the Department of Defense had recently organized its own global intelligence service, the DCS, which stood for Defense Clandestine Service.

Molly Walker had been employed by The Company for over twenty years, and she had the distinction of being one of the first graduates of the CIA University, created in 2002 in response to an agent shortage. The university offered hundreds of classes each year, training both new hires and experienced intelligence officers. Her advance training had taken place at Camp Peary, a classified facility near Williamsburg, Virginia. After two decades of service, she was a razor-sharp operative, and she would not be an easy nut to crack.

Driving to the Inn at Perry Cabin in St. Michaels', Maryland, an hour and a half east of Washington, was Walker's idea, and it definitely caught McVey by surprise. He figured she'd chosen this remote location in order to escape from the prying eyes of the capital, but as he quickly discovered, she had a much different motive. The inn was part of a lovely resort situated on a tranquil stretch of the Miles River, a romantic setting where diners could indulge in the stunning sunsets of the Eastern Shore. Tipping her hand, she'd reserved a table for two in a private outdoor space equipped with AC, music, and a specially curated menu for diners who were celebrating "special occasions."

McVey wondered what special occasion they were celebrating, but he didn't have to wonder long. After they were seated, she ordered a bottle of champagne and asked the server to dim the lights. Under normal circumstances, he would have been quite flattered by her intentions, but since she worked for the CIA, he suspected an ulterior motive.

As it turned out, he was right.

Between sips, she said, "Do you know why I chose this place?"

"Two's company, seven hundred thousand is a crowd?"

"Well, that was certainly a consideration, but mainly because I'm a hopeless romantic."

McVey waited a few moments before responding. "Are you planning to seduce me?"

"If that's what it takes."

"If that's what *what* takes?"

"I want you to reconsider my offer."

"Your job offer?"

She nodded. "I want you to come to work for the CIA."

A pang of disappointment went through him. "Jesus, you're really dedicated."

"No, I'm really determined. I never take no for an answer."

"So you went through all this trouble just to offer me a job again?"

"Part of my modus operandi."

"What's the other part?"

The question made her blush, which was McVey's intention. She hesitated for a moment, then rubbed the rim of her glass with one of her long, slender fingers. "We'll get to the other part after dinner. Right now I want to lay my cards on the table."

The pink deepened in her cheeks. "The director was extremely impressed with your resume, and he wants you to join The Company. He's willing to up the ante. You can have your pick of foreign assignments." She leaned forward and sniffed the gardenia centerpiece on the table. "How does a London flat sound? Or an apartment in Paris?"

McVey wasn't biting. "Frankly, my dear, it sounds like a foreign assignment, which means living abroad and working undercover. Two things I don't relish."

"Your starting salary would be one hundred and twenty-five thousand plus a one-time bonus of fifteen thousand."

"Very generous."

"If you were fluent in Arabic, Farsi, or Urdu I could get you a thirty-five thousand dollar bonus."

"I'm still struggling with English."

"Did I mention our excellent benefits?"

"No, but I think you're about to."

She held up a finger like a teacher demanding silence. "Health insurance, life insurance, dental insurance, and a very generous retirement package. You'll also get a federal pension. Between the package and the pension, you can live like a king."

"If I live long enough to retire."

She waved away his concern. "On top of everything else, we get ten paid holidays per year."

"What a deal."

Not used to being mocked, she narrowed her eyes and stared at him for a moment before speaking. First, she let out a long, exasperated breath. "Look, you don't have to decide this minute. Take some time and think it over. Weigh the pros and cons. Will you do that for me?"

"If you'll do something for me."

"What's that?"

"I have two small favors to ask."

"I'm listening."

"The first is relatively simple. A friend of mine is being harassed by DHS at the behest of the Chinese government. I'd like the harassment to stop."

"What'd he do to deserve such attention?"

"He stepped on a few toes in Tiananmen Square." He looked at her with a slack expression. "Beijing has a long memory."

"The bastards don't believe in forgiveness."

"So I hear."

"What's your friend's name?"

"Victor Wong."

"Easy to remember." She raised her brows in a politely quizzical expression. "Favor number two?"

"Well, the second one is tricky..."

She held up her hand and stopped him midsentence. The server had returned and was ready to take their order. She reached for a menu, then whispered, "Why don't we enjoy our dinner and then you can twist my arm?"

McVey saw this was going to be more difficult than he had imagined, but there was no point in risking another interruption. "Do you know what you want?" he asked.

"A little of this and a lot of that."

"I'm starving, too." He twisted his neck from side to side. "Why don't we swing for the fences?"

"Sounds good to me."

They dined extravagantly, ordering lobster and steak and, eventually, two bottles of Veuve Clicquot La Grande Dame. The dessert course included two culinary wonders: Pumpkin Smith Island Cake and Speculoos Lava Cake. The digestif was a generous pour of Dow's Vintage Port 2016.

Fully satiated — and a bit tipsy — they returned to the conversation they'd started before dinner. "So where were we?" Walker asked. "Before we were so rudely interrupted."

McVey propped his elbows on the arms of his chair and steepled his fingers. "I was about to mention my second favor."

"The tricky one."

"That's right."

"Lay it on me."

McVey remained silent, thinking. He was trying to come up with a diplomatic way of phrasing his request. He decided to give it to her straight and let the chips fall where they may. "Would you feel uncomfortable discussing an intelligence source?"

The way McVey put the question seemed to amuse her. She threw back her head and gave a shout of laughter; then she said with a girlish grin, "No, but I'd have to kill you afterward."

"Be serious."

"I am being serious."

McVey ignored the weak joke and turned his port glass in his hand, watching the play of the candlelight on the crystal. "What if I told you that the source was someone we've been after for a long time?"

"I'd wonder why you haven't nailed him."

"Good question."

"Do you have a good answer?"

"I think he's being protected."

"By whom?"

"The CIA."

Walker frowned, evidently troubled by the answer. After a long silence, she spoke softly, almost as if she were afraid of her own thoughts. "For your information, the agency is not in the habit of protecting criminals."

"Since when?"

She sighed, slightly miffed. "Don't judge us by the past."

"I wouldn't dream of it. Otherwise, I'd have to remind you of the CIA's human rights violations, domestic wiretapping, and allegations of drug trafficking."

Walker felt as if she was losing control of the situation, and she didn't like it. She gave him a murderous look, then said, "I suppose the saints at HHS are as pure as the driven snow."

"No, we can be heartless bastards when we have to." He smiled to alleviate some of the tension. "I think we both agree that, on special occasions, the ends justify the means."

She gave it some thought, then nodded. "For a moment, I thought you were getting on your high horse."

"Nope. I've gotten my hands dirty more times than I can remember."

She gave him an apologetic look. "I know all about your past. Why do you think I'm so anxious to hire you?"

"I thought it was because of my stunning good looks and charming personality."

That made her laugh a little, in the same sweet way she had laughed at one of his jokes during dinner. She had always found McVey humorous, and she had to admit that he was quite handsome. The server arrived with the check, and she waited until he'd moved out of earshot, then placed her credit card on the table and picked up where they'd left off. "So, tell me, who's this desperado that you're after?"

"Joseph Kemmler." He waited for a reaction, but she didn't blink an eye. "Does the name ring a bell?"

"Nope."

"Too bad."

"Did he ever use an alias?"

"No, but he's got a weird nickname. He likes to chew bubble gum, so he's known as Bazooka Joe."

"The comic strip character?"

"Yep."

She was quiet a moment, and McVey thought he saw the trace of a smile play on her lips. Then it was gone, if it had been there at all. "You're right," she said at last. "That's a weird name."

"Not as weird as Kemmler."

She fixed him with a wary look. "What makes you think we're protecting him?"

"Family tradition."

"What does that mean?"

"The agency helped his father get out of East Germany. I assume he was on your payroll for a while. Fortunately, he's no longer with us."

"I never heard of any East Germans on our payroll, but it might have been before my time."

McVey sat with his arms crossed over his chest, his eyes focused somewhere a foot or two above Walker's head. From time to time he'd draw a breath, but nothing so deep as a sigh. She was undoubtedly lying, but lying for all of her own, probably very good, reasons. In the end he believed that nothing she said was going to make any real difference. "I'm not asking you to confirm or deny that Joseph Kemmler is one of your intelligence sources. I just want to know if I need to protect my flank. A guy like Kemmler could have some nasty associates, and I don't want to be caught off guard."

"I don't understand what you're asking."

"Maybe you could check on his associates. I'd like to know if they're involved in human trafficking."

"Is that your area of expertise at HHS?"

"No, that's my area of concern. I'm part of a federal task force that includes the FBI and ICE."

"Enjoying the camaraderie?"

"We're like three peas in a pod."

"I'll bet."

McVey hesitated, allowing a small grin to slide across his face like a cloud passing in front of the moon. "I know I'm asking a lot, but I have nowhere else to turn." To his immense relief, she seemed amenable. "By the way, discretion is my middle name."

She sat back in her chair, considering what she had just heard. "If I help," she said simply, "you'll reconsider my job offer?"

"You have my word."

"That's good enough for me." Her next comment surprised him. "I think we've had too much to drink. Maybe we should spend the night here and drive back in the morning." She stood up shakily and reached for the check. "What do you think?"

"Sounds like a plan."

"I love when a plan comes together." She endowed these last words with an excess of promise and gave McVey a small, encouraging smile accompanied by a gentle lift of her eyebrows. Then she grabbed her purse and turned to leave, but before she took her first step, she glanced over her shoulder and said, "I hope you don't snore."

CHAPTER NINETEEN

Gold hadn't slept very much at all. Every time he had started to fall asleep, he had jerked himself awake, afraid of the nightmares he knew would come. Nightmares about Joseph Kemmler. The ringing of the telephone ended the possibility of sleep, and as he groped for the receiver on the stand by the bed, he was able to make out the luminous hands of the alarm clock: 6:00 a.m. who the hell was calling at this ungodly hour?

"Hello?"

"Good morning, Adam. Sorry if I woke you up. I wanted to catch you before you jumped in the shower."

"You caught me, Christine. What do you want?"

"I've been working on Plan B."

"You don't say."

"I know what we need to do."

"Press the snooze button?"

"How about meeting downstairs for breakfast at oh-eight-hundred?"

"When?"

"Eight o'clock."

Gold sighed. "Aye aye, captain."

"See you then." The connection broke.

Gold hung up and fell back into bed, wondering if the poor girl had gotten any sleep. She was taking her work rather seriously. Too serious to suit him. No telling what she'd come up with during the night.

Christine knew that Plan B was a long shot, so she braced herself for a long, tiresome lecture, but much to her surprise, Gold was completely receptive. She'd proposed finding a bladesmith, a craftsman who could shed some light on the sword in their possession. She reminded him that they were in the heart of Texas. How hard could it be to find a bladesmith?

As it turned out, it wasn't hard at all — just inconvenient. The closest bladesmith was in Boerne, a small town about thirty miles north of San Antonio. From Austin, it was a straight shot down I-35 to New Braunfels, and then another fifty miles west on Highway 46.

Boerne had been spared from the overdevelopment that had ruined many other Hill Country towns, but there were still a mite too many shops on Main Street. Most of the stores were of the mom-and-pop variety, selling Hill Country kitsch, a mixture of German and cowboy-inspired merchandise.

The town's one and only bladesmith bore the name of the proprietor, Bubba Jones, a name that was synonymous with the University of Texas football program. Back in 2006, Jones was on the Longhorn team that posted a perfect 13-0 season and then beat USC in the Rose Bowl with nineteen seconds left on the clock. Close to forty, Jones was a substantial man with ebony skin and a head shaved nearly clean to hide encroaching baldness, but he still looked agile enough to tackle a charging running back.

Gold, a coffee in one hand, the sword in the other, walked inside and introduced himself and his companion. Jones glanced at the sword, then gave them a weary smile. He looked tired and a little disheveled, though that wasn't unusual in his line of work. Gold wondered how quickly that smile would disappear when he discovered why they wanted to see him. "I hope we didn't catch you at a bad time."

Jones stared at Gold for several moments, then looked at Christine, who smiled back at him. He settled on Gold, who was looking for a spot to lay the sword. "What have you got there, pahdner?"

Gold smiled sheepishly. "I'm not sure. Might be an antique. Might be a reproduction. I really don't know. I was hoping you could figure it out."

Jones scrutinized Gold a bit longer and then shuffled over, clearing a spot for the sword on a workbench. He had a pained expression on his face. He looked down at his swollen hand, closed it and opened it again a couple of times, then said, "Just to be clear, I'm a bladesmith, not a weapons appraiser. Y'all need to remember that." He proceeded to explain that bladesmithing was an artisanal craft, much different from metal working. Simply put, it was the art of making knives, swords, daggers, and other blades using the basic tools of the trade; a forge, hammer, anvil, files, and tongs. "I've been at it a long time. Over twenty years."

Gold nodded approvingly. "You must be doing something right."

"I suppose so."

"Shall we give it a whirl?"

"Why not." He took a picture of the sword with his cell phone and then led them to the back of the shop, cautioning them to watch their steps and keep clear of the quench tank. The floor was covered with metal shavings, so they walked slowly, past a workstation that contained a vise, grinder, buffer, and drill press. The interesting part was still to come. But it was worth waiting for. Shelves had been installed on the back wall, and they were filled with hundreds of books about bladesmithing.

Jones considered himself a student of his craft, and his personal library was evidence of his devotion. Each shelf was dedicated to a specific period of swordmaking, starting with ancient Egypt and continuing with Celtic, Chinese, Korean, Japanese, Germanic, Indian, Spanish, and Middle Eastern blades.

Gold risked a quick, conspiratorial can-you-believe-this-guy glance at Christine. She was smiling, shaking her head from side to side. Neither knew exactly what to say.

Jones ran a hand over his mouth, wiping away the sweat that was glistening over his lip. "What do you think of my library?"

"Speaks volumes," Gold joked.

Jones wasn't amused. He grabbed one of the books and led them back to the front of the shop. He spent the next few minutes eyeballing, measuring, and weighing the sword. Between tasks, he told them that most swords were typically between twenty-four and forty-eight inches in length. Their weapon measured thirty-three inches.

"Definitely a sword?" Gold asked. "Not a saber?"

"Definitely a sword," Jones said. "It's got the four basic parts: blade, guard, hilt, and pommel. I'm sure you know what the blade is for: stabbing, slashing, or hacking. The guard prevents an opponent's sword from sliding down over the hilt. The hilt is the handle of the sword. The pommel is the end of the sword, the part that secures the hilt."

Gold cast Christine another sidelong glance. "I guess that settles that."

She nodded. "Check off another box."

Jones, reading their minds, said, "Y'all curious about the metal?"

"The suspense is killing me," Gold quipped.

"The blade is steel, but it might contain some chrome. Chrome was added to make the steel resistant to corrosion. I can't say for sure, but there could also be traces of cobalt and vanadium."

Gold frowned. "Why were those added?"

"Cobalt improves the cutting quality. Vanadium increases strength."

"Any other elements?" Penny asked.

"There's probably some manganese or nickel, but I couldn't say what amount."

Gold was silent for a while, thinking long and hard before he disclosed too much. He'd come this far, he might as well say what was on his mind. "We thought we might have an antique sword. Maybe an Alamo artifact. What do you think?"

Jones started to smile, but suddenly cut it off when he realized that Gold was serious. *Damn*, he thought. *The guy's a nut job.* Rather than hem and haw, he gave it to him straight. "I wouldn't get my hopes up. Genuine artifacts are few and far between."

"One in a million, eh?"

"Look, mister, there are three possibilities. Your sword is either a replica, a fake, or an authentic antique. I don't care to guess which one."

"How do you tell the difference?"

"Well, first and foremost, you look for signs of modern technology."

"Do you see any?"

"No, but the naked eye can only see so much, and I don't own a microscope."

Christine tipped up her soda cup, sucked in a small ice cube, chomped it, and looked closely at the sword. "What else do you look for?"

"I'd take note of any carvings, etchings, or signatures on the blade, scabbard, or hilt. Antique swords tend to have precise and artful decorations. Fakes and reproductions usually have poor artwork."

Christine broke into a small, weary smile. "Our sword has no artwork at all. Just some initials etched into the blade." She reached for the sword, focusing on a dark red stain near the tip of the blade. "I never noticed this before." She pointed to the stain. "Jesus, it looks like blood."

"Dried blood," Gold said. "I never noticed it either."

Jones looked over at Gold, trying to figure out if he was playing with him. A shadow slid across his face. Something deep and dark registered. He wiped his mouth with the back of a beefy hand and said, "There's blood on the tip *and* the blade."

"You're right," Gold said. "How the hell did that get there?"

Jones scowled. "Damn good question." He stepped back, eyeing them suspiciously. "You own this sword?"

"Not exactly."

"Who does?"

"I'd rather not say."

"Why? You got something to hide?"

"Nothing that would make the six o'clock news."

Jones shifted his weight from one foot to the other. "You know, I didn't catch your names."

Gold could see what was coming, so he dropped the polite facade. "My name is Clyde Barrow, and this is Bonnie Parker."

Once again, the joke fell flat. "You folks seem to be in a hurry."

"Time is money."

"Mind if I get a second opinion? I've got a friend that's a weapons appraiser."

"Be my guest."

"Y'all wait here," Jones said sternly. "I need to make a quick call."

The moment that Jones turned his back, Gold grabbed the sword and pushed Christine toward the exit. They ran to the car, tossed the sword in the back seat, and sped away. Neither said a word until they were back on Highway 46, heading east to Austin.

Gold was the first to speak. "Well, that was fun."

"What a way to start the day."

"Still want to tag along?"

She sighed heavily. "I need a cocktail."

"Little early in the day, don't you think?"

"It's gotta be five o'clock somewhere."

Gold smiled. "Well, at least he didn't try to tackle us."

"You think he called the police?"

"I wouldn't doubt it. He was suspicious from the get-go. The blood was the final straw."

She glanced over at him briefly, not wanting to sound worried but not able to help herself. "How the hell did it get there?"

Gold caught the look and sighed. "Beats me."

"You have no idea?"

"Nope."

"That's strange."

Gold looked at her, wounded by her tone of voice, wanting to say something childish like, *Hey, I didn't stab anybody!* Instead, he gave her a handkerchief and told her to scrape off some of the dried blood on the sword. "Get as much as you can."

She looked at him with a strange expression on her face. "What are you going to do?"

"Have it tested."

"God, another test?"

"I'd like to know the blood type."

"Why?"

Gold's lips twisted into a strange smile. "Blood will tell."

CHAPTER TWENTY

Gold was in heavy traffic on I-35 heading north into Austin, wondering whether to stop for lunch or just go straight back to the hotel, when his cell phone began to beep. He glanced at the screen and saw that he had an urgent message from the manager of the cargo terminal at Austin airport. Somebody was on the way to the terminal, and that somebody was coming to claim a rifle and a sword.

Showtime, Gold thought. He moved into the passing lane and floored the accelerator, reaching the speed limit in no time flat. He kept the windows rolled up and the air-conditioning on, and he listened to a George Straight radio station while he drove.

Christine shot a bewildered look at him, then said, "Where's the fire?"

"Austin airport."

"What's going on?"

"Our pigeon's in flight."

"I don't know what you're talking about, but you'd better slow down."

Gold waved his hand in the air like he was swatting away a bee. "Somebody's coming for the artifacts. We need to cover some ground."

The traffic was much less dense on I-35 as they drew closer to Austin and exited the interstate onto Highway 71. When they reached the cargo terminal, they found the manager, who discreetly pointed out the person who'd just requested the artifacts. The man was filling out forms, but even with his back turned to them, they could tell that he looked to be in his late thirties or early forties. He was on the short side, perhaps five feet seven, and could not have weighed much more than 140 pounds. His thin, brown legs emerged from oversized Bermuda shorts, but he wore an expensive guayabera shirt, brand-new alligator loafers, and a baseball cap with an emblem advertising the Miami Dolphins football team. His gold, diamond encrusted wristwatch was a Rolex.

When the man turned around, Gold's jaw dropped open. The last person he expected to see was Ricardo Paz, a colorful character he'd met in South Florida a few years earlier. Paz had been expelled from his native country of Cuba for making derogatory remarks about the Castro government. Somehow, he'd landed in a detention facility in Miami, where he was recruited by a mobster and duped into filing a fraudulent insurance claim. The harebrained scheme led to his arrest in Havana — and a lengthy stay in Villa Marista, the most notorious prison in Cuba. If not for Gold, Paz would probably still be in prison, or buried in an unmarked grave somewhere on the island.

When Paz recognized Gold, he stopped dead in his tracks, gaping at him as if he'd seen a ghost. Clearly shaken, he stood there, shifting from one leg to another, trying to act nonchalant. *"Santa mierda,"* he said under his breath. "My old amigo, Adam Gold!"

Gold studied him with suspicion. *"Buenos dias, Señor Paz."*

Paz laughed nervously. "Your Spanish still sucks. In the afternoon, we say *buenas tardes.*"

"I'll try to remember that when I visit you in prison." He took Paz aside and spoke to him in a low voice. "What the hell are you doing here?"

"What does it look like I'm doing?"

"Working your way back to a cell."

"Whoa, take it easy, man. I'm on the path of the straight and narrow."

"The only thing straight and narrow about you is your *pene.*"

"I got news for you, amigo. I'm a legitimate businessman, and I make a damn good salary. Six figures, to be exact."

Gold gave him an annoyed look that said, *really?*

"Okay, okay," Paz said. "Five figures. But the future looks bright."

"The light you see? It's coming from an interrogation lamp. You're about to be grilled like a Cuban sandwich."

"Hey, what's your problem? I haven't done anything wrong. I'm a law-abiding citizen. I swear on my mother's life."

"Your mother's dead."

"Whatever. You got no cause to hassle me." He stared ahead stonily and began to pout, evidently offended by Gold's comments. After a short silence, he said, "Maybe you should look before you leap." He whipped out a business card and handed it to Gold. "I got three offices. Miami, Boca Raton, and Fort Lauderdale. I'm what you call a magnet."

"Your English still sucks. The word is magnate."

"Whatever. Read it and weep."

Gold read the card slowly, the wrinkles across his forehead growing thicker with each line. "What the hell is a consignment facilitator?"

"A person who accepts merchandise and facilitates the transfer to a third party."

"Wow, that's impressive. Did you have to pass a test?"

"No, but you need a license."

"So does my dog."

Paz cursed softly. "Jesucristo, why do you care what I do for a living?"

"Because, as usual, you're up to your ears in trouble."

"What kind of trouble?"

"Are you here to pick up some artifacts?"

Paz felt his stomach twist into a wrenching knot. He started to say something, then changed his mind. He glanced at Christine, then turned his attention back to Gold. "Hey, who's the *mujer hermosa?*"

"Excuse me?"

"The good-looking broad."

"None of your business."

"Your new girlfriend?"

"No, peabrain, just a colleague."

"I liked your last girlfriend. The Indian broad I met in Cuba. Sally-something. She helped me get out of prison."

Gold sighed. "She wasn't my girlfriend."

"No problema. I don't judge."

"Speaking of judges, you might have to face one."

"Why? What have I done?"

"Tell me about the artifacts. The rifle and the sword you came to pick up. How did you get involved in their transfer?"

"Why do you care?"

"Because they fall into the category of evidence."

"Evidence of what?"

"Insurance fraud."

Paz's heart did a little flip in his chest. He'd already had one confrontation with Gold several years before, and he had no interest in having another. "Fuck," he whispered under his breath. "I had a bad feeling about this sale."

Gold looked at him squarely. "How'd you get involved in this mess?"

"The usual way. Some guy called me up and asked me to handle the transfer of some valuable artifacts. He was willing to pay me five grand. All I had to do was deliver a sword and a rifle and then pick up a cashier's check for the balance due. I swear to God, I had no idea that fraud was involved."

Gold gave him a penetrating stare, glanced at his watch, and shrugged. "I believe you, Paz." A ghost of a smile played around Gold's mouth. "Tell me about the seller."

"The guy's name is Kemmler. Joseph Kemmler. He buys and sells antiques. He's from your neck of the woods. Kind of a creepy dude, but a lot of dealers are like that. Anyway, this was our first transaction."

"How did he find you?"

"I'm not sure. Maybe he saw one of my ads. I'm all over the Internet."

"Just a random act, eh?"

"Shit happens."

"Especially when you're around."

Paz sighed heavily, closing his eyes on the exhale. When he opened them, he took another weary breath. "I know why he hired me. He needed somebody who was fluent in Spanish. The buyer's from Mexico."

"Tell me about him."

Careful, Paz warned himself. He was about to implicate a powerful man with some dangerous friends. He breathed deeply and felt a thick knot in his stomach. "Do you really need a name?"

Gold's scowl deepened, his voice suddenly harsh. "Yeah, I really need a name."

"You're putting me in an awkward position."

"You were born in an awkward position. What's his name?"

"Jesus, Gold, you're like a dog on a bone."

Gold's eyes now bored in on him. "I'm not asking for myself. My colleagues need the name." He pointed to a group of men — undercover federal agents — who were watching them intently. "You see those guys? They're all federal agents. HHS, DHS, FBI, and maybe a CIA agent or two. They've all got one thing in common: they're chomping at the bit to make an arrest. So if I were you, I'd start talking."

Paz made a skeptical face. "Seriously? Those guys are federal agents?"

"Every man Jack of them."

"They're not wearing suits."

Now here is an idiot, Gold thought. "They're undercover."

Sweating, breathing hard, Paz stared at Gold for the longest moment, then lowered his head and looked at the floor. The wheels were turning, but there was no way to know what he was thinking. A long silence stretched between them before Paz finally realized that he was stuck between a rock and a hard place. He smiled with regret and a trace of sadness, then said, "What happens after I tell you his name?"

"You get a card."

"What kind of card?"

"A get-out-of-jail-free card."

"I'm free to go?"

"Free as a bird."

"What about the artifacts?"

"You can have them."

Paz's bullshit bell clanged. "Are you playing games with me?"

"I don't have time to play games. Give me the buyer's name and you can go on your merry way."

Paz wrestled with it for another minute or more. Finally, he threw caution to the wind and said, "The guy's name is Miguel de la Cruz. He's a Mexican national, but he lives in San Antonio. I'm supposed to deliver the artifacts to his house."

Gold nodded as if that made perfect sense. "Well, don't let me stop you."

"I can leave?"

"A deal is a deal."

Paz glanced at the undercover agents. "What about them?"

"They won't get in your way."

"You sure?"

"You have my word."

For one fleeting moment, Paz thought it was a trick, that he'd be arrested as soon as he claimed the artifacts. When Gold accompanied him to the claim area, he breathed a sigh of relief and cheerfully signed a release form. They muttered their goodbyes, and Paz walked out of the cargo terminal with a big smile on his face.

Christine's reaction was delayed a bit. A dry chuckle caught in her throat, but there was no humor in it. "What was that all about?"

Without providing too much detail, Gold told her that Paz was on his way to San Antonio. "He calls himself a consignment facilitator, but he's just a delivery boy."

"What do we do now?"

"Follow him."

"The game's afoot!"

Gold's expression grew sober. "I'm glad you're enjoying yourself."

"Better than being chased by a linebacker."

"You've got a point."

They left the cargo terminal through a side exit, assuming the agents would follow them from a safe distance. Three Hispanic teenagers were huddled in the parking lot, pulling on joints, and they smiled nervously when they spotted two adults walking toward them. Their eyes showed no fear, only amusement, and that was troubling. Just as troubling were their facial tattoos, which appeared to be gang related. Almost instinctively, Gold dropped into a protective position behind Christine. Suddenly one of the teens yelled something in Spanish, then ran toward them. When Gold turned, he saw a pistol pointed in his direction.

Gold heard the gun explode but felt nothing. The bullet had missed him, slamming into the rental car, shattering the windshield and showering the parking lot with splinters of glass. The second shot also missed, but only by a hair. Fighting down panic, he lunged toward the shooter and jabbed two fingers into his right eye. The teen howled, then tumbled backward, covering his face with his hands.

A moment later, Gold heard hurried footsteps and the sound of urgent voices. A contingent of federal agents swarmed into the parking lot, guns drawn, and handcuffed the three perpetrators. It took a few moments for Gold to regain his composure. Almost as an afterthought, he checked to see if he'd been hit by flying glass. Luckily, he didn't have a scratch on him.

Christine Penny was a different story. A sizeable shard of glass had struck her in the shoulder, knocking her to her knees. By the time Gold reached, her side, she was bleeding profusely and starting to lose consciousness. He immediately applied pressure to the wound, and he may have saved her life by stanching the flow of blood. A quick-thinking agent nudged him out of the way and used his belt as a tourniquet, looping it around the wound.

While Gold tried some comforting words, two other agents lifted Christine into a van, keeping the makeshift tourniquet in place. She was still conscious. Her eyelids fluttered and her shoulder hurt, but she was awake, alert, aware.

Gold jumped into the van and continued to console her, hoping there was no residue of anxiety in his eyes. The last thing he wanted to do was scare the poor girl to death. He drew a breath, collected himself, let the breath out. His expression neutral, he patted her reassuringly on the leg, then said, "Hang in there, Chrissy."

She gave him a long and piercing look, then whispered, "What a way to go."

Gold grimaced slightly, making a face. "The only place you're going to is the hospital."

"I was referring to the van." She chuckled good-naturedly. "Would a roomy Suburban be too much to ask?"

CHAPTER TWENTY-ONE

Later that afternoon, Christine was moved into a private room at Seton Medical Center, one of Austin's premier hospitals. The state-of-the-art facility was located on West 38th Street, about sixteen miles from the airport. A team of surgeons had skillfully removed a three-inch shard of glass from her right shoulder, stitched her back up, and prescribed a regimen of nonsteroidal anti-inflammatory drugs and opioids. The drugs, as anticipated, made her feel more comfortable, but the morphine made her drowsy. She'd barely remained awake during Gold's first visit, but later that night she was back to normal, in full control of her senses.

Especially her sense of playfulness.

When Gold sat beside her, she dimmed the room lights with a handheld control and asked him to check her bandages. In order to do this, he had to unbutton the top of her gown and gently lift it to one side. Once this was done, her ample cleavage was fully exposed, and wound or no wound, she looked magnificent. Her next request, whispered into Gold's ear, was even more surprising. She asked him to lie beside her and hold her until she fell asleep.

Feeling guilty, Gold obliged, and he had to admit that she felt good in his arms. Not knowing what to say, he kept quiet, allowing her to ramble on about whatever subject came to mind. For some strange reason, she zeroed in on her favorite adult beverage, the speakeasy-inspired Negroni. In her view, which had to be blurred by the drugs in her system, a "proper" Negroni cocktail had to have equal parts of Campari, sweet vermouth, and gin. An orange garnish was preferable to a lemon twist, but both were acceptable.

Just before she dozed off, she tried to convince Gold that the cocktail contained some valuable medicinal properties. The bitters were excellent for one's liver, but the gin was bad. So they balanced each other.

Never argue with a bedridden woman, Gold told himself. Especially a woman who was under the influence.

Shortly after midnight, the lights in the hallway dimmed, and the entire floor became eerily calm and quiet. So quiet you could hear a syringe drop. Gold was still lying on his side, facing Christine, when he felt her stir, then squeeze closer. The next thing he knew, she reached over and unbuttoned his shirt. Then she ran her hands over his chest.

"You saved my life," she whispered softly.

Gold stared into her eyes, wondering where this was going. He made a vague gesture with his hands to suggest that it was all in a day's work. "I also put you in harm's way."

"I forgive you."

"I hope so."

"Need proof?" She unbuttoned the rest of her gown and pulled it open, exposing her stunning breasts. "Convinced?"

Gold was fumbling for a reply when she reached for his hands and put them on her breasts. He caressed them, feeling her nipples harden. Rather than say something stupid, he kissed her, and she kissed him back. They were about to cross the Rubicon, and neither thought of retreating. She pressed her breasts against his chest, and they kissed while she directed his hand between her legs, and he felt her warm thighs, then her vagina, which was moist. She made the kiss last. Gold closed his eyes and began to swim in sensation. There was a feeling of skin on skin as Christine slid against him and up the length of his body. He could smell her hair. He could taste her lips and her tongue.

"God," she whispered, "I hope I'm not dreaming."

Gold gave her a reassuring smile. "Would you like me to pinch you?"

"I'd rather have another kiss."

"That can be arranged."

They kissed again, completely naked now. Gold found himself distracted by her smooth, creamy skin, the lovely swell of her breasts, the curve of her neck, the fresh scent of her hair and skin. He felt light-headed, almost as if he had taken a narcotic. How could he hold her so close and not want to do more?

She laughed seductively, leaned forward, and breathed into his ear. "You're just what the doctor ordered."

"It takes two to tango."

"Shall we dance?"

"Are you up for it?"

"Where you lead, I shall follow."

Gold slid his hand under her buttocks and kissed her again, but this time with abandon. Before he realized what was happening, she was drawing him inside her and he was trapped in the slow pull and push of her rhythm until, moments later, he exploded and collapsed, spent but yearning for more.

Now for the hard part, Gold thought. Thinking of something to say that didn't sound corny or trite. He stayed silent for a full minute, then stood but said nothing. He looked at her, and she had her eyes closed, so he drew the sheet and blanket around her. He kissed her gently on the forehead, but she didn't move a muscle.

To Gold's surprise, she had fallen asleep. He studied her for a moment, marveling at her ability to flip the switch and nod off. He wished he could do the same.

A lumpy couch and hourly visits by the night nurse prevented Gold from getting a good night's sleep, but he didn't really care. There were more important things on his mind. He kept thinking about the teenage assassins with the facial tattoos, and he wondered if Paz had anything to do with the shooting. He hoped to God he didn't, and deep down inside, he knew that Paz was many things, but a murderer wasn't one of them. Maybe the trigger-happy teens had been following Paz, not Gold, and had misread the situation. Maybe they thought Gold was a security guard or a cop. Anything was possible.

Gold was half asleep when, at seven the following morning, a male nurse woke him up. The nurse had tried not to make too much noise, but he kept fiddling with the monitoring machines, filling containers, refolding the already folded bathroom towels and bed sheets. As Gold rolled off the couch, he tried to recapture his dream, but the details were instantly lost to him, leaving him with nothing but a vague sense of dread. He was more alarmed when he noticed that Christine was not in the room. He threw a questioning glance at the nurse but got no response. By now he was understandably agitated and confused, but he kept a civil tone. "Where's our patient?"

"They brought her downstairs for an X-ray."

"Jesus, I didn't hear a thing."

"You were sleeping like a baby."

"Must have been that comfortable couch. How's she doing?"

"She seemed to be in good spirits."

Gold breathed a sigh of relief. "Thank goodness."

"She must have liked your bedside manner." He winked, then chuckled. "You misbuttoned your shirt."

"Thanks for the notice."

"Want some breakfast?"

"Just coffee."

"Be right back."

The only thing worse than hospital food was hospital coffee, but Gold managed to down two cups before Christine returned from the X-ray unit. She was wide awake and smiling, but she remained silent while the nurses made her comfortable and reattached an IV. When the nurses left, she waved him over and told him about her morning, which had begun in the X-ray unit at the crack of dawn. Just to be on the safe side, she was also given an ultrasound exam, a neurovascular exam, a blood test, and a urine test. Fortunately she passed them all with flying colors, and according to her surgeon, she was on the road to recovery.

Gold was delighted by the news, and he told her so. "You had me worried for a while."

She leaned over to reach for a cup of water, and her cleavage opened wide. Gold's eyes crawled right in. He couldn't help it. "Were you here last night?"

"I never left your side."

"Where'd you sleep?"

"On the couch."

"How sweet."

Gold felt himself blush. "I was happy to do it."

"Did you get any sleep?"

"Yeah, I dozed off for a while. How's your shoulder feel?"

"Sore, but I'll be good as new in a few days. The nurses are calling me Wonder Woman."

Gold didn't have to wonder if she was a woman, but he wisely kept that thought to himself and said, "The name fits"

She sat up, a bright light in her eyes. "You think so?"

"Well, you're certainly a marvel."

She got the joke and giggled. "I didn't feel marvelous yesterday. The last twenty-four hours have been a complete blur."

"You can thank Morpheus, the Greek god of dreams. Morphine is named after him." He stroked her hair, fondly, almost absently, as one would a child's. "Do you still feel light-headed?"

"No, but I've got a little buzz."

"Don't be concerned. Morphine can stay in your system for up to twelve hours."

"There goes my discharge."

"They can't let you leave until the drugs are out of your system."

"No, I guess not, but you don't have to stay."

"I don't mind."

"Well, I do. You've got a job to finish, and you won't get anything done sitting around here. Seriously, you don't have to play nursemaid. I'll be just fine."

"I feel guilty leaving."

"I'll feel guilty if you stay. Who's gonna catch the bad guys?"

Gold knew she was right, but that didn't make it any easier to leave. "I'm sure gonna miss that couch. The coffee, too."

"Jesus, you're a glutton for punishment."

"Look who's talking. You're eating the food."

She reached for his neck, drawing him to her, and kissed him on the lips. "Thanks for watching over me."

In a low, amused voice, Gold said, "It was my pleasure."

At four o'clock, after logging about forty-five minutes of troubled sleep, Gold gave up and went downstairs to use the hotel gym. He stretched and lifted weights for an hour, then returned to his room and took a long, hot shower. Emotionally drained, he decided to order room service and watch television for the rest of the evening. The six o'clock news had just ended when the telephone rang.

"Where the hell have you been?" Irene Kaminski shouted into the phone. "I've been trying to reach you for two days." She listened for a reply from the other end. "You still there?"

"Yeah, I'm here."

"Well?"

Gold gave her a moment to calm down, then said, "I had to visit a sick friend."

"Did you forget to take your phone?"

"No, I didn't have a chance to call. Sorry about the failure to communicate." Another short pause. "You sound a little... stressed."

Kaminski's voice went up an octave. "I've got plenty to be stressed about, in case you've forgotten why you're in Texas."

"Not likely. Would you like an update?"

"Did you think this was a social call?"

Gold winced, but he swallowed the snide remark on the tip of his tongue. Without mentioning Christine Penny, he gave her a detailed account of the last two days, starting with his visit to the Texas Land Office. She was not surprised to learn that they had no record of any donation from Kemmler. That act of charity was just too good to be true. When she heard about Fredericksburg — and the flintlock rifle — she responded with an "I-told-you-so" attitude, and now she was ready to tear somebody's head off.

Somebody like Kemmler or Katz.

"What about the sword?" she asked.

Gold braced himself for a terse response, then told her about his trip to Boerne. "The sword was also fake."

"Two fake artifacts. Imagine that. What is this world coming to?" She took a deep breath, composed herself. "Have the items been claimed?"

"Yep."

"By whom?"

"Are you sitting down?"

"Uh-oh, this should be good."

"Do you remember Ricardo Paz?"

"The Cuban con man?"

"He claimed both artifacts."

She hit the roof. "Are you kidding me?" She cursed into the receiver. "How the hell did that idiot get involved in this scam?"

"Long story."

"Give me the condensed version."

Gold marshalled his thoughts and gave her an abbreviated explanation of how Paz got involved with Kemmler. He did not mention the airport ambush, which he knew would only give her agita. When he finished talking, there was a long silence on the other end. "Are you taking notes or something?"

"No, just thinking. Who's keeping tabs on Paz?"

"I'm sure the feds are following him."

"Do you know anything about the buyer? What was his name?"

"Miguel de la Cruz."

"What's his story?"

"I have no idea."

"Well, find out, and make it quick. I want to wrap this thing up before our next board meeting." Another pause. "Keep me informed of your progress — or lack thereof."

Gold grunted goodbye and hung up.

CHAPTER TWENTY-TWO

Gold was dreaming when, at seven-thirty the following morning, he was awakened by a loud knock on his door. He stumbled out of bed, wove his way toward the door, and turned on the light in the bathroom. As he put one of his bleary eyes against the peephole, whoever was on the other side of the door pounded on it again. The vibration was strong enough to slap his cheek, and now he was really pissed off. He stepped back from the door and yelled, "Who the hell is it?"

"Just open the goddamn door."

Gold thought he recognized the voice and tried to take another look through the peephole. The only thing he could make out was a big gray shoulder standing in the hallway. "Is that you, McVey?"

"No, it's housekeeping. Open the door, Gold."

"This better be important," Gold said as he opened the door. "Don't you ever sleep?"

McVey brushed past him and walked over to the bed. "What the hell is wrong with you? I tried to call your room and I kept getting a busy signal. Who were you talking to?"

"Nobody. I took the phone off the hook."

"Why?"

"I was trying to get some sleep. People do that in a hotel."

"I've been banging on your door for the last five minutes. Everybody on your floor woke up but you."

"I'm sure they appreciate the wake-up call. What time is it?"

McVey looked at his watch. Almost eight o'clock. Time to rise and shine." He opened the curtains. "Get cleaned up and I'll meet you downstairs. Try not to dawdle."

"Dawdle?"

"Just hurry up."

"What's the rush?"

"We got trouble."

"Trouble?"

"Right here in River City." He walked back toward the door, shaking his head. "I'll explain after you clear the cobwebs. Try not to fall asleep in the shower."

"Try not to slam the door on your way out."

By the time Gold arrived, McVey was on his third cup of black coffee. "You clean up nice." There was something subtly patronizing in his voice. "Pull up a chair and make yourself comfortable."

Gold plopped down on a chair and sat with his hands at his sides, gazing off somewhere. Then a shadow crossed his face, a flinch as though he had been slapped, and everything changed. His mind had flashed back to the image of Christine Penny lying in the airport terminal lot, blood oozing from her shoulder. He noticed the alarmed look on McVey's face and said, "I need some coffee."

A worried frown flickered across McVey's face. "You all right?"

"Yeah, I'm fine."

"You don't look fine."

"I was thinking about an old friend."

"Christine Penny?"

Gold's face twisted into a look of anger and surprise. "I guess you've heard the news."

"Unfortunately. How's she doing?"

"Coming along nicely."

"She's in good hands."

Gold cleared his throat. "She got lucky. A glass shard went through her shoulder, but it missed the brachial artery by a quarter of an inch."

"Whew, that was close."

"Too close for comfort."

McVey paused, his hand nervously massaging his chin. After a server took Gold's order, he leaned forward and said, "What the hell happened?"

Gold hesitated, struggling for an answer. "I'm not sure... we were ambushed. I had just finished talking to one of your men and we were on our way to the car when all hell broke loose. As you probably heard, there were three gangbangers — all with facial tattoos — waiting for us in the parking lot."

"Wait a minute," McVey said abruptly. "Didn't those tattoos look out of place?"

"They didn't look ominous, if that's what you mean. Just silly. Two of them had dots or teardrops under their eye. The shooter had something that looked like devil horns. I thought it was a macho thing. I guess I was wrong."

There was something undeniably disturbing about Gold's description, but McVey remained calm and spoke in a professional tone. "The dots are worn by gang members. They mean *mi vida loca*, my crazy life."

"What about the devil horns?"

McVey rubbed his forehead with the butt of his hand before responding. "I'm not sure. I'll have to do some research."

"Let me know what you find out."

"Go on with your story."

"When we walked past the three stooges, one of them said something in Spanish. I turned around and saw him pointing a gun in my direction. Before I could react, he fired a couple of shots but missed. I wasn't about to give him a third shot, so I lunged at him and poked a couple of fingers in his eye. I think he fell to the ground, and before I knew it, the cavalry arrived. They handcuffed all three of them, then whisked them off in a van." A heavy silence fell between them. It was broken a few seconds later by a server delivering a tray of coffee and some pastries. "Want some breakfast?"

McVey gave the faintest trace of a smile. "No, but help yourself."

Gold poured himself a cup of coffee but passed on the pastries. Christine Penny's image drifted suddenly through his mind: long red hair, sculpted cheekbones, magnificent breasts, and green eyes. There was something about her that intrigued him, something he couldn't shake. Thinking about her was distracting, and he hated being distracted. "When I saw that Christine was hit, I ran to her side and tried to stop the bleeding. One of your men took over and applied a tourniquet. They brought her to a local hospital, and the rest, as they say, is history."

Another faint smile. "Is that where you've been spending your time?"

"I slept there last night."

"No wonder you look like shit."

"I feel worse than I look. I should never have gotten her involved in this mess. I don't know what I was thinking."

"No sense crying over spilled blood."

Gold shot him a look. "Not funny."

"Sorry, but I don't have time to hold your hand and whisper words of comfort." He took a deep breath and plowed forward. "Tell me about Ricardo Paz."

Gold's head had ached from the moment he woke up. Now he was holding it gingerly in his hands, thinking about the ramifications of painting too dark a portrait of Paz. He squeezed his eyes shut, then opened them. He cleared his throat and drummed his fingers on the table for a minute. This was a card he'd hoped he wouldn't have to play, but he really had no choice. "Do you remember the cigar claim I handled?"

"The one in South Florida?"

"Yeah, the one that led to Capone Island."

"Vaguely."

"One of our insureds smoked a box of expensive Cuban cigars, claimed they were destroyed by fire, and demanded we pay for the loss. We agreed to pay the claim, but we informed our insured that he would also be charged with arson — for lighting the cigars. Needless to say, we never paid a penny."

"Yeah, now I remember. That was quick thinking on your part."

"The claimant was Ricardo Paz."

McVey's expression turned contemplative, then he shook his head. "Small world."

Gold went on to explain how Paz became involved in their present investigation, suggesting that the hapless Cuban emigree was little more than a delivery boy. "I wouldn't waste too much time worrying about him, but you might want to check out the buyer. The guy's name is Miguel de la Cruz. He lives in San Antonio."

McVey made a note of the name. "I'll run it through our computer and let you know what I find."

Gold eased back in the chair and poured himself another cup of coffee. "I assume you're tailing Paz?"

"Watching him like a hawk. He's still in Austin, holed up at a motel on South Congress Avenue."

"I wonder why he's still in town."

"Maybe he likes the Mexican food."

Gold sat motionless for a while, then said, "You mentioned something about trouble. What's up?"

McVey leaned in close and whispered, "Marvin Katz is missing."

"Missing?"

"Gone with the wind."

"What are you talking about?"

"Nobody's seen hide nor hair of him for several days. He hasn't called home and he hasn't contacted his office. He seems to have vanished off the face of the earth."

The blood seemed to drain from Gold's face. "Jesus, that's not good."

"Mrs. Katz is on the verge of a nervous breakdown. She called the police and told them that her husband had been kidnapped, and they were obligated to contact the FBI. So now a missing person's case has become a federal case. It's just a matter of time before the press starts snooping around, and the last thing our investigation needs is publicity."

"You worried about spooking Kemmler?"

"Kemmler's a cockroach, and cockroaches run for cover when you shine a bright light on them."

Gold started to say something to reassure McVey but couldn't seem to find the words. Not knowing what to say, he asked about Katz. "When was the last time he was seen?"

"Last Thursday. One of our surveillance teams spotted him in Manhattan — on his way to Kemmler's shop."

"What time was it?"

"Seven p.m."

"Did they see him go into the shop?"

McVey nodded. "They took photographs."

"I'd like to see them."

"I figured you would." He pulled out an envelope and slid it across the table. "The photos are a little blurry, but you can still make out his face."

Gold looked up, puzzled. "What are all these spots?"

"Rain drops. There was a big storm that night."

"Heavy rain?"

"Came down in buckets."

Gold flipped through the photographs, studying them closely. The last one seemed to interest him the most, and he stared at it for quite a while. Poor lighting made it difficult to capture much detail, but it appeared to be a photograph of Katz walking down East 69th Street — away from Kemmler's shop. There was something about the image that looked out place. *What the hell could it be?* In spite of his weariness, he kept at it and it soon became clear that he was turning something over in his mind. Finally he looked up and said, "I don't think this is Katz."

"Excuse me?"

"I don't think this is Marvin Katz."

McVey paused, at a loss for how to respond. "What the hell are you talking about?"

"Take a closer look." He placed the first and last photographs side by side. "Notice anything?"

"Yeah, Katz is wearing a hat and rain coat." He folded his arms very tightly. "So what?"

"So he seems to have shrunk an inch or two. Check it out. He looks taller in the first photograph."

McVey glanced at the photographs, then moved his hand in a dismissive gesture. "I don't see any difference. Besides, he's wearing the same hat and coat. He's even carrying the same umbrella."

"An umbrella that's blocking his face."

They exchanged a long look, which was interrupted only when the server brought over a fresh pitcher of coffee. When they were alone, McVey said, "All right, let's have it. What are you suggesting?"

Gold locked gazes with him and, in a firm voice, said, "Let's look at the facts. It was dark, and it was raining. Raining hard. The subject was wearing a hat and a coat and holding an open umbrella. Your surveillance team assumed it was Katz, but you can't see his face. I don't think it was him. I think it was somebody else. Somebody dressed as a decoy."

"I hate to burst your bubble, but if you're suggesting that it was Kemmler, you're wrong. He left his shop at midnight. We've got the photos to prove it."

"I didn't say it was Kemmler."

"Well, who the hell could it be?"

"Chatty Cathy."

"*Who?*"

"Kemmler's assistant. The brunette that's always yacking on the phone. She's about the same height and weight as Katz, and they have the same hair color. I'd bet the farm that it was her."

"Why would she go through the trouble of posing as Katz?"

"To make you believe that he left on his own accord."

"So what are you saying? He was actually kidnapped?"

"No, I think he was murdered."

"*Murdered?*"

"I'm afraid so."

McVey gave a little half laugh of disbelief, then looked away in exasperation. "You've been watching too many episodes of

Dateline. Don't you think the police searched the premises after Mrs. Katz raised a stink? NYPD got a warrant, and we followed them inside. There were no dead bodies. Apart from us, it was business as usual."

"What does that mean?"

"There were customers in the shop. Merchandise was coming and going."

"What sort of merchandise?"

"I don't know, the usual crap. Chairs, tables, armoires. Those sort of items."

"Did your men check the merchandise before it left the shop?"

"Check it for what?"

"A dead body."

McVey rolled his eyes. "You need more sleep."

"For your information, the average armoire is about five feet wide, seventeen inches deep, and five or six feet high. Similar to a coffin. In other words, the perfect size to hide a body."

McVey remained skeptical, but he had to admit that it was certainly possible. "You seem pretty sure of yourself."

"Why don't we test my theory?"

"How do we do that?"

Gold told him about the blood he'd found on Kemmler's sword in Boerne. He was positive the blade had been clean when Kemmler showed it to him in New York, and he could only think of one way the blood got there. He was certain that Kemmler had stabbed Katz with the sword. "I took a sample of the blood we found. I'd be willing to bet that it belongs to Katz. We need to get it tested."

"No problem there."

"We also need to know his blood type, so we can make a comparison. Maybe you could contact Mrs. Katz. I'm sure she'd be willing to help."

"If she doesn't bite my head off first."

Gold grinned. "It's worth the risk. If the blood types match, it's all over for Kemmler."

"What a pleasant thought."

"By the way, make sure you don't lose track of Paz. We need to retrieve the murder weapon."

McVey gave him a wicked smile. "Why do you think I put a tracking device in the handle?"

CHAPTER TWENTY-THREE

Joseph Kemmler had a problem. A big problem. He had just realized the awful truth about murder. Killing someone was the easy part. Even a prominent attorney like Marvin Katz. It didn't matter. The hard part was disposing of a body without leaving any traces or trail. Nothing the authorities could later use to track him down and throw his ass in jail.

Decisions, decisions. Incineration or interment? Burial on land or at sea? Whole or dismembered? There were pros and cons of each, but not much time to decide.

Unfortunately, decomposition begins several minutes after death, through a process called self-digestion. After the heart stops beating, cells become deprived of oxygen, and they begin to emit some toxic by-products.

Kemmler knew enough about death to know that a corpse could emit a bewildering array of more than 400 chemicals and gases including carbon tetrachloride, a highly toxic chemical formerly used in fire extinguishers; freon, a refrigerator coolant; and benzene, which was a crucial component of gasoline.

He had to move quickly, but moving a corpse was no easy task. Contrary to popular belief, body weight did not increase after death, but lifting a fully grown adult still required an enormous amount of strength. He'd be trying to lift two hundred pounds of dead weight. But that wasn't the only problem. Due to the complete loss of muscle tone, the limbs and head sprawl every which way, making it difficult or impossible to transport a dead human body without assistance.

Burying Katz presented a unique set of obstacles. In addition to transporting dead weight, Kemmler had to consider the possibility of future identification. He could dress the corpse in old clothes and drop off the body in a bad part of town, but a clever crime scene investigator might see through that ruse and turn their attention elsewhere.

If Katz went underground, the corpse had to be ruined, and that required a great deal of effort. To prevent recognition, Kemmler would have to pulverize the teeth, burn off the fingerprints, and disfigure the face. A time-consuming project that required special tools and a certain level of expertise.

Dumping the body in the Hudson River was also an option, and strangely enough, it was a rather common occurrence. Around sixty bodies were discovered there each year, a majority of them reportedly originating from New York City. Amazingly, 25 percent of unsolved homicide victims were pulled out of the river annually, making it the most popular dump site in America.

The river was a viable option but far from perfect. There was always a chance that a dead body — even weighted down — could float to the surface and be found. The police referred to them as "floaters," and they were most common during the summer months, when warm water produced bacteria in the body. The bacteria would then produce enough gas to raise the dead. Not a pretty sight, and big trouble for the murderer.

Salt water was a much better choice, but that involved boats or beaches, and both were risky. Too bad, because a body tossed into the ocean would have the flesh peeled away in about a week, and shortly thereafter, the remains would be devoured by fish, crabs, and sea lice.

An hour or two went by before Kemmler realized that dismemberment was the only safe bet. Safe but inherently dangerous. Disposing of pathological waste — tissues, body parts, and carcasses — was nasty business, and the risk of contamination was high. So was the risk of getting caught, which happened all the time. If convicted of dismembering a body, a person faced a mandatory minimum sentence of six to thirty years in prison — without the possibility of probation.

What am I getting into here? Kemmler thought, and he was shaken by a sudden, reasonless terror of seeing the police at his door. "Damn," he whispered to himself, cursing his predicament. One mistake and it was back to prison. Back to Attica or Sing Sing or some other hellhole.

What were the chances of getting caught? he asked himself.

Too damn good.

Maybe it was time to ask for help. Time to seek guidance. There was a man — a frequent customer — who understood such matters. He was a former mobster who'd disposed of many bodies, someone who took pride in their work. If the price was right, he'd probably be willing to reveal the tricks of the trade.

Pay it forward, so to speak.

What could possibly go wrong?

There weren't many old-school mobsters left in New York City, and the few that were still above ground were old, sick, or out on parole and behaving themselves. Joe DeCarlo was all three. Giuseppe DeCarlo, aka Joe the Hammer, had once been the underboss of the Genovese crime family, a notorious hit man, and the scourge of the OCGS — The Organized Crime and Gang Section of the Justice Department. During his tenure, the Genovese family became synonymous with racketeering, murder, extortion, illegal gambling, drug trafficking, loansharking, and prostitution. He'd become a "made man" in his twenties, initiated into the mob after beheading a snitch who had violated the Oath of Omertà, the Mafia code of silence and honor.

Now in his early eighties and suffering from diabetes, DeCarlo spent most of his time in a luxurious Park Avenue penthouse overlooking Central Park. From his lofty perch, he spent long hours peering through a telescope, watching the world go by thirty-three floors below. Visitors were few and far between, and those who spent any time with the old man thought he might be losing his mind. Either that or he was putting on a show for the feds — trying to convince them that he was senile.

Truth was, nobody knew for sure, and nobody was about to ask if it was just a ruse. Even now, a question like that could lead to a grisly death.

When Kemmler reached DeCarlo's door, he took a moment to compose himself and check his appearance in the mirrored hallway. The last thing he wanted to do was look or sound desperate. To a man like DeCarlo, desperation signaled weakness, and the weak never fared well in the brutal world of the Mafia.

The woman who answered the door was slender, with fair skin and brown eyes a shade darker than her hair. Her look was neither friendly nor hostile. Mostly it was solemn. She spoke with a pronounced Russian accent and asked Kemmler to wipe his feet before he entered the foyer. While this was happening, she frowned, cocked her head, and gave Kemmler the once-over. "You look familiar," she told him. "Have we met before?"

Like an embarrassed child, Kemmler mumbled, "Two years ago. You came into my store. You were looking for a rodeo poster."

She searched her memory. Then she remembered. He owned a cute little place on East 69th Street. "*Da,* that's right. You sell cowboy suveniry"

Kemmler bristled. "Western Americana."

"How's your business?"

"I can't complain."

"Nobody listens anyway."

"True."

She heaved a big sigh, obviously bored, and pointed him toward the living room. "You'll have to excuse me. I have a pilates class. Make yourself at home."

Kemmler had been to the penthouse several times before, so he had no trouble finding the living room, or the lord of the manor, who was gazing through a telescope. He waited a moment, then cleared his throat to announce his arrival. "Find a new planet?"

DeCarlo turned around, clearly annoyed by such a silly question. He forced a smile but didn't offer his hand. "Planets are boring. I've been watching a couple of horny *mulignans.* They can't keep their hands off each other." He fumbled in the pocket of his bathrobe, fishing out a cigarette pack and a lighter. "You ever get it on with a black chick?"

"No, I haven't had the pleasure."

"Pleasure is the right word." He lit a cigarette and took several deep drags, which caused a brief coughing attack. After exhaling a cloud of smoke, he said, "There's an old saying. Once you try black, you never go back."

Kemmler was tempted to ask about the Russian woman, but he decided not to go there. Instead, he took a quick inventory of the room, surprised to see so many medical supplies and devices in full view. Most of the items were related to the treatment of diabetes, and these included insulan syringes, pens, and a pump. He also spotted a blood sugar meter, ketone test strips, and a large supply of glucose tablets. Maybe he should have bit his tongue, but he couldn't restrain himself. "I'm just curious. Should you be smoking?"

DeCarlo threw out a dismissive puff of air through his lips. "You gotta die sometime." After a beat, he chuckled. "It's either cancer or diabetes. Who gives a shit which one." His mouth curled into a sneer. "I always thought I'd go out in a hail of bullets."

"The day ain't over yet." Kemmler meant that as a lighthearted comment to ease the mood, but it didn't seem to work. "Mind if I sit down?"

DeCarlo looked contemptuously at him, thinking that he was being fresh. *Dumb bastard*, he said to himself. *Who the hell does he think he's talking to? In the old days, civilians were more respectful.* He fixed him with a flat, disgusted glaze. "What can I do for you, Kemmler?"

"I've come to ask a favor."

"A *favor?*"

"Do you remember those wanted posters I found for your grandson?"

"Yeah, I remember. Billy the Kid and Jesse James. What about 'em?"

"They were very difficult to find. I spent a lot of time and energy tracking them down, but I did it out of respect for you and your family. If you recall, you were very grateful."

DeCarlo tried to stifle a yawn. "Get to the point."

"You told me that your grandson was elated, and that if I ever needed a favor, all I had to do was ask. Well, I guess that day has come."

"Me and my big mouth." He ran his fingers across the top of his head, as if brushing back the hair that had not graced his scalp for many years. "What is it you want me to do?"

Kemmler lowered himself into a nearby chair that was obviously too small for him, adding to his already evident discomfort. "I'd like you to help me get rid of someone."

"Who?"

"Marvin Katz."

"Who the hell is Marvin Katz?"

"A Jew lawyer. He used to represent me."

DeCarlo held up his hand, stopping him. "Wait a minute. You expect me to whack some sheister because you found a couple of posters?" He pulled himself up straight in his chair, his attention now riveted. "You must be out of your fucking mind."

Kemmler answered in a small voice. "Katz is dead. I killed him. I'm only seeking advice. How do I get rid of the body?"

It took a moment for the question to register, and DeCarlo chuckled. "You whacked your own lawyer? *Marone*, you're crazier than I thought. What the hell did he do? Lose a case? Send you a bill? *Che cosa?* He must have done something."

"He threatened me."

"What was he going to do, hit you over the head with a legal brief?"

Kemmler was silent for a moment, considering whether it was a good thing or bad thing that DeCarlo was making fun of him. He slowly unwrapped a piece of bubble gum and worked it for several chews before speaking. "A man of honor always keeps his word. I believe that's part of your code."

DeCarlo scrunched his face in concentration for a second. He assumed that Kemmler was referring to the Oath of Omertà, which, in his opinion, was a fucking joke. The mob had more rats than a cheese factory. Inwardly he sighed. He'd given the man his word, and like it or not, he was obligated to be a stand-up guy. He looked at Kemmler as if he were a simple child, then said, "You want to keep it whole or cut it up?"

"Excuse me?"

"The body. How do you want to move it?"

Kemmler stopped chewing. "I'd prefer to keep it intact."

"You got access to a boat?"

"No."

"Too bad."

"I suppose I could rent one."

"Too risky. Too much paperwork."

"What do you suggest?"

DeCarlo was frowning deeply, sitting all the way back in his chair, his hands in his lap, his legs straight out and crossed at the ankles. "You have to bury the corpse. You got two good choices. Pelham Bay Park in the Bronx or the Fresh Kills Landfill on Staten Island. They're both good places to dump a stiff but too popular to suit me. If you want a remote area, you need to look out of state."

"Any recommendations?"

DeCarlo exhaled and clasped his hands behind his head. "You ever been to Texas?"

CHAPTER TWENTY-FOUR

While Joe the Hammer talked, Bazooka Joe took notes — mental notes — grateful to be sitting at the feet of the master. Within minutes, it became clear how DeCarlo had become the underboss of the Genovese crime family at such a young age. In mob-speak, he was *molto intelligente*, a man who knew his shit. Under normal circumstances, he would not have shared his expertise with a guy who wasn't connected, but since he'd given his word, he began to spill his guts. The way he saw it, the problem with Pelham Bay Park was that it was too accessible, making it a convenient place to ditch a corpse. Back in the day, which meant the '80s and '90s, over 65 bodies had been discovered in the 2,700-acre park. Some were found floating in a turtle cove, others buried in shallow graves, and almost all of them had missing fingers or limbs — a sign that they were mob or gang related murders.

DeCarlo gave the faintest trace of a smile. "How'd you like to have a picnic in that fucking place?"

"Not on my bucket list."

"Mine either." He laughed. It was a dry, hacking cackle, the best he was capable of, but he choked it out nonetheless. "In my humble opinion, you'd be better off dumping the body in the Meadowlands in New Jersey or in the marshes off Fountain Avenue in Brooklyn. Even Long Island has a couple of good spots. I've heard some chatter about Ocean Parkway, where they found those four prostitutes." He looked at Kemmler with a quizzical expression. "By the way, did you have anything to do with those murders?"

Kemmler looked up, eyes wide with surprise. "I hope you're joking."

"Yeah, I'm just pulling your leg."

"I would never pay for sex."

"No, of course not." He studied the tip of his cigarette for a moment, then said, "Dumping is easy, but sooner or later the body will be discovered by some hiker or jogger. You can count on that. Those annoying pricks are all over the place. New York, New Jersey, Connecticut. They're like a fucking plague." He glanced around, lowered his voice another notch. "You won't have that problem with a dumpsite, but you do have to worry about garbage pickers."

Kemmler shut his eyes an instant to organize his head. "So what are you saying? Stick with Fresh Kills Landfill?"

"No, I didn't say that. Don't put words in my mouth. I said it was a possibility, but personally, I wouldn't go near the place."

Kemmler asked a question he thought he knew the answer to. "Because they closed the landfill?"

"Yeah, that's one problem, but there's something else to consider. In this thing of ours we have rules about respect, and some of us think of Fresh Kills as hallowed ground."

"Hallowed ground?"

"Because of 9/11."

"I don't understand."

DeCarlo leaned forward, eyes bulging a little more as his face drew taught. "After the attack, those *gavones* at City Hall used the landfill as a burial site for personal effects and human remains from Ground Zero. One area, called West Mound, contains about a million tons of body and building parts." He shook his head. "Only a *chooch* would disturb the dead. Which brings us back to Texas. If you've got a hard-on for landfills, that's where you need to go. They got about two hundred of 'em down there. He leaned back into his chair, let out a heavy breath. "Even better, they got the best dumping strip in the country. A place that only gives up its dead in little pieces."

When DeCarlo didn't elaborate, Kemmler said, "Tell me about it."

DeCarlo took in several deep drags, which in a strange way seemed to settle his breathing. After exhaling a big cloud of smoke, he said, "Ever hear of the Highway of Hell?"

"No, but I like the name."

"Yeah, its got a certain panache."

"What is it?"

DeCarlo explained that the Highway of Hell was a fifty-mile stretch on Interstate 45 in Texas. From what he'd heard, the highway ran between Houston and Galveston, through a desolate and remote section of the state. So far, thirty bodies had been found, all of them badly decomposed. "The weather sucks. It's always hot and humid. Damp as a washcloth. Bodies deteriorate almost overnight."

"Sounds interesting."

"From what I hear, most bodies don't have a chance to deteriorate."

"Why's that?"

"The area is filled with alligators, coyotes, and vultures. Those bad boys will pick a skeleton clean." He shivered theatrically. "Not a nice way to go."

"Certainly not."

"I could help you get the body to Texas."

"Really?"

"I got a teamster friend who could handle things. Of course, there'd be a slight charge. A modest amount of *scharole*. Nothing you couldn't afford."

Kemmler's expression showed that he was interested but still worried about something. "Texas is a border state."

"So?"

"I'm worried about the border patrol. Don't they have checkpoints along the interstate?"

"Not around Houston and Galveston."

"Are you sure?"

"You need to brush up on your geography. Those cities are three hundred and fifty miles from the US-Mexico border. They don't search vehicles in that part of the state."

"That's nice to know."

"Bottom line, the odds are in your favor."

DeCarlo had no idea how right he was. Even if the mortal remains of the late Marvin Katz were found, the chances of identification would be slim to none. In all likelihood, he would become an "orphan case," the law enforcement term for an unidentified body that nobody had claimed. According to the Department of Justice, the remains of about 40,000 unidentified bodies were stored in evidence rooms or buried in graves across the country, with another 4,400 discovered every year. The longer they remained unnamed, the less attention they received from the police, and after a while, they simply became another grim statistic.

Kemmler was ready to pull the trigger, but he had one last question. "You mentioned a slight charge. What did you have in mind?"

"Twenty-five large."

"Twenty-five thousand?"

"That a problem?"

"You call that slight?"

"A small price to pay for your freedom."

Kemmler could feel his blood pressure rising. He took a moment, then spoke calmly. "We need to move fast. We don't have much time."

"I agree."

"It would take a few days, maybe a week, to raise that much cash."

"Then you'd better get started."

"Joseph, please, there must be another way."

"What do you have in mind? A down payment?"

"I could come up with five thousand."

DeCarlo shook his head, the smirk spreading across his lips. "Not the way we do business."

"Couldn't you make an exception? For old times' sake?"

"If it was up to me, I'd take a down payment — with a little vigorish on the side — but my teamster friend never works on credit."

"Maybe you could twist his arm."

DeCarlo exhaled sharply and gave Kemmler a look that said his patience was gone. "Not gonna happen, so fuggedaboutit."

Kemmler fumed for a few seconds, then nodded. "What about a loan? You know I'm good for the money."

"You want me to finance the deal?"

"If you don't go crazy with the vig."

DeCarlo took out another cigarette and rolled it thoughtfully between his fingers. He didn't reach for a match. He threw his head back and grinned, obviously enjoying himself. "How does twenty percent sound?"

"Five thousand sounds high."

"The best I can do. I'll give you a month to pay me back."

Kemmler thought about that for a bit, then said, "Well, I guess I have no choice."

"Good. Let's talk about collateral."

"Are you serious?"

"Who loans money without collateral?"

Kemmler gave him a small, disbelieving frown. As much as he hated to admit it, DeCarlo was right. "I could send over some furniture."

"I don't have room."

"Would posters suffice?"

DeCarlo cracked a small smile. "How about a painting?"

Kemmler gave him a cautious look. "Did you have one in mind?"

"The last time we saw each other, you tried to sell me a Wieghorst painting. I forget the name of it, but there were a couple of cowboys and some horses outside of an old shack."

"*Old Mexico Rancho.*"

"Yeah, that was the name. I think you wanted forty grand."

"Sounds about right."

"That would cover your nut."

You're stating the obvious, Kemmler thought. He eyed the old man. He had a sinking feeling in the pit of his stomach. DeCarlo was asking for painting that was dear to his heart, a painting by his favorite artist. Olaf Wieghorst was recognized as the "Dean of Western Painters," and his work was often compared with that of Remington and Russell. Many of his pieces hung in the great public and private collections of western art, and owning one was a rare privilege.

DeCarlo smiled ruefully, well aware of this fact. "Well, what's it gonna be? Deal or no deal?"

Kemmler slumped in his chair. "I'll bring it by tonight."

"I'll be here."

"You will be careful with it, won't you?"

"I'll guard it with my life."

"What about... Katz?"

"Where'd you leave him?"

"In my freezer."

DeCarlo let out a howl of delight and slapped his thigh. "Remind me never to come to your house for dinner!"

"I didn't know what else to do."

"Well, at least he won't stink up the truck."

Just then another thought raced through Kemmler's mind. Maybe there was a way to kill two birds with one stone. A way to get rid of another nuisance. He let his thoughts spill out as words. "How would you feel about a twofer?"

"Non capisco."

"Two for one."

"Two for one *what?*"

Kemmler's eyes took on a furtive cast. In a quick pass, they scanned the living room, then came back to DeCarlo. "I might have another corpse."

DeCarlo's jaw went slack. "What the fuck are you talking about?"

"There's another guy on my hit list. A real pain in the ass. I was wondering if we could make a package deal."

"A package deal? Do I look like the fucking post office? I can't believe you want to whack somebody else."

"The timing seems right."

"I'm glad you think so. Who's the lucky guy?"

"A nosy investigator."

"You want to kill a private eye?"

"No, an insurance investigator. The guy's been busting my chops about a claim, so I thought I might get rid of him. Throw him in the truck with the other Jew."

For a moment DeCarlo didn't respond. *He can't possibly be serious*, he thought, but Kemmler's gaze was absolutely steady. He smiled at him, willing to play along until he could twist things to his advantage. "First a lawyer, then an insurance investigator. Who's next, your fucking dentist?"

"What can I say? I'm antisocial."

That's putting it mildly, DeCarlo thought. He'd seen some stone-cold killers in his time, but for them it was strictly business. Kemmler was different. He seemed to enjoy the idea of killing, as if it was some sort of game. "Tell me about this investigator. Who does he work for?"

"A local insurer."

"Which one?"

"The Anchor Insurance Company."

DeCarlo maintained a show of indifference, but inside he was worried. "What's his name?"

"Adam Gold."

Showing a hint of anger, DeCarlo leaned forward and said, "Never heard of him."

"I'm not surprised. A man of your stature wouldn't know a clown like him."

"I know a few clowns."

"Not like this one. This guy's in a league of his own."

"When were you planning on taking him out?"

"Well, if we can do a twofer, as soon as possible."

DeCarlo looked at Kemmler as if he were a simple child. The poor bastard had no idea that he'd just given the aging mobster a chance to making a different sort of killing — one that involved a Wieghorst painting. Pulling this off was going to be tricky but manageable, as most betrayals were. He sat ramrod straight in his chair, then said, "I need some time to think."

Kemmler felt a knot tighten in his throat. "We don't have much time."

"You just keep the freezer running. I'll talk to my teamster friend, and I'll let you know what we decide."

"Fair enough."

"In the meantime, don't forget my collateral."

"I won't forget." He stood up and offered his hand, which DeCarlo accepted and shook. "It's always a pleasure doing business with a gentleman."

DeCarlo smiled to himself. These small-time criminals were so easy to play. So enamored by the allure of the mob. It was like taking candy from a baby. While Kemmler was playing checkers, DeCarlo was playing chess, and his final move would be one for the books.

CHAPTER TWENTY-FIVE

All in all, Kemmler found himself thinking, the meeting with DeCarlo had gone quite well, and except for the collateral nonsense, everything was hunky-dory. All he had to do now was pack a suitcase, grab the Weighorst painting, and head uptown. The body of Marvin Katz would be picked up after dark, and then he'd be gone to Texas. Another day, another identity, and he'd soon be kicking up his heels on a far-off tropical island.

Goethe was right, he thought. *"One ought, every day at least, to hear a little song, read a good poem, see a fine picture, and, if it were possible, to speak a few reasonable words."*

A good plan, well executed, was the key to a clean getaway, and Kemmler was sure that he'd thought of everything. There were no loose ends. No overlooked details. Nothing to worry about.

Nothing except one old adage...

Hell hath no fury like a woman scorned.

Kemmler needed a drink, a glass of schnapps, before he started packing. He slowly lowered himself into a well-used cushioned chair. On the table next to it was a brandy glass, a bottle of peach schnapps, and an overloaded ashtray. The house smelled of cigarettes and old age, but he didn't care. He had more important things on his mind. He poured himself a full glass, chugged it down, poured another. He was so absorbed in his thoughts that at first he didn't notice he had company.

Chatty Cathy, whose real name was Elena Mendoza, was standing over him, and she looked miffed. She had brushed her hair and washed her face but had put on only a white robe. Kemmler had almost forgotten how attractive she was. Small and dark and exotic-looking in some way, he guessed she had a hidden Spanish bloodline mixed with some modern-day Mexican genes. Whatever the mix, her shiny black hair framed an oblong face that was beautiful and sorrowful at the same time.

Elena had been hired six months earlier, after dropping off a resume and flirting like a sorority girl during spring break. Back then, she was all smiles, and there was no hint of a dark side. Unlike her employer, she never discussed her past, and Kemmler was unable to shake the notion that she was hiding something.

Kemmler studied the serious look on her face and said, "What is it?"

"Where the hell have you been?"

"Here and there." He slid his hand under her robe and ran his fingers up her leg. "Did you miss me?"

She pulled back, irritated — she was in no mood for silly games. "You were gone all day."

"Something came up."

"Something or *someone?*"

"Frailty, thy name is woman!"

"Don't start that shit. I hate when you talk down to me."

"Elena, my dear, you're too sensitive. I wasn't talking down to you. I was quoting Shakespeare."

She dismissed his explanation with a wave of her hand. "Save that crap for those uptown whores."

Kemmler sighed. "Those uptown whores are the reason you have a job."

"Spare me."

"Somebody woke up on the wrong side of the bed."

"Is that where you've been? In bed with one of those whores?"

Kemmler kept a meaningless smile in place as he finished his drink, then lit a cigarette. "Jealousy does not become you, Elena."

"Jealousy?" She laughed unpleasantly. "I could never be jealous of a *maricón*. A man with a foot fetish is not much of a man."

"I don't have a fetish. I'm simply intrigued by other people's feet."

"Maricón!"

Kemmler instantly lost his smile and lowered his voice. "What's wrong, dear? That time of month again?"

"Vete a la mierda."

"Speak English."

"Go fuck yourself."

Kemmler took another drag on his cigarette; exhaling, he studied the cloud of smoke as if it held some interest. His voice was somber, almost hesitant. "What's stuck in your craw?"

"I want to know where you've been."

"Don't you trust me?"

"Are you serious? You stabbed your own lawyer with a fucking sword. You murdered the poor man in cold blood. How could you do such a thing?"

"Believe me, he had it coming."

Suddenly she laughed. It was a bitter sound. "What about me? Did I have it coming, too? You forced me to wear his damn clothing. You made me an accessory to a crime."

Kemmler held up a hand, silencing her. "Calm down, Elena. You have nothing to worry about. Everything's under control."

Elena wasn't buying. *"Under control?"* she said harshly. "What the hell are you talking about? There's a goddamn body in your freezer."

"Not for long."

"What does that mean?"

Kemmler couldn't keep her in the dark forever, but he would have preferred to wait a few more days. He began to play with the ashtray and gave her one of his patented scowls. He was thinking. He took a deep, steadying breath, then gave her a brief recap of his meeting with DeCarlo, and by the time he finished, she was shaking, her face set with worry. "Now what's wrong?"

"You're taking a corpse to Texas?"

"That's the plan."

"You're out of your mind."

"You think so?" He told her about the Highway of Hell, the fifty-mile stretch of interstate that ran between Houston and Galveston. She wasn't shocked — or impressed — by the thirty decomposed bodies found in the killing fields. "Why the blank stare?"

"There are better places in Mexico. Places where the dead are never found."

Kemmler sat up, rigid. "How would you know?"

An alarm went off inside Elena's head as she stared at him with a slack expression. *Damn*, she thought. Why had she mentioned Mexico? Mentally cursing herself, she managed a trembling smile. "I know such things because I read *El Mundo*, the Spanish language newspaper. They publish stories about the cartels. Very bad hombres."

Kemmler let this register a moment before asking the next question. "Were you born down there?"

She folded her arms across her chest. "Why do you care where I was born?"

"I don't care. I'm just curious." He glared at her. "Humor me."

"Mind your own business." She started to turn away, but Kemmler grabbed her wrist. He tightened his grip and twisted, sending flashes of pain through her arm. "Ouch!" she yelled. "You're hurting me. Let me go."

Kemmler loosened his grip. "I asked you a question."

"Yes, *bastardo*, I'm from Mexico. I was born and raised in Tijuana." She swallowed hard, her face now ashen. "What the fuck is your problem?"

"I just want to know if you're an illegal alien. I don't want any trouble from the INS."

She mumbled something incomprehensible in Spanish, then said, "I'm as much of a citizen as are you, and I'll tell you something else. If you ever hurt me again, I'll cut your throat."

A tiny smile appeared on Kemmler's face. "Get dressed. We have work to do."

"*Work?*" She shook her head in disbelief. "*Estás loco.*"

"No, I'm not crazy. You and I are going fishing."

"Now you're scaring me."

"Allow me to elaborate. I'm going fishing. You're the bait. I want you to call a guy named Adam Gold and tell him you've got news about Marvin Katz. Say it's urgent. Invite him over for a drink. I'll take it from there." He smiled weakly. "You think you can handle that?"

"What are you planning to do?"

"What do you think?"

"Jesus, don't tell me you want to kill him."

Kemmler smiled coldly. "The thought crossed my mind."

"Why? What the hell did he do?"

"Nothing yet, but he's a nosy bastard. He could stumble upon the truth and ruin my plans."

"Does this have something to do with your precious artifacts?"

"An astute observation, my dear. You're not as dumb as I thought."

"I don't understand. You've shipped the sword and rifle. How could this man cause trouble?"

"Yours is not to reason why; yours is but to do and die."

"Speak English."

Touché, Kemmler thought. He momentarily toyed with the idea of explaining Tennyson's poem "The Charge of the Light Brigade," but decided against it. She was too dumb to appreciate such a literary reference. After a moment of strained silence, he said, "Gold's an investigator. He investigates insurance matters. Do you understand what that means?"

"Not exactly. Why don't you explain it to me?"

"Some other time."

"No, right now."

"Don't be a pain in the ass, Elena."

"I'm not leaving until you explain."

Kemmler rose angrily from his chair and glared down at her. "Go put some clothes on, and wear something sexy."

"What do you think I am, your slave?"

"No, just a cheap *puta* who will do what I tell her. But I won't tell her twice."

"Drop dead."

"I've warned you about talking back."

"Bésame el trasero."

"What did you say?"

"Kiss my ass."

An undecipherable expression flitted across Kemmler's face. "Don't push you luck, Elena."

"What are you going to do, fire me?"

"Hopefully it won't come to that."

She chuckled contemptuously. "You still haven't figured it out, have you, asshole? I have no intention of helping you kill this man Gold. Not now, not ever. I'm finished with your abuse. I'm leaving, and I never want to see your ugly face again. *Comprende?*"

Kemmler's dark eyes showed no amusement as he smiled. "You're hurting my feelings, Elena."

"You have no feelings. You're just a one-eyed freak who likes to beat up women." He didn't rise to the bait of the insult, so she kicked it up a notch by poking him in the chest with her finger and raising her voice. "Let me tell you something else. You chew gum like a fucking cow. You're disgusting."

"Don't push me, bitch."

"Vete a la mierda. Do you remember what that means?"

Kemmler hadn't hit her in several weeks, but now she was asking for it. Begging for a beating. Seeing the almost animal-like rage on his face, Elena instantly knew she had crossed the line. For whatever sick reason, Kemmler was about to hit her. Of that, she had absolutely no doubt.

The first blow struck her in the face and broke her nose. Blood began to pour out of her nostrils. The second punch landed on the side of her head, and she saw stars. She gasped, then held up her hands in a defensive position. What happened next was purely reflexive. She didn't even stop to think, but simply reacted. With one sweep of her hand, she grabbed the bottle of schnapps and slammed it into Kemmler's knee. Through the rushing of her own blood, she heard him groan, but there was rage fueling him, and he just kept punching.

Punch after punch until the room went dark.

All of a sudden she felt his hands around her throat. She drew one final breath, then whispered, "Oh my God, don't. No, please."

CHAPTER TWENTY-SIX

Surveillance was never a barrel of fun, even when the guys on stakeout were old friends. Gold and McVey had learned this lesson once or twice before, and now they found themselves on another unenviable watch. They had spent the previous day — and half the night — parked outside the South Congress Hotel, waiting for Ricardo Paz to make a move. For some reason, he remained in his room, content to while away the hours with a bottle of Havana Club rum. They had no idea why he was killing time, but one thing was clear. He was in no hurry to get to San Antonio.

McVey had enjoyed the camaraderie, but he had no interest in spending another day in the parking lot. Neither did Gold. They both had better things to do, so they agreed to pass the baton to a couple of HHS agents.

For his part, McVey was anxious to get back to Washington and speak with one of his colleagues about the facial tattoo that Gold had described. He also wanted to touch base with Molly Walker, hoping that she was ready to fill in the blanks about Kemmler's involvement with the CIA.

Gold had a full plate, too. In order to save time, he'd offered to take the dried blood sample to Seton Medical Center for testing.

When that was done, he planned to take Christine Penny to the airport and make sure she got off safely. After that, he'd check in with the HHS agents who were keeping an eye on Paz.

McVey nodded approvingly. "I'll arrange a private jet for your friend. It's the least we can do for her."

"I'm sure she'll be pleased. By the way, it would also be helpful if you called the hospital and got the ball rolling."

"Will do. I'll let you know who to contact."

They sat in the parking lot for one more hour, and before they went their separate ways, McVey shed some light on Irene Kaminski's obsession with Kemmler. Most of his observations were based upon his conversation with Ernst Mueller, his old friend from the German embassy. They could have talked longer, but McVey had a plane to catch.

The clock, as they say, was ticking.

Gold exchanged his damaged rental car for a government vehicle, then drove to Seton Medical Center with the blood he'd found on Kemmler's sword. He had the good fortune of meeting with Dr. Jeremy Sheinberg, the chief phlebotomist of the venipuncture unit. Dr. Sheinberg explained that testing Gold's sample was right up his alley — a procedure he'd undertaken a thousand times before. He went on to say that the antigens A and B, which determined the classic blood groups, were relatively stable substances. Therefore, it was possible to determine their presence in dried blood stains and thus identify the group of blood that produced the stain.

Gold was thrilled to learn that 95 percent of dried blood samples were successfully checked in the lab.

"I usually draw the sample," Sheinberg said. "Then we test for a laundry list of medical conditions, anything from high cholesterol to diabetes."

Somewhat curious, Gold asked how a person became a phlebotomist, which was a word he could barely pronounce. Surprisingly, the only educational training needed was the completion of a certificate or diploma program. A college degree was not required. Sheinberg was an M.D., but many of his colleagues were not. Most of them had enrolled in a six- to eight-week course, then completed a state-approved internship, which required forty hours on-site at a hospital or medical facility.

Gold shook his head admiringly. "I could never handle your job."

"Does the sight of blood make you queasy?"

"Only if it's mine."

Sheinberg flinched reflexively, forcing a smile. "I assume that's not the case today?"

"Fortunately not." He put his attaché case on a table, opened it, and took out the sample of dried blood. "I wasn't sure if dried blood could be tested the same way as wet blood."

"Blood is blood," Sheinberg replied. "In case you're curious, your blood type is determined by genes inherited from your parents." He put on a lab coat and began to prepare the sample for testing. "There are four main blood types; A, B, AB, and O.

Each can be Rh positive or Rh negative, so now we have eight blood groups." He looked at Gold and smiled. "Are you with me?"

"So far, so good."

"If red blood cells contain RhD antigen, a protein, then they're RhD positive. If not, they're RhD negative. Antigens are molecules that are capable of stimulating an immune response. They're often confused with antibodies, which are Y-shaped proteins produced by B cells of the immune system in response to exposure to antigens." He paused and looked at Gold thoughtfully. "Am I going too fast?"

For a moment, Gold's eyes glazed over and he stood utterly still. Finally, he blinked, then said, "Is there a test at the end of med school?"

Sheinberg was amused by the question. "Hermatology is a fascinating subject. Did you know that there are one hundred fifty billion red blood cells in one ounce of blood?"

"Nope."

"Two and a half trillion in one pint."

"Amazing."

"Humans have red blood, but there are other colors."

"You don't say."

Sheinberg nodded his head vigorously. "Crabs have blue blood. Earthworms have green blood. The blood of a starfish is yellow."

Gold restrained an urge to make a smart comeback, hoping class was just about over. "What can you tell me about my sample?"

"Let's take a look." He transferred the sample onto an absorbent filter paper, then proceeded to cut out a disc-shaped piece with a manual hole punch, dropping it onto a flat-bottomed microtitre plate. Scrunching his face in concentration, he added a precise amount of a phosphate-buffered saline solution, then placed the solution into a microcentrifuge tube for two minutes of centrifugation. The eluates were then analyzed and examined under a compound microscope. "Wow, that's interesting."

"Something wrong?"

Sheinberg straightened up, thinking. "I'm just curious. Where did you get this sample?"

"Evidence from a crime scene."

"What sort of crime?"

"I'm not sure. Probably a murder."

"Too bad."

"I beg your pardon?"

"The blood type is very rare. AB-negative. I would have definitely asked for a donation."

Gold looked at him for a moment, then turned his attention to the microscope. "When you say rare, what do you mean? How rare?"

According to Sheinberg, 38 percent of people had O-positive blood, the most common blood type. A-positive was the second most common, accounting for 34 percent. All the other blood types were in single digits, ranging from 1.5 to 8.5 percent. AB-negative, the rarest blood type, was found in less than 1 percent of the population.

"*Less than one percent?*" Gold asked.

"Somewhere around zero point six percent."

Gold shot him a dubious look. "Are you sure about that?" Straightaway, he knew he'd said the wrong thing. He turned away. "I don't know what to say." It was hard to put into words but he tried. "You just made my day."

"I'm glad I could be of service."

Gold felt hairs bristle on his arms and neck. He never expected to find such a rare blood type on Kemmler's sword, and if Katz had the same blood type, his killer was one step closer to a cell on death row. *It ain't over till the fat lady sings*, he reminded himself. The authorities would still need a body to make the charges stick.

Sheinberg looked questioningly at him. "Has the victim been autopsied?"

"No, not yet."

"Well, when an autopsy is performed you might discover some underlying health problems."

"What sort of problems?"

"A person with AB-negative blood is more likely to develop type 2 diabetes and coronary heart disease. Some studies have also shown a link to cancer."

Gold made a mental note of that, and then another question crossed his mind. He wondered if there were any connections between blood type and personality. "I've always heard that personality traits were inherited through blood."

Sheinberg barked a quick, short burst of laughter. "An old wives' tale," he said. "*Old* being the operative word. That idea dates as far back as Aristotle. Hippocrates, the father of medicine, also thought there was a link, and he even suggested that bodily fluids produced four personality types: sanguine, choleric, melancholic, and phlegmatic. Temperament theories are a dime a dozen, but none of them are based on actual science."

Gold digested his answer for a moment, then shook his head in disgust. "So much for old wives."

Sheinberg's face softened, and he said in a calmer tone, "There's one other anomaly about AB-negative blood. People in that blood group seem to have a higher risk of developing cognitive and memory problems that lead to dementia. Do you know if your victim had any signs of mental deterioration?"

"Just the opposite," Gold said. "He was sharp as a tack. In fact, he may have been too smart for his own good."

"I know the type," Sheinberg said. "No pun intended."

Gold snatched up his ringing cell phone, listened, asked questions, and listened some more. He clicked off and glanced at his watch. A note of distress sounded in his voice. "Sorry, but I have to run."

"No problem."

"Can I get a copy of the blood test results?"

"I'll leave it at the front desk."

"Thank you, doctor."

"Any time."

Gold was embarrassed by the abrupt departure, but it couldn't be helped. There was no time for a long goodbye. He'd just received an urgent call from Irene Kaminski, and she was the bearer of some very bad news. The police had recently found the badly burnt body of Marvin Katz in a dumpster, and all hell was breaking loose in the city. A major investigation was now underway and there were rumors about a contentious insurance claim — and a company called Anchor Insurance. Kaminski had told him, in no uncertain terms, that it was time to get back to the office. He could return to Texas after the heat died down.

Upstairs, Christine Penny lay on her freshly made bed, hands folded behind her head, long legs crossed at the ankles, daydreaming. She was dressed in the same clothes she'd been brought to the hospital in, but with the blood washed out. Her legs felt a little wobbly, and there were occasional spots floating in front of her eyes, but her doctor had said that both conditions would eventually pass. All she had to do was take it easy and get plenty of rest, and she'd be good as new in a couple of weeks.

"I spoke to your doctor," Gold said. "He gave you the all clear to fly."

She nodded as if to say, "I'm not surprised." She'd always known this moment would come, but she wasn't happy about it. "Maybe I should get a second opinion."

"I don't think that's necessary."

"It wouldn't hurt."

"It wouldn't help, either."

She sat up, folded her arms across her chest and just stared at him. Gold thought that maybe she had figured out where he was going with this, and she didn't like it. "Are you sending me home?"

Keeping his voice under control, Gold explained the situation. He told her about the urgent call and why he had to return to New York ASAP. "When the boss says jump, I ask how high."

"I understand."

"I hope so."

She faked a short-lived smile. "Are you coming with me?"

Gold made a thumbs-up gesture. "I'm your chaperone."

"You're the one who needs supervision."

"Yeah, you're probably right. Are you ready to leave?"

"My bags are packed."

"I'll take them down."

She looked around the room, then gave him a smile that was hard to read. "Believe it or not, I'll miss this place."

"Even the food?"

"Everything."

Gold felt himself reddening. He came over to the bed, bent, and kissed her lightly on the hair. "Don't worry, dear. I'll make sure you get plenty of airline grub."

She gave him a droll look. "You're a mensch."

CHAPTER TWENTY-SEVEN

After the Bombardier Challenger leveled off, a flight attendant came around and offered the passengers food and drink, but both Gold and Penny declined. Instead, they watched a movie about a zombie apocalypse and then folded their seats down flat — one of the perks of a private jet — and went to sleep. By the time the flight touched down at Newark Airport and offloaded the passengers and crew, it was ten minutes past six, Eastern Standard Time. Two SUVs, driven by federal agents, were waiting at the arrival gate. One took Christine Penny back to Bangor, Pennsylvania. The other took Gold to Lower Manhattan, where he hoped to meet Irene Kaminski. But his hopes were dashed when he learned that she'd been summoned to an emergency board meeting.

C'est la vie, he thought. *Tomorrow's another day.*

After dark, when the office workers went home, the Financial District had a whole different feel. Without all the hubbub and sunlight, the concrete canyons were dark and forboding, and the area was anything but inviting. Gold was not accustomed to having John Street to himself, and if the truth be told, it felt spooky. There wasn't a cab in sight, so he decided to try his luck on William Street, two blocks north. He'd only walked a few yards before a long, black limousine drove by, stopping at the corner. The car pulled up to the curb, and a man wearing a gray turtleneck and a black leather jacket got out, walked over to Gold, and extended his hand. "Nice to see you again," he said matter-of-factly, though his expression said something altogether different. "Do you remember me?"

Gold shook the man's hand, trying to place him. He rubbed his chin for a few seconds but couldn't come up with an answer. He considered lying but decided against it. Too dangerous. The man was tall and potbellied, with thinning black hair and a lengthy scar on his right cheek. His penetrating dark eyes marked him as a man of above average intelligence, but they were cold, guarded, and calculating — the eyes of a Mafia hit man. Struggling to remain calm, Gold said, "I know we've met, but I can't remember where or when."

"Casa D'Angelo. Boca Raton. Three years ago. You were at the bar, stuffing your face with a giant meatball. Your second course was either pappardelle or risoto."

Trying to be funny, Gold said, "Did you forget what I was drinking?"

"Brunello di Montalcino."

"You've got a hell of a memory."

"Comes in handy in my line of work."

"Which is?"

"Waste management and disposal."

Gold swallowed hard. "What do you need to remember?"

"Garbage routes. Dump sites. Incinerator locations. That sort of thing." He somehow managed to flash a smile that lacked even the slightest trace of warmth. "You have no idea how stressful my job can be."

"I'll bet."

"Well, it's a dirty job, but somebody's gotta do it."

"I didn't catch your name."

"We don't need to go down that road." He walked back to the limousine and opened the rear door. "But we do need to take a drive. Get in."

Gold cleared his throat and did his professional best not to look scared. "My parents told me never to get into a car with strangers."

"You're a funny guy."

"Occasionally."

"I hope I don't have to twist your arm."

Gold was a man with a healthy respect for instinct. It was no substitute for evidence, but it was usually helpful. His instinct said that if somebody intended to kill him, he'd already be dead. All things considered, it would probably be best to go along for the ride. "Where are we going?"

"La Grenouille."

"The French restaurant?"

"No meatballs tonight."

They drove up FDR Drive at breakneck speed, exiting onto 1st Avenue and then over to East 52nd Street. When Gold stepped out of the limo, a rough looking character led him inside and pointed to a table at the back of the restaurant. A tuxedoed maitre d brought him to the table, pulled out a fauteuil chair, then returned to his station. Out of the corner of his eye, Gold saw Joe DeCarlo come out of the men's room and head his way. He was using a cane, but he didn't seem to have any problem with balance or stability. He lowered himself into a chair and smiled broadly, affording Gold a repugnant view of his cigarette stained teeth.

"*Buona serata,*" DeCarlo mumbled. "How ya been?"

Gold took a sip of water, tapped his lips with his napkin, and dropped it on the table. "What a pleasant surprise."

"I'm glad you could join me."

"To be honest, it was an offer I couldn't refuse."

"Do you need to call home?"

"No, I'm good."

"Have you ever eaten here?"

"Nope."

"Too pricey, huh?"

"No meatballs."

DeCarlo stifled a smile. "The meal's on me, so order whatever you want. I can vouch for the food. Everything's good. The only thing I haven't tried are sweetbreads. The thought of eating animal organs makes me sick."

"I know what you mean. Offal is awful."

"You're a funny guy."

"So I've been told."

DeCarlo called over a waiter, asked for two menus, then ordered a bottle of 1945 Lafite Rothchild, something Gold never thought he would taste. "Fucking wine's expensive, but it's worth every penny."

"I'd be happy with a beer."

"No way, Jose. We're celebrating."

"What's the special occasion?"

"I just made a killing in the market."

"Wall Street's the place to be."

"Not the stock market. The art market. I just got my hands on another Weighorst."

"Your favorite artist."

"Damn right. You've been to my place. You've seen how great they look on a wall."

Gold had only entered the lion's den once, but he remembered how good they looked. "Which painting did you acquire?"

"*Old Mexico Rancho*. Oil on canvas. Gold leaf frame. A real beauty."

"Congratulations. Did you buy it at an auction?"

"No, I went through a dealer."

Gold scratched his jaw with the menu. "I might have seen that painting somewhere."

DeCarlo waved off Gold's remark. "I don't think so. It was in a private collection."

"How many Weighorst's do you have?"

"Ten."

"Trying to corner the market?"

"I wish I could. I love his work. I don't know how to explain it, but his paintings speak to me."

"What do they say?"

"Depends on the piece, but the artist gives you a glimpse of his soul, and that's some heavy-duty shit."

"Spoken like a true enigma."

"Yeah, that's me. A man of many puzzling parts."

"Which part are you playing tonight?"

DeCarlo sat ramrod straight in his chair. He spoke formally with a deep, melodious voice. His posture and tone conveyed his "I am a serious man" persona. "Tonight I play an important role. *Un uomo che paga i suoi debti.* A man who pays his debts."

This should be good, Gold thought.

They sat for a while in completely awkward silence. Well, it was completely awkward for Gold. DeCarlo seemed fine with it. Gold didn't like the silence. It made him feel as if he might blurt out something he would regret. He drew a deep breath, then exhaled noisily. They had played this game before, and Gold was sure the rules weren't going to change now. DeCarlo would take his time, drink some wine, gather his thoughts. There was no point in pressing him.

When the waiter finally returned, he went through the whole nine yards with the wine. He sniffed the cork, decanted the wine, poured two glasses. DeCarlo shooed him away, then said, "Salud."

"L'chaim," Gold said. He took a tiny sip and nodded slowly, duly impressed by the quality of the wine. "Rich, long finish."

"One of a kind."

"I'm glad I didn't order a beer."

"Yeah, I bet you are."

Gold took another sip and did some quick calculations. The bottle contained twenty-five fluid ounces, which was five glasses of wine. The bottle cost four thousand dollars, which meant that each glass cost eight hundred bucks. Whoever said crime didn't pay was an idiot. Sensing the time was right, he said, "Tell me about this debt you owe."

DeCarlo allowed the silence to stretch until Gold shifted again beneath his stare, then he said deliberately, "You pulled my bacon out of the fire. Three years ago. I got tangled up with that cop killing. The detective that Nicky Russo clipped. I forget his name."

"Lou Feretti."

"Yeah, that's the guy. Poor bastard got shot with a spear gun."

"Yes, I remember."

"Anyway, you vouched for me, straightened things out with the powers that be. I never got a chance to thank you for being a stand up guy."

"You helped me find Russo. Pointed me in the right direction. My friend collected the reward."

"What did you get? Oogotz!"

"So this is my reward? A lovely dinner and the pleasure of your company?"

"Not exactly. I got something else in mind. A little surprise that will make your day." He waved at the waiter, who made a beeline to the table. "Let's order. You can open your gift after dinner."

They dined on warm lobster salad, followed by expertly prepared chicken breast in a truffle sauce, with haricots verts and pomme souffle. Neither of them ordered dessert, but the maître

d' sent over a complimentary tray of petit fours. He also sent a
bottle of anisette. Between sips, DeCarlo said, "You ready to tear
up my IOU?"

Gold forced a smile. "The suspense is killing me."

"Funny you should use that term." He reached into his pocket
and took out an envelope, which he placed directly in front of him
on the table. A wicked little smile turned one corner of his mouth.
"What do you think is inside?"

"Hopefully not the check."

"Like I said before, you're a funny guy."

"Should I take a peek?"

"Be my guest."

Gold opened the envelope and extracted a photograph — two
photographs, actually, a head-on shot and a profile — of a man,
apparently after being arrested. A mug shot of Joseph Kemmler.
Bristling, he said, "What a thoughtful gift."

"I thought about it long and hard."

"I can't imagine what you were thinking."

"I kept asking myself the same question. Should I show Gold
a photo of the guy who's planning to kill him or not? Maybe I
should mind my own business. Maybe he won't believe me. Maybe
I should let the chips fall where they may." He leaned forward
across the table, his bony hands clasped. "You think I did the
right thing?"

Gold felt his stomach go hollow. He caught his breath,
cleared his throat, tried to swallow. "How do you know what he's
planning?"

"The dumb bastard confided in me."

"You friends or something?"

"Hell no. He's a business associate. Nothing more, nothing less."

"A business associate?"

"I've bought some artwork from him. A couple of paintings and a sculpture or two. He gives me first dibs, but I don't like the son of a bitch. He's got a big mouth and a violent temper." He refilled his glass with anisette. "I don't remember how your name came up, but you're on his shit list, so watch your back."

Gold leant back slowly in his chair as he absorbed what DeCarlo had told him. A pained expression crossed his face. "Did Kemmler say why he wanted to kill me?"

"No, but he's a fucking Kraut, and you're just another Hebe he'd like to whack."

Gold glared at him and literally spat out the words, "What do you mean *another* Hebe?"

"You've been out of town, so you might not know that a shyster named Melvin Katz is MIA."

"I think you mean Marvin Katz."

"Whatever. I happen to know that Katz is on his way to the bone orchard."

"Where?"

"The cemetery. Although in his case, it won't be much more than a hole in the ground."

"Wait a minute. Are you saying that Katz is dead?"

"Dead as a doornail. Kemmler stabbed him with a fucking sword."

Gold played dumb, hoping to learn as much as he could from the old man. "Did Kemmler confess to the crime?"

"He not only confessed, he asked me to help him get rid of the body. I didn't want any part of that shit, so I sloughed him off on a teamster who does some moonlighting. You ever heard of the Highway of Hell?"

"No."

"It's down in Texas. Somewhere near Houston. Great spot to dump a corpse." He gazed into what was left of his anisette. "You know, when you took down Russo you became a big shot. A man among men. You could do the same thing with Kemmler. All ya gotta do is make a phone call." With some difficulty, he got up from the table and tossed an envelope in Gold's direction. "Do yourself a favor. Reach out and touch someone."

CHAPTER TWENTY-EIGHT

As usual on a hot summer's day, South Congress Avenue was a sea of sweating tourists. They milled elbow to elbow, dressed in T-shirts and shorts, flushed faces shaded from the Texas sun beneath floppy hats and gimme caps. From his perch above, on a rooftop bar, Ricardo Paz surveyed the crowd, wondering when the hell Miguel de la Cruz was going to call.

Let sleeping dogs lie, he told himself. Sometimes no news was good news, and this might be one of those times. He'd never met Señor de la Cruz, but he'd heard that the man had a mercurial temperment — and a weird fascination with poisonous insects. Nobody seemed to know much about the mysterious Mexican's past, but there were rumors that he was connected to the Mexican Mafia. Also known as *La eMe*, Spanish for "the M," the Mexican Mafia was the deadliest and most powerful gang on the West Coast. By most accounts, they currently had four to five hundred official members and over a thousand "associates" engaged in various forms of illegal activity.

One bad hombre, Paz thought, not the sort of man you'd want to rile. Even so, he was tempted to leave the artifacts in his motel room and catch the next flight back to Miami. He'd never done such a thing before, but there was a first time for everything. Of course, if de la Cruz was actually mobbed up, it could also be the last time he did such a thing. In the end, he decided to cool his heels and pray that the telephone would ring.

As fate would have it, his prayers were soon answered, and later that day, he was on his way to San Antonio — followed by two unmarked cars and a small contingent of federal agents.

Señor de la Cruz lived in the King William Historic District south of downtown, close to the San Antonio River. The entire area had once belonged to the Mission San Antonio de Valero, commonly known as the Alamo. The original settlers were Coahuiltecan Indians, brought to the region by a Franciscan missionary in 1718. The tribe was relocated in the early 1800s, and their land was subdivided into lots and sold at public auction. Before long, streets were laid out and German immigrants began to arrive en masse, and the area became known as "Sauerkraut Bend."

The main street was named in honor of King Wilhelm I, the King of Prussia. Over time it became the epicenter of a fashionable neighborhood, the thoroughfare where wealthy movers and shakers built impressive houses designed in the Greek Revival, Victorian, and Italianate styles. During the 1930s and 1940s, the neighborhood declined, but it wasn't long before investors saw the potential of restoring the fine old houses, and soon thereafter, the King William environs became San Antonio's first designated historic district.

Many of the most impressive homes were on King William Street, including a limestone gem owned by a foreign investor named Miguel de la Cruz. The de la Cruz property was situated on a corner lot, surrounded by old-growth trees and manicured gardens. The villa was 150 years old, but extensive renovations had restored it to its former grandeur. Unfortunately, even new wallpaper and a fresh coat of paint couldn't hide a faint musty smell, a lingering annoyance caused by mold, mildew, and poor air circulation.

Inside, a hard-looking man was standing in the foyer, his arms crossed, impatience etched on his face. "Ricardo Paz?" he said brusquely, straightening his tie. "I'm Carlos Mendoza, head of security. Follow me, please."

It suddenly occurred to Paz that he could probably just drop the rifle and sword on the floor right this minute, run back to his car, and drive away. The idea was appealing, but it was a little late for that sort of thing. Mendoza had to be armed, and he was probably a damn good shot.

They walked through the house and into the backyard, security cameras recording their every step. Paz followed a few feet behind, admiring the grounds but wondering where the hell they were going. Finally, they came to a stone cottage that had been converted into a private chapel. Paz was told to go inside and make himself comfortable in the first row of pews. Señor de la Cruz would be joining him shortly.

Heart racing, Paz entered the chapel and took a seat in the first row of pews. Looking up, he saw a stained glass window depicting images of Jesus and the Virgin Mary. A beam of sunlight shone down on a brass crucifix mounted upon a marble altar. Next to the altar was the "Presider's Chair," the chair that was used by a priest conducting Mass. Someone had bolted the chair to the floor, which Paz thought was strange. Other than that, the de la Cruz family chapel was a comforting sanctuary, an oasis of spirituality in the middle of America's seventh largest city.

Suddenly, a side door opened and a middle-aged man walked in, someone outside closing the door behind him. The man was short, maybe five-foot-five, dressed impeccably in a suit and tie. He scrutinized Paz, directly meeting his eyes as he took a seat beside him. Paz opened his mouth, then closed it again, opting against saying whatever was on his mind.

The man leaned in close and said, "The Lord's my shepherd, I'll not want. Yet there are things that I want. For instance, a rifle and a sword." The muscles around his mouth twitched in an imitation of a smile. "I'm Miguel de la Cruz. Welcome to my humble abode." He glanced at the duffle bags that Paz had brought with him. "I trust you have my artifacts?"

Paz found himself grinning manically, and he couldn't douse it out. "Yes, I brought the rifle and the sword. Would you like to see them?"

"Not right now."

"Most buyers like to inspect the merchandise."

"I understand, but that won't be necessary. You see, I conduct business in an honorable way, and I expect others to do the same. I won't tolerate deception, dishonesty, or deviousness." He sighed and rubbed the bridge of his nose. "If the artifacts are not genuine, I'd be disappointed. Not because I spent two million dollars, but because I was made to look foolish. A man in my position cannot afford to look like a fool."

Paz stopped grinning, his bottom lip quivering slightly. "I'm just the middleman, but I'm sure everything's on the up-and-up."

With his typical calm demeanor, de la Cruz said, "I certainly hope so. I've never been able to handle disappointment. Allow me to demonstrate what I mean." He stood up and walked over to the side entrance, then opened the door and waved to someone outside. "I think you'll find this quite instructive."

Paz didn't like the way he said that, with a hint of malice, his eyes narrowing ever so slightly. "I don't mean to be rude, but I'm pressed for time."

"Well, this won't take long, and like I said, you'll find it instructive." He stepped aside, allowing Mendoza to drag in a bound and hooded prisoner. *"Atarlo a la silla.* Make sure he can't move."

Mendoza tied the prisoner's hands and feet to the Presider's Chair, then yanked off his hood. Paz's eyes almost popped out of his head. *Dear God,* was all he could think. Then the shock of recognition punched his gut. *I know him.* Dammit, it was the gangbanger with the devil horns tattoo. He'd been severely beaten and bore little resemblance to the cocky kid who'd been strutting around the cargo terminal.

Paz watched de la Cruz closely, wariness gathering inside him. *"Qué pasa, amigo?"*

"Mexican justice," de la Cruz answered. "Are you familiar with the laws of my country?"

"I'm from Cuba," Paz said. *"No sé nada. No quiero saber."*

"You don't want to know?"

"Not really."

"Knowledge is power."

"Ignorance is bliss."

Characteristically, de la Cruz wasn't deterred. He explained that unlike the United States, where an offender is presumed to be innocent until proven guilty, Mexico based its laws on the Napoleonic Code, which presumed an offender guilty until proven innocent. As if that wasn't bad enough, prisoners were never told that they had a right to remain silent. Nor were they offered free legal counsel. There was no habeas corpus. No right to a speedy trial. By and large, a defendant was at the mercy of the court.

When de la Cruz was done rambling, Paz said, "Why are you telling me these things? We're not in court."

"True, but this is where *I* hold court and where I pass judgement. The prisoner has been found guilty of disobeying my orders. A great disappointment. Now he must be punished."

Paz eyed de la Cruz thoughtfully, trying to remain calm. "What did he do wrong?"

"He was supposed to keep an eye on my property. Instead, he tried to kill the man you were talking to at the airport."

"Adam Gold?"

"I'm not sure of his name, but you were talking to him — perhaps arguing — inside the cargo terminal. After you left, the young *idiota* tried to assassinate Gold and his female companion. He was arrested, but I was able to post bail."

"What happened to the other two?"

"Not your concern."

"They were only teenagers."

"Street urchins. Illegitimate and expendable." He shook his head in a slow, disapproving way. There wasn't an ounce of pity in his eyes. "To be honest, I'm partly to blame. I hired children to do a man's job. I won't make that mistake again." A disgusted look settled on his features. "Shall we proceed with the demonstration?"

A great sense of impending doom settled in Paz. He could almost hear himself saying *I told you to run.* Now it was too late. Too late to run and probably too late to save devil horns' life. But it was worth a try. "Look, I don't mean to be pushy, but would you mind taking a peek at the artifacts — just to be on the safe side?"

"Are you trying to distract me?"

"No, I just want to be sure — absolutely sure — that I brought the right items."

"Don't you trust Mr. Kemmler?"

"I never met the man."

"You've never met?"

"We've only spoken on the phone."

"That's odd."

"I haven't met many clients. We usually do business over the phone or on the Internet. Saves time and money."

"I would think a two million dollar deal would require a face-to-face meeting."

"Not in this day and age."

A boyish grin crept across de la Cruz's face. He studied Paz with cautious eyes. He didn't believe him for a second, but he decided to play along. A few more minutes couldn't hurt. "Very well," he said at last. "Let's take a look at the artifacts."

Paz composed himself, smoothed his hair, opened the duffle bags, and placed the rifle and the sword on the pew. He hovered over the artifacts for a few moments before saying, "Two antique weapons. A valuable addition to your lovely home. I hope you're pleased."

"Beyond words," de la Cruz said. "I've been waiting for these a long time. Most of my adult life."

"They must be of great importance."

"*Sí, muy importante.* Would you like to know why?"

"I certainly would."

"I thought so." He blew air out through his nose in a long sigh. "I'm willing to explain their importance, but then it will be time to carry out the sentence of the court. Understood?"

The sick feeling in Paz's stomach intensified. He was quiet a long moment, not sure how to respond. "I think I should mention something."

"*Qué?*"

"I have vasovagal syncope."

"What the hell is that?"

"I faint at the sight of blood." He saw a momentary flash of what he knew was disappointment on de la Cruz's face. "I've had it since I was a kid."

"You needn't worry. Blood-letting is passé." He laughed and rubbed his hands in glee. "I have a much better way of inflicting pain."

CHAPTER TWENTY-NINE

Miguel de la Cruz was only thirty-five years old, but he was often mistaken for being in his late forties. Premature baldness made him look old, and he was not a particularly attractive man. He had a sagging jawline, high cheekbones, a crooked nose, and a mouth that twisted into a perpetual smirk. He had carried in with him a small tote bag, and now he placed it on the altar and withdrew a glass jar, which contained a live scorpion. He tapped on the side of the jar, stirring the arthropod, then handed it to Mendoza. He was pretty calm for a man who was about to carry out a death sentence.

Sounding a little frustrated, de la Cruz said, "The artifacts are symbolically important, but I believe they might restore the pride of my people. Try to imagine how you would feel if the United States had successfully invaded Cuba, making your homeland part of their empire. Your Hispanic culture would be of little interest to the rulers of Norteamérica. They would have no use for your customs, your language, your religion, or your history. In time they would steal your land and auction off your possessions to the highest bidder. When that was done, they would add insult to injury by renaming your towns and cities and building magnificent homes that only they could afford." He threw Paz the look of a school principal dressing down a rowdy pupil. "Look around you, Mr. Paz. The evidence is everywhere." He leaned over the altar, obviously agitated. "Do you know where you're standing?" Paz shook his head, hoping that would suffice. "You're standing on the graves of my ancestors."

Every hair on the back of Paz's neck stood straight up, and his skin actually goose-pimpled for the first time in years. "I don't know what to say."

"I know that sounds strange," de la Cruz said. His face softened, and he said in a calmer tone, "Allow me to explain."

Paz nodded glumly. "Take all the time you need."

Surprisingly, de la Cruz was not only a successful businessman but also a student of history. He reminded Paz of their shared Spanish ancestry and the fact that the United States had gone to war against Cuba and Mexico. Struggling to remain civil, he went on to tell Paz that Mexico had achieved independence in 1821, but soon thereafter Anglo-American settlers began to pour into the region. By 1836, the Texians were strong enough to declare their own independence and create the Republic of Texas. Nine years later, the republic was annexed by the United States and became a state.

"Those were dark days," de la Cruz said. "My ancestors were among the thirty families who originally founded the Presidio San Antonio de Bexar, on the west side of the river. From this small settlement grew a great city, but much of it was stolen by the Anglo-Americans." His eyes darkened. "We were not the only ones to suffer a great humiliation. You might be interested to know that twenty-five Cuban families were sent to San Antonio in 1730, and they also lost everything. So you see, Mr. Paz, we have much in common."

With one exception, Paz thought. *I'm not living in the past. I don't have a chip on my shoulder.* Not knowing how to respond, he settled for a platitude. "No sense crying over spilled milk."

"You're missing the point," de la Cruz said. He looked at Paz as if he were a simple child. "We're not talking about spilled milk. We're talking about spilled blood. The slow, torturous bleeding of our ancestors. The forced assimilation. The constant humiliation. Even in victory we were mocked and shamed." He gestured toward the artifacts. "Take a good look at those weapons. They once belonged to famous Texians. The so-called heroes of the Alamo. Now they're mine, and I intend to display them throughout Mexico. They will serve as a constant reminder of our great victory. Our children will see that Mexican troops prevailed and learn that Santa Anna was the true hero of the Alamo." He laughed harshly, then leaned across the altar and whispered, "I might become a national hero. Wouldn't that be ironic?"

Paz saw something in de la Cruz's eyes that frightened him. "You're going to piss off a lot of people in Norteamérica."

"That's part of the plan. A big part, actually." He stared at Paz for a moment, contemplating how much to reveal, what was safe to tell him. For just a moment he felt so euphoric he wanted to tell him everything, and the hell with what he would later repeat. But he didn't. Control came back. "It pains me to think how close I came to losing the artifacts." He glanced at the young man in the chair, meeting his eyes for only a second, but that was long enough for him to understand the depth of de la Cruz's anger and to be frightened by it. "Speaking of pain, the time has come to carry out the sentence of the court." He told Mendoza to proceed, and the head of security gagged the young man's mouth with duct tape.

Paz's shoulders slumped visibly as the world seemed to settle on him. "Do I have to watch this?"

"I'm afraid so," de la Cruz answered. "It's part of the lesson plan." He unscrewed the glass jar and raised it to eye level, studying the scorpion inside. "Do you know what my enemies call me? *El acosador de la muerte.* The death stalker. I don't care for the name, but it keeps my employees in line and prevents my enemies from becoming too bold. I came by this name a few years ago, when I discovered how to strike fear in someone's heart. A man in our village was selling drugs to children, so I put a scorpion in his boot. The man died a painful death, and I acquired a new nickname." He jiggled the jar ever so slightly. "This little beauty is the deathstalker scorpion. *Leiurus quinquestriatus.* Also known as the Palestine yellow scorpion. A very deadly fellow."

Paz was quiet, thinking. "What are you going to do with that insect?"

"Watch and see." He handed the jar to Mendoza. "By the way, scorpions are not insects. They're classified as Arachnida, the distant cousin of spiders. They have eight legs, while insects have six. As you can see, they also have two body segments and a prominent stinger. The stinger is the part you want to avoid. It's filled with a powerful mixture of neurotoxins, making it one of the most dangerous species of scorpions. The cause of death is usually pulmonary edema. Liquid accumulation in the lungs, which leads to respiratory failure or cardiac arrest."

Paz's eyes widened perceptibly. "Did you find that thing around here?"

The question seemed to amuse de la Cruz. "No, you can't find them in North America. They prefer much warmer climates, places like the Middle East or North Africa."

"Thank God," Paz said. "I'd hate to step on that tail."

"Well, they're not all bad. By volume, their venom is the most expensive liquid in the world. Believe it or not, it's priced at thirty-nine million per gallon."

Paz tried a smile that mostly failed. "Maybe you should put him in a safe place."

"I've got a better idea. Let's see if he's in a good mood." He made a slashing gesture across his throat, and Mendoza dumped the scorpion down the shirt of the young man in the chair. Shuddering, de la Cruz glanced at Paz, then whispered, "Now for the fun part."

Almost immediately the young man felt a warm sensation in his chest. It spread like a wave of numbness over his entire body. He tried to scream, but the duct tape muffled his words. His eyes bulged, and his muscles began to spasm, accompanied by a sudden burst of pain in his joints. After several stings, his breathing became labored and his face lost color. Soon he began to emit a gurgling sound. He seemed to be choking on his own saliva.

Paz let his repulsion show. He glared at Mendoza, then at de la Cruz, shaking his head. "For God's sake, put the poor kid out of his misery."

"Seen enough?" de la Cruz asked.

"More than enough."

"Don't forget to spread the word."

"Whatever you say."

For a long time, de la Cruz said nothing at all. The tense silence stretched. With a deep sigh, he pulled a Glock 9mm pistol out of his tote bag and placed it on the altar. "I took the liberty of putting a suitcase in the back seat of your car. Inside, you'll find two million dollars in cash. Small bills. Kemmler's request. Make sure it's delivered in a timely fashion. Any questions?"

Paz glanced at the young man, now slumped over and barely breathing. "What are you going to do with him?"

"You wanted me to put him out of his misery." Slowly, deliberately, he placed the pistol to one side of the young man's head. Slowly, deliberately, he pulled back the hammer. "Give my regards to Mr. Kemmler."

Paz turned to leave and a wave of dizziness and nausea nearly buckled his knees. He kept his head down, waiting it out, trying not to throw up. When the feeling passed, he ran out of the chapel, wondering what the young man's final thoughts would be as the bullet tore through his head. A loud explosion ended all speculation.

God, he couldn't wait to get back to Miami.

Dreaming of home, he got back on the interstate, hoping to reach Austin before rush hour. With any luck, Kemmler would be waiting for him, and they could wrap up their business and go their separate ways. The sooner the better, he thought. These crazy bastards made Castro look like a saint.

Needing gas, he pulled into a station in San Marcos, a pleasant college town halfway between San Antonio and Austin. As he stepped out of his car, another vehicle pulled beside him and two men got out, identifying themselves as Texas Rangers. They asked a few routine questions, which Paz refused to answer, citing his constitutional right to remain silent. From experience, he knew it was a good idea to talk to a lawyer before agreeing to answer questions. The rangers did not appreciate his attitude, and they informed him that he'd been pulled over for a traffic violation, which meant that he was required to show a license, vehicle registration, and proof of insurance.

The traffic violation, failure to signal, was bogus, but they insisted upon the required documents. Paz was able to produce a valid driver's license, but he'd inadvertantly left his rental car agreement in his motel room, and inside the agreement were the other two items.

The rangers were sympathetic, or at least they appeared to be, but they still had a job to do. Without the proper documents, they had no choice but to make an arrest. They read Paz his rights, slapped on a pair of handcuffs, and brought him to the ranger station in Austin.

For the life of him, Paz could not understand why he was being arrested for a simple traffic violation. He had no idea how far from simple things were about to become. In compliance with state law, he was fingerprinted, photographed, and placed in a holding cell while his background was being checked. After two hours of twiddling his thumbs, he was assured that he would be allowed to make a phone call, but that right was never granted.

Dinner time came and went, but nobody except an untalkative guard paid him any mind. He was starting to wonder if the state of Texas had adopted the Napoleonic Code. Finally, just before lights out, a beefy ranger showed up, carrying the suitcase with the two million dollars inside. He introduced himself as Major Wilson and asked Paz if they could chat a spell.

Paz was in no mood to be interrogated, but after five hours of sitting on his duff, he was willing to answer a few basic questions. Surprisingly, Wilson only had one question: "Mind telling me why you're driving around with two million dollars?"

"None of your business," Paz snapped. "I'd like to make a phone call."

"I'd like to win the lotto," Wilson replied. "I don't think either one of those things are gonna happen."

"I know my rights."

"Well, good for you, son. That'll come in handy if we have a civics exam. Until then, I suggest you lossen your reins. If you pitch a hissy fit, I'm leavin'. Catch my drift?"

Paz was tempted to ask Wilson if he would mind speaking English, but he decided not to antagonize him. "If you must know, I'm bringing the money to a client. Is that against the law in Texas?"

"Depends how, where, and when you got the *dinero*."

"I don't have to tell you squat."

"No, you sure don't."

"I'm glad we agree on something."

"Just so you know, I'm fixin' to contact the FBI."

"Be my guest."

"Well, bless your heart. I was hopin' you wouldn't mind." He wedged a healthy chew under his lip and offered the plug to Paz, who shook his head. "I'll give those old boys a call when I get a chance."

Something in Wilson's tone sounded like a warning, but Paz was angry enough to ignore it. "When will that be?" he said with deliberate rudeness.

Wilson shrugged weakly. "Beats the hell out of me."

CHAPTER THIRTY

On the day after Paz was arrested, Gold met Irene Kaminski at the offices of the chief medical examiner on 1st Avenue. The OCME was the principal mortuary of the city, the place where all human remains that fell under their legal mandate were stored and examined. In addition to their regular customers, they received all unidentified and/or unclaimed remains found throughout the five burroughs. Under law, the OCME had jurisdiction to investigate certain deaths, which was why a keen-eyed medical examiner was struggling with the issuance of a certain death certificate.

The examiner, whose name was Lowenstein, happened to be an old friend of Irene's, and he'd read that she had a business connection to the deceased — a murder victim named Marvin Katz. Lowenstein was a large man with burly shoulders and a protruding stomach. He had a pleasant, round face and alert brown eyes, and — unlike the other examiners who spent their days and nights carving up corpses — he had a likable, welcoming aura.

When Kaminski and Gold walked into his office, they found him sitting at a roll top desk, studying the photographs of a recently autopsied body. A can of diet soda sat forgotten among stacks of X-rays and reports that cluttered the desktop. He looked up when Kaminski knocked on the door frame. "Good morning, Irene. Welcome to the inner sanctum."

Kaminski introduced Gold, then found a couple of usable chairs. "How do you work in here?"

"What do you mean?"

"The place is a pigsty."

Lowenstein swatted the words away. "For your information, pigs are not dirty animals. In fact, they're actually quite clean. They've gotten a bad reputation because they like to roll around in mud to cool off. You see, my dear, pigs are unable to sweat."

"You know a lot about pigs for a man who doesn't eat pork."

"I've always been something of a ham."

Kaminski rolled her eyes. "So what's up, sawbones?"

"Nothing that will brighten your day."

She eyed him speculatively. "Uh-oh, I don't like the sound of that. Should I brace myself?"

Lowenstein shrugged and put down the photographs, which he hadn't looked at since they sat down. After examining a hangnail for about twenty seconds, he finally said, "Marvin Katz."

"What about him?"

"I just finished the autopsy."

"Something wrong?"

He tugged at an ear, placed his glasses on his wide nose, and cleared his throat. "What religion was Katz?"

"I think he was Jewish."

Gold nodded. "A nonpracticing Jew."

"I thought so," Lowenstein said. "The body was burnt to a crisp, but I recovered a piece of jewelry. A religious item. Oddly enough, it wasn't a Star of David." He reached into his lab coat and pulled out a Virgin Mary pendant. "The pendant was attached to a gold necklace, which hung around the neck of the deceased." He handed the pendant to Kaminski. "If you'll look on the back, you'll see the owner's initials: E.M."

"Wait a minute," Kaminski said harshly. "Are you saying..."

Lowenstein cut her off mid-sentence. "Listen to me. I don't know who I autopsied, but I don't think it was Marvin Katz. To be perfectly honest, I couldn't determine the gender."

"How could that be? I thought there were anatomical differences between men and women."

"Several differences. A male skeleton is heavier and possesses a narrow pelvic cavity, broader shoulders, and a longer rib cage. Generally speaking, males also have larger skulls and longer leg bones. Unfortunately, the bones were virtually destroyed by the dumpster fire, which lasted several hours and reached an incredibly high temperature in the continuous flame region — somewhere between one thousand and fifteen hundred degrees Fahrenheit."

Kaminski gave him a dubious look. "The fire burned for several hours? In the heart of Manhattan? Where the hell was the fire department?"

"They arrived promptly, but firefighters have an old saying. Risk a lot to save a life, risk a little to save little, and risk nothing to save nothing."

"So they just sat back and watched?"

"They were required to take certain precautions. You must remember, a dumpster fire can be just as dangerous as a structural fire in certain circumstances. The firefighters had no idea what was inside the dumpster. The flip top was closed. It might have contained hazardous materials."

Little worry lines invaded Kaminski's polished image, creasing out from her mouth in rays of subsurface strain. "This is not good."

"No, but I do have some good news. Most of the victim's teeth survived the fire. I also found evidence of dental restoration. Metal screws, implants, and a couple of gold fillings. I brought everything to our forensic odontologist and asked him for a complete evaluation. We should have a report later today."

Kaminski paused, then she was struck with an idea. "What about a DNA test?"

"I can order one, but it will take some time."

"How long?"

"One or two weeks."

"Too long. What about a blood test?"

"Already done. I found some blood on the victim's clothing."

Gold gave him a long, hard look. "How did the clothing survive the fire?"

"The clothes were outside the dumpster."

"Outside?"

"Sounds weird, but that's where they found them."

Gold stiffened, then smiled at him. It was a small, sad smile. "Did you get the results of the blood test?"

"Just before you got here." He reached under a pile of lab reports and pulled out a sheet of paper. "The victim's blood type was identified as O positive."

"The most common blood type."

"Correct."

"Good to know."

Lowenstein paused, acutely aware of how intently Gold was watching him. It made him a bit uncomfortable. "It would be helpful if we knew Mr. Katz's blood type."

"Yes, it certainly would."

Kaminski cocked her head to one side as she tried to sum up the situation. She'd just been dealt a wild card, and she wasn't sure how to play it. "So what do we do now? Wait for the dental report?"

Lowenstein met her eyes again briefly, then he abruptly got up and walked over to the window that ran along one side of the room. He stood there for a few seconds before nodding to himself and turning around. "I need to keep my boss in the loop. I'll let him deal with the police. Somebody should tell Mrs. Katz that her husband might still be alive."

Gold's tone was businesslike. "I'll handle that chore."

Lowenstein gave him a sideways look that was difficult to read. "You're a good man, Charlie Brown."

Outside, a storm was abating; the thunder and lightning were and fading in the distance, and the rain had become little more than a drizzle. Gold and Kaminski had driven to a Greek diner for some coffee and Danish pastry, and while they were waiting to be served, Kaminski said, "You were awfully quiet back there. Something on your mind?"

Gold stared at a spot on the table, motionless, off in another world. He rubbed a kink out of his neck, sighed, then said, "Do you know why they found those clothes outside the dumpster?"

"No, I haven't a clue."

"They were left there to fool the police. They were Katz's clothes, but he didn't put them there. The killer did. The monster who murdered Elena Mendoza."

"Who's she?"

"The person they found in the dumpster."

"You knew her?"

"Only in passing. She was Kemmler's assistant."

Kaminski's mouth fell open. "He killed his own assistant?"

"I'm afraid so."

"Why would he do that?"

"I'm not sure. Maybe she knew too much. Maybe she stepped out of line. Anything's possible."

"How can you be sure it's her?"

"Her initials are E.M. The same initials that were on the Virgin Mary pendant." He lowered his voice, just a notch. "I spoke to McVey this morning. He mentioned her name and told me that she'd been missing for several days. Now we know why."

"God, that's awful. I wonder if she had a family."

"I'll ask McVey to check on that. In the meantime, we need to have a talk about Marvin Katz." They ordered, but they waited until the server was out of earshot before returning to the subject at hand. "There's no need to visit Mrs. Katz. We have nothing good to tell her."

"What do you mean? We know her husband wasn't in the dumpster."

Gold dropped his head, lifted it, and felt a thick knot in his stomach. "Marvin Katz is dead. Kemmler killed him. I'm sorry, I haven't had a chance to bring you up to date."

Kaminski was struck dumb by what she heard. "How do you know he's dead?"

"A little bird told me."

"Don't play games."

"A jailbird." He leaned in close. "Joe DeCarlo."

"The mob boss?"

"He gave me all the gory details."

"Why would he tell you such a thing?"

"He said he was repaying a debt, but I know that old rascal. He just wants to get rid of Kemmler and expand his art collection. He told me about a painting he'd recently acquired. A piece by an artist named Olaf Weighorst. *Old Mexico Rancho*. Kemmler had that painting in his shop, and it wasn't for sale."

"All the same, how can we take the word of a mobster?"

"We don't have to take his word. We've got an ace in the hole. Several aces."

"What does that mean?"

"McVey spoke to Mrs. Katz, and she confirmed that her husband's blood type was AB, Rh negative, the rarest blood type in the United States."

She looked at Gold questioningly. "What does that have to do with the price of tea in China?"

"There was blood on the sword that Kemmler shipped to Texas. I had it tested and it was AB negative. A perfect match. Which means that Kemmler stabbed Katz."

The light slowly dawned in Kaminski's eyes. "What do you think Kemmler did with the body?"

"I know exactly what he did." He pushed an envelope across the table. "Courtesy of Joe DeCarlo. He gave me this when we had dinner together. Take a look inside."

Out of the corner of her eye, she saw the server heading their way, so she waited until they were served before opening the envelope. Inside, she found a handwritten note:

FREIGHTLINER REGRIGERATED TRUCK
White/ Texas Plates
VIN # 3ALADFW0FDGK0320
I-81S/I-75S/I-59S/I-10W

Kaminski didn't look up. She spoke quietly and didn't give away anything by her eye or body movements. "What do we have here?"

Gold inhaled heavily. "The vehicle that Kemmler's using to transport the body, and the route he's taking to Texas."

A moment of stunned silence passed.

She sipped at her coffee. "Remind me to send DeCarlo a bottle of champagne."

"I might send him a case."

"Should we contact the police?"

"I don't think so. They might screw things up. I think we should let McVey call the shots. He's got some loose ends to tie up in D.C., and then he's heading back to Texas. I'd like to join him, finish what we started." He popped a piece of Danish into his mouth and chewed on it thoughtfully. "We still don't know Kemmler's endgame. I'd like to be around when his plan falls apart."

"I'd like to see that myself."

"Yeah, that's something else we need to talk about."

CHAPTER THIRTY-ONE

Greek diners were good for a nosh, but not the best place to have a heart-to-heart talk. Ralph Bunche Park was a much better choice, and only a few blocks north of the diner, directly across from United Nations Plaza. The park, squeezed between 42nd and 43rd Streets, had been named in honor of the first African-American to win the Nobel Peace Prize. From end to end, it covered less than a quarter of an acre, and its most famous monument was the Isaiah Wall, which contained the famous quotation from Isaiah 2:4: "They shall beat their swords into plowshares and their spears into pruning hooks; nation shall not lift up sword against nation, neither shall they learn war anymore."

Like most New Yorkers, Kaminski had never been to the park, and she was embarrassed to admit that she unaware of its very existence. They sat by the stainless-steel obelisk that stood in front of the wall, waiting for a group of Japanese tourists to finish taking photographs. When they were finally alone, Gold said, "I used to come here when I needed a place to unwind. I like the ambiance."

"Kind of far from the office."

"Worth the trip."

"How'd you get up here?"

"Subway. Number 4 train to Grand Central Station."

She nodded her head in a slow, approving way. "I like this spot. It's peaceful."

"It should be. It's the city's first Peace Park."

"Did you bring me here to make peace?"

"Are we at war?"

"No, but something's got you stirred up. I can see it in your eyes."

Gold faked a short-lived smile. "Well, now that you mention it, I do have something on my mind."

"Spit it out."

"Joseph Kemmler."

"Kemmler?"

"The guy makes my skin crawl, but you seem to hate everything about him. Your hatred is more than intense hostility; it's all-embracing, almost obsessive."

She turned away. "I have my reasons."

"Yeah, I know, but you've been keeping them to yourself. I'm starting to think you don't trust me."

"Don't be ridiculous. I trust you with my life."

"Maybe so, but there are parts of your life you don't like to share. I wouldn't repeat anything you told me, you have my word." He put his hand on her shoulder and looked her in the eye. "Need I remind you that, in our business, your word is your bond?" In his own clever way, Gold was referring to one of the unique aspects of the insurance industry. A verbal agreement — or binder — was just as valid as a written one, and it was based upon the same principles of trust and understanding. "The key word is trust."

Not to be outdone, Kaminski replied, "Need I remind *you* that a binder is only good for ninety days?"

"What are you saying, my time's up?"

She leaned back and appraised him, slowly and carefully. "You're like a dog on a bone today." Now she paused for a moment, wondering if she was missing something, if there was something else going on. She finally decided she couldn't worry about it. "Which parts of my life are you concerned about? You already know about my physical, financial, and occupational circumstances. Are you curious about my emotional and spiritual well-being?"

"You're on the right track." He watched her for several seconds, tempted to push further. He had sensed an opening, a subtle sign from her that maybe she was ready to open up. There was only one way to find out. "Tell me about your family. Your parents. Your aunts and uncles. Your cousins. Did they all live in Austria?"

Kaminski shifted uncomfortably at the mention of her family. "My God, you're a nosy son of a gun."

"I get paid to be nosy."

"Why do you care about my family?"

Gold placed a reassuring hand on her shoulder. "Because I care about you, and I think there's something you're not telling me. Something about Walter Kemmler, Joseph's father." He paused and leveled his gaze at her, waiting for the impact of his words to kick in. He didn't have to draw the picture any more clearly. "I've heard he was a rotten SOB."

She regarded him for another brief moment. "Who said that?"

"A gent named Mueller. A friend of a friend."

"How would he know?"

"He works at the German Embassy. Foreign intelligence officer."

Kaminski's mouth hung half-open in shock, although she quickly recovered. "When did I give you permission to pry into my life?"

"When you began to trust me with it. What do you think friends are for, Irene? To sit on their hands and do nothing? Sorry, that's not me."

"I don't know whether to give you a lecture or a raise."

"I'd settle for an explanation."

There were times — and this was surely one of them — when Kaminski wished she was at Dickenson Bay on Antigua, sipping a piña collada and soaking up the sun. She'd been blindsided by Gold, her favorite investigator, and now she had to decide how much to tell him. She swore under her breath and shook her head. Then she said, "Walter Kemmler was a vicious bastard, no different from his father or his son. I hope he rots in hell with the rest of his family." She got a little better control of her anger and said, "Fifty years ago, during the Cold War, my aunt and uncle owned a small bookstore in Berlin. They had barely survived World War II, so they were poor and struggled to make ends meet. Like many Germans, they had become apolitical. Totally disinterested in the politics of the day. Strangely enough, that's what got them in trouble with the secret police. They were lax about promoting Stasi propaganda, and after several warnings, they were targeted for *Zersetzung*, a program of biodegradation. Kemmler and his comrades destroyed their reputations, self-confidence, ability to make a living, and personal relationships. They were crushed under the heel of Stasi, then discarded like trash." She fiddled with her bracelet, avoiding eye contact. "They had no way to escape, so they remained in Berlin for a while, and then one day they reached the breaking point. They ran toward the wall, hand in hand, pretending to flee. They were both shot dead." She shook her head, tears welling up in her eyes. "I never met my aunt and uncle, but I heard their story a thousand times. My mother was never the same after her sister's death. I can't say that I blame her."

Gold swallowed, unsure how to proceed. "I don't blame you either. You have every right to hate Kemmler."

Kaminski, her mouth set tight, let out a long, slow breath through her nose. She did not like to be reminded of the past, but surprisingly she felt a sense of relief. She was glad she'd gotten it off her chest. "Any more questions?"

"No, I think we're done here."

"Not quite. I still have a bone to pick with you."

Gold was incredulous. "With me? How could that be? I just got back."

She dabbed her eyes with a tissue, then said, "I received an email from Seton Medical Center in Austin. A surgical bill. Imagine my surprise when I saw the amount due. Fifteen thousand dollars."

"Fifteen thousand?" He whistled softly. "I thought they put an end to surprise billing."

"I might put an end to your career. What the hell is this about?"

Knowing he was trapped, Gold told himself that confession was good for the soul. A good career move, too. "Do you remember Christine Penny? Red hair, green eyes, big smile? She was an underwriter in our Inland Marine department."

Kaminski sighed. "What about her?"

"She retired several years ago."

"Good for her."

"After she left the company, she moved to Pennsylvania and became an appraiser of antique weapons. I figured she might know something about Kemmler's rifle and sword, so I looked her up. Always good to get a second opinion."

"You brought the artifacts to her house?"

"No, I didn't have to. She was at a convention in Nashville, so I stopped there on my way to Texas."

"What does this have to do with the surgical bill?"

"Well, I'm getting to that. You see, Christine's always been a team player, so she volunteered to help with the investigation. I didn't have the heart to say no."

"You mean brains, don't you? How could you do such a stupid thing?"

"Not my finest hour."

"You can say that again. Did you bring her to Boerne and Fredericksburg?"

"Yeah, I did. She was actually a big help."

"Now she's a big expense. I assume she's the one who had surgery?"

"It was a minor operation."

"Fifteen thousand is minor?"

"You know hospitals. They overcharge for everything."

Another deep sigh. "How was she injured?"

"Flying glass."

"Car accident?"

"Er, no, but there was a car involved."

She shot him a look. "Let's have it."

It annoyed Gold to be spoken to like an unruly child, even though he guessed he deserved it. He *had* endangered the life of a former employee. A good comeuppance was in order. But first it was time to come clean. He started with the trip to Fredericksburg, then gave her a blow-by-blow account of the fiasco in Boerne. She almost blew a gasket when she heard that Penny was at the airport when Paz claimed the artifacts.

"Good Lord." She shook her head in slow wonder. "What were you thinking?"

"I wasn't thinking. I should have dropped her off at the hotel." He squirmed a little, then in a lower voice, he said, "After Paz left, we walked outside and were ambushed by a group of street thugs. I'm not sure why they were there or who sent them. In any case, a couple of shots were fired and Christine got hit by flying glass."

Kaminski cringed. "Were they apprehended?"

"On the spot."

She breathed lightly, getting a grip on her emotions. "Thank God she wasn't shot. If she'd been hit by a bullet, you'd have a lot of explaining to do. The board of directors would be furious. We'd both be out of a job."

"Yeah, it was a foolish mistake."

"Do you think she'll file suit?"

"Not a chance. Like I said before, she's a team player."

"You'd better hope so. I've got enough problems." With surprising gentleness, she said, "Maybe we should send her some flowers."

"I'll take care of it when we get back to the office."

"Send something nice. Money is no object."

Gold's expression lightened. "I hope you'll remember that when you pay the hospital bill."

Looking solemn, she said simply, "If I had a sword or a spear, you'd be in trouble."

CHAPTER THIRTY-TWO

The CUT Bar and Lounge was one of Georgetown's classiest watering holes and McVey's favorite place to grab a cold beer. The cozy bar was tucked inside the Rosewood Hotel in the Northwest section of the city, and the bartender, an Irish lad, knew how to pour a proper pint of Guiness. While McVey sipped his beer, the bartender hovered in the background, reorganizing some of the 2,500 bottles that were on display. With the drapes partially drawn, it was pleasantly dark, no one knew or recognized him, and he could while away the hours in a perfectly calibrated atmosphere of relaxed sophistication.

Molly Walker, the CIA recruiter, enjoyed the plush, green furniture, and she thought she remembered a time when a middle-aged piano player sang the kind of songs that were worth listening to. Molly had ordered a shot of Woodford Reserve on the rocks, then walked to the window to stare down at the canal. The water was murky brown beneath blue skies; there were a couple of kayakers and a group of canoeists paddling close to the shore. They seemed to be having a jolly good time. She turned around to face McVey, then said, "How far does the towpath run?"

McVey was quiet for a moment, thinking. "Almost two hundred miles. All the way to Cumberland, Maryland."

"Good place to jog?"

"I wouldn't know. I don't run unless I'm being chased."

She ignored the weak joke and returned to their table, turning her glass in her hand, watching the play of the lamplight on the crystal. A moment later, her complexion changed from pale to flushed. "I suppose we should talk about you-know-who. I know you're anxious to tie up a few loose ends."

McVey sat rigid, his face showed nothing. It rarely did. But his voice took on a sharp edge. "Let's get something straight. I'm not interested in tying up loose ends. I want to tie a knot around Kemmler's neck. So I need to ask. Are your people good with that, or do they intend to protect him?"

"I'm happy to report that Joseph Kemmler has become persona non grata at Langley."

"Since when?"

"Since he went from an asset to a liability. I can't provide much detail, but let's just say that he strayed off the reservation and got greedy. He went into business for himself and got used to the high life." She took a sip of her bourbon, then said, "How ya gonna keep 'em down on the farm after they've seen *Paree?* You know what I mean?"

"Too big for his britches, eh?"

"Something like that. In any case, he's fair game." She raised her glass to make a toast. "Happy hunting."

McVey absently adjusted his tie and nodded approvingly. "You just made my day."

"Maybe you can make my night."

"I'll try my best."

She looked directly at him and smiled sweetly. "You always do."

"What are friends for?" He smiled back at her and realized that he had missed looking at her. She was somewhere around forty but seemed both younger and older somehow. The flawless skin. The perfect features. She was almost too pretty to be in the espionage trade. When he told her that, she blushed. "I'm serious, Molly. You're a beautiful woman."

"How many drinks have you had?"

"Just one. This is me talking, not the alcohol."

Her smile was dazzling as she looked up at him through thick lashes, flirting. "If you were a gentleman you'd offer to buy me dinner."

"Where would you like to go?"

"Upstairs."

"The back porch?"

To McVey's surprise, she laughed, hard and long. She had to wipe her eyes before attempting an answer, and when she finally did, she prefaced it with, "I think you and I are going to work well together. No, silly, I mean *upstairs*. In a room."

"You want to get a room?"

"Do you have something better to do?"

"I can't think of anything better."

"Why don't you get us a nice suite. Something overlooking the canal."

"What about dinner?"

"We can order room service."

"I was planning to take you to a fancy restaurant."

"I'd rather stay here. To tell you the truth, I love to eat in bed." She laughed, dispelling the tension. "What do you think, sport?"

"I think you're on to something." He winked at her and stood up, signaling to the bartender. "Why don't you order another round. I'll be right back."

"I'll be here."

"Try to behave yourself."

"Sure, you say that now."

They were barely inside their suite before they began to kiss, and their inhibitions were soon abandoned. McVey lifted her off the floor, crossed the room, and dropped her on the bed like a sack of potatoes. She fell limp and loose, bouncing off the mattress. She pulled her blouse over her head and threw it aside, then unhooked her bra, slipped it off, and let it drop to the floor. "Come here," she whispered. She held out her hands, and he took them. She put his hands on her breasts, and he caressed them, feeling her nipples harden. He unbuttoned his shirt and pressed his bare chest against her breasts, which were soft and warm. Still kissing, he took off her skirt and pulled her panties down to her thighs. He bent over and kissed her lips, her breasts, and her stomach. She arched her back and began to moan.

He stood slowly and undid his belt and trousers.

They remained in bed for several hours, making love, making small talk, and making up for lost time. They had a lot to talk about, but there were limits. Places they couldn't go. Truth was, when your lover was a spy, you could never ask, "Where have you been all my life?" Those were the rules, and there was nothing they could do about it.

McVey kissed her on the back of the neck, then said, "A penny for your thoughts."

"I don't have any. I'm just basking in the afterglow."

"You weren't just glowing. You were on fire."

"Look who's talking. You've given new meaning to the term *room service*." She turned to face him. "I'm so glad you decided to join the agency."

"I thought it was time for a change."

"Have you given notice?"

"No, not yet. I want to wrap things up with Kemmler." He glanced at his watch, surprised to see how late it was. "Are you hungry?"

"For what?"

"Food."

"I'm starving."

"Me too."

"Why don't you order dinner while I take a quick shower?"

"What would you like?"

"Surprise me."

The food arrived thirty minutes later, and as she'd requested, McVey had surprised her. He'd ordered a veritable feast from Das Ethiopian, a popular Ethiopian restaurant on 28th Street. He'd also set the table, and when she sat down, he proudly presented

the evening meal. In addition to a double order of *injera*, a spongy
textured flatbread, he'd ordered two main courses, chicken *doro
wat* and steak tartare. The side dishes were assorted vegetables, red
lentils, yellow split peas, and *tikil gomen*, a mixture of cabbage,
potatoes, and carrots.

In keeping with male tradition, he'd ordered enough food to
feed Coxey's Army.

Molly smiled for the requisite few seconds, then her expression
turned dour. "What do we have here?"

"Ethiopian cuisine."

"Is this our dinner?"

"First time?"

"How can you tell?"

"You look confused."

"Where's the silverware?"

"No forks or knives. No spoons, either. You tear off a piece of
bread and scoop up what you want."

"Charming."

"Only use your right hand."

"Excuse me?"

"Using the left hand is frowned upon. Improper etiquette."

"You'll do well overseas."

"Is that where I'm heading?"

"Time will tell."

Between bites, McVey told her that he had Ethiopian food
once a week. She was surprised to learn that he had once lived
in Little Ethiopia, an ethnic enclave between 9th and U Street, in

the Northwest section of the city. She was even more surprised to learn that somewhere between 200,000 and 300,000 Ethiopian immigrants resided in the D.C. Metropolitan Area. "Washington has the largest Ethiopian community outside of Africa."

"Have you been to Africa?"

"Once or twice."

"Would you like to go back?"

"Are you offering me a post?"

"No, but if you're interested in that part of the world, I could mention it to someone."

"Right now I'm only interested in Kemmler."

"Which reminds me..." She walked over to the bed and retrieved a small notebook from her bag. "I spoke to our body adornment expert, and he was able to identify those facial tattoos you asked about. As you thought, the teardrop tattoo is closely associated with gang and prison culture. It indicates that a person has served time, been humiliated, or killed a fellow inmate. Our expert believes that teardrops on the left side of the eye indicate that the person has murdered someone. Each teardrop represents one murder. Teardrops on the right side of the eye often represent sadness, sorrow, or pain related to being in prison." She flipped the page, stared hard at him and spoke slowly. "You know about the dots, the *mi vida loca* nonsense. The devil horns are the ones that worry me. Those are often associated with Mara Salvatrucha."

"MS-13?"

She nodded glumly. "Your friend is lucky to be alive. Those bad boys play for keeps."

The MS-13 gang was well-known to McVey and every other law enforcement officer in the nation. Originally set up to protect Salvadoran immigrants, the gang had mutated into a violent criminal organization that was active in many parts of the United States as well as Canada, Mexico, and Central America. Members were frequently identified by their distinctive tattoos, and they were famous — or infamous — for their mindless cruelty.

The gang was also notorious for recruiting minors, who were targeted while traveling to school, church, or work. Aspirants, regardless of age, were savagely beaten for thirteen seconds as part of their initiation into the gang, a ritual known as a "beat-in."

Molly said gently, "Did you say they shot at Gold?"

"From close range. Both shots missed."

"I'm not surprised. Guns are not their forte. They prefer machetes. They seem to enjoy hacking off limbs." Straightaway, she realized that was a callous remark. "I wonder what those gang bangers were doing at the airport."

"I'm not sure. Maybe they were sent there."

"By who?"

"I don't know, but I have a feeling — a gut feeling — that they might have been sent by the guy who bought the artifacts. A Mexican businessman named Miguel de la Cruz." He pushed out a loud yawn, leaned back and closed his eyes for a second. "Does the name ring a bell?"

"No, but I'd be happy to run his name through our computer network."

"Thanks, but that won't be necessary. I contacted the Federal Ministerial Police in Mexico City and requested a background report. I should have it tomorrow morning, and then I'm off to Texas."

"Just be careful. You might be walking into a hornets' nest."

"Wouldn't be the first time. By the way, how do you know so much about MS-13?"

"I spent some time in counterterrorism, and I helped the DOJ formulate a policy on gang activity. They recently began to file terrorism charges against high-ranking members of MS-13. They've also increased gang deportations."

"Better late than never."

"I could say the same thing about us, so watch your back. I wouldn't want to lose such a promising recruit." She stared at him, frightened to find his face a mask, his eyes muted and dull. "Are you all right?"

"Yeah, I was just thinking about Adam Gold. The man has a knack for getting himself into trouble."

"No wonder you get along so well. You're like two peas in a pod."

"Not quite." He glanced down for a moment, shifting his hard gaze away from her and placing the palms of his big hands flat against the top of the table. "I carry a Sig Sauer sidearm, and I've had to shoot a few bad guys. I may have to shoot another one in Texas, and that makes all the difference."

CHAPTER THIRTY-THREE

The background report from the PFM — The Federal Ministerial Police — provided some eye-opening information about Miguel de la Cruz, the so-called businessman from Mexico. Unlike the cartels, he was not involved in the smuggling and distribution of cocaine, heroin, methamphetamine, fentanyl, or any other illegal drug. Señor de la Cruz had made a fortune managing Mexico's pervasive corruption, a significant risk for any American company operating south of the border. As the head of a vast criminal enterprise, he raked in millions of dollars in bribes, payment for construction permits and licenses. Those who objected quickly discovered that their prostestations were futile. Truth was, collusion between the police, judges, and criminals was endemic, and to make matters worse, gifts and "hospitality" were not forbidden by law.

During the three hour flight to Austin, McVey learned that the judiciary at the local level was often controlled by drug cartels and that nearly two-thirds of Mexicans believed that most or all police officers were corrupt. Unfortunately, there was plenty of evidence to support this belief, including a chilling example mentioned in the report. In September 2014, dozens of Mexican police officers were accused of kidnapping forty-three students in the town of Iguala and handing them over to a local drug gang to later be killed under the order of a high-level politician.

Iguala, a small village in the state of Guerrero, was also the birthplace of Miguel de la Cruz.

Reading the report generated by the PFM's central database took some time, but it was well worth the effort. While McVey was scribbling notes on a pad, he came across an old photograph made a startling discovery. An intrepid *Federale* had captured the entire de la Cruz clan on film, identifying each member by name on the bottom of the photo. Miguel de la Cruz, the family patriarch, was standing in the center, surrounded by his wife and children, two brothers, and his only sister, identified as "E. de la Cruz."

McVey stared at the photograph for several minutes, wondering if his eyes were playing tricks on him. Upon closer examination, he realized that he was not seeing things. He recognized one of the people in the group. His heart was beating like a drum in his chest as a slightly chubby, round-faced man came over to him and announced that they would be landing shortly. Time to put tray tables up and bring seats forward.

As they made their final approach, McVey reflected that if people actually made their own luck, he would give himself an A+ for what he was making today. Maybe the old adage was true. Maybe the best luck of all is the luck you make for yourself.

Whatever the case, he knew he'd found a four-leaf clover.

Downtown Austin was already emptying out in the daily lemming rush for the suburbs by the time McVey reached the ranger station. He suppressed a smile when he saw Gold twiddling his thumbs outside the "secure interview room." Gold was shaved, showered, and dressed in a crisp white shirt, striped red tie, blue linen blazer, and tropical-weight tan slacks.

McVey stared at him, caught off guard by his dapper appearance. "Well, you're a sight for sore eyes."

"About time you showed up."

"We had to stop for gas."

"Very funny."

McVey's voice was flat and emotionless. "I'm just curious. Are you applying for a job?"

"Never hurts to look professional."

"You look like a used car salesman."

Gold gave a snort of laughter. "You look worn out."

"Long night."

"Business or pleasure?"

"Not your concern." He glanced at his watch. "Are you ready to talk to Paz?"

"Ready, willing, and able."

"Try not to agitate him."

"Are we going to do the good cop/bad cop routine?"

"No, but we might do bad cop/worse cop. Let's see how things go."

"I'll follow your lead."

The moment Paz laid eyes on Gold, he let out a lengthy string of expletives in Spanish. McVey walked into the interview room behind Gold, coffee in hand, and took a seat at the table, turning his chair a little sideways so he could comfortably cross his legs in front of him. Paz got up and started pacing, his hands on his hips. "Jesucristo, I should have known. You keep showing up like a bad *peso*."

"Bad penny," Gold said.

"Who gives a damn. What the hell are you doing here?"

"I came to rescue you."

"*Rescue me?* First you destroy my livelihood, then you want to save me? Man, you've got big cojones." He gave McVey a withering look. "Who the hell are you?"

McVey kept his expression polite and as casual as possible. "I'm your friendly federal agent." He flashed his badge. "Have a seat, Mr. Paz."

Paz sat down, a little surprised he hadn't been handcuffed or read his rights again. He took that as a good sign. Maybe his present nightmare was about to end. "I don't know what's going on, but I know my rights. These cowboys down here have no regard for the law. I haven't been allowed to make a damn phone call. I'm not sure, but I think that's a violation of the Fourteenth Amendment."

McVey's face was an absolute blank, but only for a second. "I'll look it up and get back to you. In the meantime, if I hear you right, you're saying they got the wrong man?"

"Damn straight they got the wrong man. I'm a law-abiding citizen."

McVey tilted his head as if he found Paz's assertion amusing. "Maybe you can help us catch the right man. What do you think?"

Paz fidgeted with his hands and seemed nervous. That was not altogether surprising; most people were when they found themselves inside an interrogation room. "What do you want me to do?"

McVey turned over a few pages of the PFM report, extracted the photograph of the de la Cruz family, and pushed it across the table. "Do you recognize the man in the middle?"

Paz's eyes widened slightly, but other than that he showed no surprise. "I don't think so."

"Take a closer look."

"No, I never seen him before."

"You sure?"

"Positive."

McVey looked at Gold. "Your friend's a bad actor."

Gold nodded. "Bad liar, too."

Paz managed a weak smile in return, a smile that abruptly vanished. He felt a sudden sinking sensation, now painfully clear on why he was being questioned. His mouth went dry, and he found it hard to speak. "Can I get a can of soda?"

"In a moment," McVey said. "First I want the truth. Tell me about your meeting with Miguel de la Cruz."

"What meeting?"

McVey gave him a penetrating stare. "Stop wasting my time. You've been under surveillance since you came to Texas. We know you went to San Antonio, and we know you met with de la Cruz. We'd like to know what you ladies talked about. If you don't answer my question, we're out of here, and you can take your chances with Major Wilson."

Gold shook his head, smiling as if McVey had said something funny. "I wouldn't want to get on the bad side of that old boy."

Paz sat still for a moment, breathing hard, fighting down panic. He felt something roiling in his stomach and realized the jig was up. He gave them an aw-shucks-you-got-me smile and raised his hands in mock innocence. "I was only trying to protect my client."

McVey gave him a blank stare. "If I were you, I'd worry about protecting myself. You're on thin ice, amigo."

Gold watched Paz's eyes grow large and fearful as he processed what was said. There was now a growing look of terror in them. "Not a lot of ice in Cuba, but you get the point, don't you, Ricky?"

Paz glared at Gold for a heartbeat, then calmed. "You could cut me some slack. For old times' sake."

Gold looked at McVey, "Isn't that a line from *The Godfather?*"

"Tessio's line," McVey answered. "He was talking to Tom Hagen. *Can you get me off the hook, Tom? For old times' sake?*"

"I thought it sounded familiar."

"Tom couldn't help. Tessio was killed."

"No doubt brutally."

Paz leaned back slowly in his chair as he absorbed what they were suggesting. He looked as shocked as if he'd been slapped. His mouth turned upward briefly in a parody of a smile. "What do you want to know?"

Switching to an offhand, almost friendly tone, McVey said, "Every little detail."

Paz spent the next half hour anxiously recounting his version of the meeting with Miguel de la Cruz. McVey and Gold listened silently and kept a mental list of all the incongruities and conflicts in the story. When he got to the part about the death-stalker scorpion, their faces abruptly drained of all color. They could scarcely believe their ears, but they knew that Paz was telling the truth. Nobody could make up such a bizarre tale.

Gold stared at Paz, uncomprehending. "How do you torture someone for making a foolish mistake?"

Paz grasped at the only explanation he could come up with at the moment. "The son of a bitch is crazy. *Un lunático completo.*"

"How did you arrive at that conclusion?" McVey asked sarcastically.

"You guys need to be careful. You're dealing with a sick motherfucker."

Gold shook his head, marveling at the capacity for simple meanness in some people. He'd listened intently, and now his face clouded over with dismay. Still shaken by the scorpion story, he took a beat before he said, "What the hell is so important about those artifacts?"

Paz laughed for the first time, but it was not a pleasant sound. "You don't get it, do you? Those artifacts are the Holy Grail. De la Cruz has been waiting for those stupid weapons his whole life. They're part of his grand scheme."

McVey hesitated, reluctant to push too hard. But he had to push. "What do you mean, his grand scheme?"

Paz rose and started pacing in a small, tight circle. He gave them the details, as much as he remembered them, of Cruz's plan to display the Alamo artifacts throughout Mexico. "He's got a bug up his ass about the way his ancestors were treated."

"I can relate to that," McVey said.

"So can I," Gold said. "So what's the end game? He wants to rub shit in our face?"

"That's the general idea."

Gold gave a sad little laugh. "The poor bastard is going to be crushed when he learns they're fake."

A worried frown flickered across Paz's face. "The artifacts are fake?"

"Phony as a three-dollar bill."

"Good God, I hope you're joking."

"I'm afraid not. Kemmler sold Cruz a bill of goods. The rifle and sword are worthless."

"Jesucristo, that's bad news. Very bad."

"I wouldn't want to be in your shoes," McVey said, sipping his lukewarm coffee. "Cruz doesn't strike me as the forgiving type."

Paz sat down slowly, shaken. "I had nothing to do with the scam."

"Au contraire," Gold said. "You delivered the fake artifacts."

"And picked up the payment," McVey added.

Paz opened his mouth as if he were about to explain, then shut it. Tight. Finally, he said, "I didn't know they were fake."

Gold sighed and gave him a sympathetic look. "I know that, and you know that, but who knows what Cruz will think? As you said before, the man's a lunatic."

"Oh God, what am I going to do?"

McVey played dumb. "If I were you, I'd get my affairs in order."

"My affairs?"

"Just in case."

"Just in case *what?*"

"Do I have to spell it out?"

Gold made a slashing gesture across his throat. "Time to pay the piper."

Paz began to bite his nails, an old childhood habit absently resurrected as he pondered his fate. He was understandably agitated and confused, but he managed to keep his wits about him. In fact, he was able to suggest a deal. "Why don't you guys straighten things out with Cruz, and I'll give you Kemmler."

McVey stirred his coffee absently. "What do you mean, give us Kemmler?"

"I'm supposed to meet him in two days. I'll give you the time and place. You let me go back to Florida."

"What about the money?" Gold asked. "Who gets the two million?"

"We could split it. Right down the middle. Fifty-fifty."

McVey chuckled.

Gold patted Paz consolingly on the shoulder. "You get your standard commission. Not a penny more."

Paz theatrically used his finger to clean out his ear. "I'm sorry, Gold, I thought I heard you say my standard commission, not a penny more."

"You heard right."

"After all I've been through?"

"After all you put *us* through."

"That doesn't seem fair."

"Fair or not, it's our final offer. Take it or leave it."

There was a full thirty seconds of silence — an embarrassed silence, as if Paz had been caught with his hand in the cookie jar and had one chance to make amends. In his darker moments, much more frequent of late, he sometimes found himself wondering what he'd done to deserve such lousy luck. Life wasn't fair. Not fair at all.

CHAPTER THIRTY-FOUR

Early the next morning, Gold and McVey drove to San Antonio to meet Miguel de la Cruz. The Mexican businessman had agreed to meet them at the Riverwalk, a popular tourist attraction that ran through the heart of the city. Under normal circumstances, de la Cruz would not have granted a meeting, but he was willing to make an exception when he heard that it was a matter of life and death. Maybe his life and death.

The hastily arranged meeting took place on one of the open-air barges that drifted down the river at a leisurely pace, allowing a pleasant view of the botanic gardens that flanked the walkway. The gardens contained philodendron, banana plants, and palms. Over the years, the Department of Parks and Recreation had added seventeen thousand assorted trees, shrubs, and vines, so there was now a distinct jungle-like atmosphere.

Shortly after nine o'clock, a barge pulled up to the Little Rhein Steakhouse and Gold and McVey climbed aboard. Miguel de la Cruz was sitting at the bow, and across from him stood Carlos Mendoza, head of security. A heavyset man with a florid, fleshy face was driving the barge. He wore solid black — shirt, slacks, coat, and tie.

Mendoza made his way to the stern and indicated that he needed to frisk them, which they allowed him to do. Mendoza's emotionless expression didn't waver, although Gold detected a slight tension in his voice. *"Estan limpios,"* he said to de la Cruz. *"Sin armas."*

Out of the corner of his eye, Gold studied Mendoza. He was a big man; he outweighed Gold two to one. His broad and brawny chest was so large it fairly rippled out of his black guayabera shirt.

Mendoza nudged them forward, and they sat directly across from de la Cruz. McVey drew in a tiny breath, giving himself a moment to think. "I like your office," he said at last.

De la Cruz regarded him for a moment, then managed a brief smile. "First visit?"

"First river trip."

"I think you'll find it interesting." He gestured to the driver, and as they got underway, he lit a cigarette. "I'm not much of a tour guide, but I'm proud of our beautiful city — and our Mexican heritage."

"So I've heard."

"Sí, you mentioned that we had a mutual friend."

"Two mutual friends."

De la Cruz conjured another smile, just as faint as before, and this time there was a hard, flat shine to his eyes. "How is Mr. Paz?"

"As well as could be expected. He recently suffered a financial setback."

"You don't say."

"Nevertheless, he sent his regards."

"I'm pleased to hear that. I thought I'd made a bad impression." He smoked his cigarette and thought about it. "I have a tendency to dwell upon the past. Sometimes I can be too verbose."

Gold forced a smile. He didn't feel remotely friendly, but it was part of the act. "Good wine needs no bush."

"I beg your pardon?"

"William Shakespeare." De la Cruz's glare caught him off guard, and he realized he'd hit a nerve. "Of course, there's nothing wrong with being proud of your heritage."

"I've always been proud of mine, Mr. Gold."

"You should be."

De la Cruz smiled again, revealing teeth as neat and compressed as the rest of him. He was groomed as always, every hair in place, suit immaculate, no sign of feeling the heat. As they drifted past Crockett Street, he waved his arm in a circular motion. "Look around, gentlemen. All this land once belonged to my ancestors. The land on both sides of the river, as far as the eye can see. Over the years, we lost it all, most of it stolen by Anglo-American settlers. *Que sera sera.* One day the shoe will be on the other foot."

"Not today," McVey said. "I'm afraid I've got some bad news."

"Your life and death situation?"

"I understand you've recently purchased a rifle and a sword, Alamo artifacts that once belonged to Davy Crockett and Colonel Travis."

De la Cruz gave him a long, hard look. "What if I did?"

"I'm afraid you made a bad investment."

"I beg to differ. I have big plans for those artifacts."

"Yeah, I know. You want to put them on display and gloat about the Alamo."

"Do you blame me?"

"I'm not in the blame game, but I can tell you one thing. If you flaunt those weapons, you'll look like a fool, and your enemies might take that as a sign of weakness."

De la Cruz took a deep breath and decided to hold his tongue. He struggled with his temper. "Whatever do you mean?"

"The artifacts are fake," Gold said. "Joseph Kemmler's a con artist, and he sold you a bill of goods." He gave de la Cruz a business card. "We provided transit coverage, so we wanted to know if they were genuine. Our experts agreed that they were fake. Solid reproductions, but hardly worth two million dollars."

Gold watched Cruz's face, already hard, turn to stone. The eyes narrowed, the lips went tight, the jaw muscle by his ear quivered. His hand went to his side and he pushed in as though trying to ease some pain. Then, for a long, frozen moment, he ceased to move entirely. Finally, he asked, "You're sure?"

Gold looked him straight in the eye and said, "Positive."

De la Cruz, eyes narrowed to slits, nodded slowly. "How disappointing."

"I can imagine.

"No, I don't think you can."

"The man's a crook, plain and simple. You weren't his first victim."

"No, but I intend to be his last. You know, it's funny, but I never trusted him. Not for a moment. I actually sent one of my best people to keep an eye on him. Oh well, live and learn."

McVey resumed speaking, his voice low but clear. "Just for the record, Paz had nothing to do with this scam. Kemmler took advantage of him, too."

"I understand. He was only the middleman." He accepted another cigarette from Mendoza and took a moment lighting it. "I'm willing to overlook his involvement, but I want my money back. I hope that won't be a problem."

"Ay, there's the rub," Gold said. "The money's gone."

"Gone?"

"Every penny."

"I do hope you're joking."

"Easy come, easy go."

Cruz eyed them closely for several seconds without saying anything. He could feel the anger surging through his body. To his credit, he managed to stay calm. "Do I detect police corruption?"

"Think of it as a charitable contribution," Gold said. "The support of a worthy cause."

"The cause being two crooked gringos?"

"It's only money," McVey said. "You can't take it with you."

"Ah, but you intend on taking it, right?"

"To the victor go the spoils."

Mendoza weighed the words he'd just heard, clearly unhappy. He had carried with him a leather briefcase and now he opened it on his lap and withdrew a small automatic pistol. A silencer squirreled to the barrel. He looked at de la Cruz with a questioning expression on his face. *"Deboría dispararles?"*

De la Cruz shook his head. "No, don't shoot them. I'm sure we're being watched. I can almost feel the crosshairs on my chest."

Mendoza gave a small, defeated laugh. *"Otro día."*

"Put the gun away, Carlos."

Gold heard Mendoza mutter an obscenity under his breath, and he suspected it was directed at them. "Well, that was exciting."

De la Cruz looked at Gold, all trace of amusement lost from his face. "Your first Mexican standoff?"

"I've led a sheltered life."

De la Cruz made a skeptical face. "We have another first. Law-abiding citizens holding up a bandito. What is this world coming to?"

"I'm not sure, but my partner wants to tell you where your money is going."

McVey looked at de la Cruz, who was doing an admirable job of concealing his displeasure over what had just transpired, then gazed out across Alamo Plaza. He made a show of deliberation. "Do you remember the mass kidnapping in Iguala?"

"Of course I remember. I was born in the village of Iguala."

"Forty-three students were kidnapped from the Ayotzinapa Rural Teachers' College. They were taken into custody by local police and handed over to Guerreros Unidos — the "United Warriors" drug cartel — and killed. Not the type of incident a village would ever forget."

"A horrible tragedy," de la Cruz said. "But I must point out that there was evidence that the 27th Infantry Battalion of the Mexican Army was behind the kidnapping and murder."

"Either way, the village has suffered greatly. Wouldn't you agree?"

"Without question."

"We thought it would be a good idea to donate two million dollars to the families of the victims. Naturally, we made the donation in your name."

Cruz lapsed into a brooding silence. He could see that McVey was serious. He had been bracing himself for something like this since the American had called him. Surprisingly, he was rather complacent. He even managed to smile, a cautious effort that did not quite extend to his eyes. "That's a lovely gesture, amigo. *Muy generoso*. I might have to revise my opinion about Norteamericanos."

"No hard feelings?"

"Well, I wouldn't go that far. Two million dollars is a lot of money to lose. Somebody should be held accountable."

"I agree," McVey said. "Somebody needs to learn a lesson."

"Do you have any suggestions?"

Gold blurted out, "I know the perfect guy."

"Do you know where to find him?"

"Believe it or not, he's on his way to hell."

CHAPTER THIRTY-FIVE

The good news, Gold thought driving east on I-10, was they'd met with Miguel de la Cruz and walked away unscathed. The fact that they were still in one piece was something to celebrate. Truth be told, they'd taken a big risk, and when Mendoza pulled out a pistol, things might have gone south. An uneasy feeling crept over Gold the more he thought about how close they'd come to being shot. He wondered if his partner in crime felt the same way.

Gold glanced at McVey, who was fiddling with his service pistol, then said, "Why didn't you bring your gun yesterday?"

"I didn't want to," McVey said.

"Why?"

McVey held the weapon in his right hand and looked down the sight to the floor. He then held it up and studied it again. It was a SIG Sauer P226, the official sidearm of the Navy SEALs. "I knew they'd search us, and when they came up empty-handed, they'd think we were under surveillance."

"Bit of a gamble, don't you think?"

"Life is a gamble."

Gold snorted. "No wonder you don't play poker."

McVey's face went blank for an instant before a cracked smile flittered back. "Speaking of yesterday, what's with you and the Shakespeare quotes?"

"I didn't want de la Cruz to think we were uneducated boobs."

"You were starting to sound like Victor Wong."

Gold waved the thought away. "Did you ever take care of his problem?"

"Yeah, I spoke to someone. I think the harassment will stop."

"Thanks for your help."

"Any time."

"By the way, I've been meaning to ask you something. Why was de la Cruz willing to let Paz off the hook?"

"You heard him. He realized that Paz was just a go-between."

"Yeah, but he also witnessed a murder."

"Not quite. The kid with the facial tattoo was still alive when Paz left the chapel. Paz told us he heard a shot, but he didn't see who pulled the trigger. Lucky for him, he'd be of little or no use as a witness."

Gold frowned slightly. "Sometimes dumb luck is the best luck."

McVey agreed, but his mind was on someone who was shit out of luck: Joseph Kemmler. Thanks to Paz, they knew exactly where and when the rendezvous was supposed to take place, so all they had to do now was block the final scene and remember their lines. They both knew this day would come, but now that it was finally here, they wondered how it would actually end. Had they devised an intelligent plan? Had they overlooked any details? Were the supporting players ready to play their parts?

It was now a little after three o'clock, and in less than an hour, Kemmler would be driving through League City, looking for a ramshackle building near one of the deserted oil fields. The building would have a single tenant: Rosario's Motel y Cantina, the type of place that Norman Bates would've loved. Kemmler would probably be in a foul mood, having spent the last three days in the cramped cab of a refrigerated truck. The road trip had begun in New York City and had taken him and his teamster driver through or around the cities of Harrisburg, Knoxville, Chattanooga, Birmingham, New Orleans, Baton Rouge, and Houston. The distance between New York City and Houston was slightly over 1,600 miles, mostly on the interstate, which could be a death-defying experience in and of itself.

When the white freightliner pulled into Rosario's parking lot, Kemmler jumped out of the cab and began to stretch his aching legs. Three days on the road was more than enough for him, and he was anxious to pick up his money from Paz and dump the body in the back of the truck. As planned, he went into the cantina while the driver remained outside. The road-weary teamster was eyeballing his tires when he felt the muzzle of a gun being jammed into his neck.

"Don't turn around," McVey said. "Leave the keys on the front seat and start walking."

"Walking where?" the teamster asked.

"Away from here."

"You're robbing the wrong guy, pal."

"Start walking."

"You gotta be joking."

"You want to die laughing?"

"I gotta bum knee."

"Hit the road, Jack." He cocked the hammer near the teamster's ear. "And don't you come back."

The moment Kemmler entered the cantina, he knew that something was very wrong. There was only one customer, sitting in a booth with his back to the door, and not a single server in sight. The lighting was bad, but he could see that the kitchen was dark and deserted. He paused to light a cigarette, then shook the match out and looked around the room through the haze of drifting white smoke. What the hell was going on? He instinctively looked over his shoulder in the general direction of the parking lot, but all was well out there. He muttered something, took a few tentative steps toward the booth, then stopped dead in his tracks. "Sorry I'm late, Paz. Rush hour traffic."

The man in the booth grunted, but did not turn around.

Kemmler came closer. "Must be siesta time."

Gold turned around and gave the murdering bastard his very best, ultra-friendly smile. "Right you are. Two to five P.M. Depending on the locale."

Kemmler looked at him wide-eyed, utterly shocked. He was silent for a few moments, trying to get his anger under control. "What the hell are you doing here?"

"I heard the enchiladas were great."

Kemmler eyed him warily. "Where's Paz?"

"On his way back to Florida. By the way, he asked me to give you something." He pointed to a suitcase lying on the counter. "That's a nice, roomy bag you have there. Lots of storage space."

"I suppose you looked inside."

"Nah, I had no reason to look. I could tell it was empty. Light as a feather."

"In other words, you stole my money."

"*Your* money?"

"Payment for the artifacts I shipped."

"Which were fake."

"Says who?"

Gold shook his head and rubbed a butter knife on his sleeve to remove some water spots. "I don't have time to play games, but I'm curious about one thing. Why in the world did you decide to swindle Miguel de la Cruz? The man's a notorious criminal."

"A criminal with a score to settle and lots of money. I'd heard about his wounded pride and figured two million dollars would be chump change to him."

"Jesus, Bazooka Joe, you're dumber than I thought."

Kemmler glared at him. "I don't like that name."

"I think it has a nice ring."

"So what now, genius? Are you going to charge me with insurance fraud? I doubt de la Cruz would be willing to testify against me in a court of law. Not his cup of tea. Too much publicity."

"Yeah, you're probably right."

"Of course I'm right. I'm always two steps ahead."

"It's not easy dealing with a criminal mastermind."

Kemmler sat down, calmly unwrapped a piece of bubble gum, and began to chew in a loud, annoying way. He was grinning from ear to ear. His voice was smooth, casual, and had a faint German accent. In comparison, his words were shockingly ugly and cold. "I don't understand Jewish people. You keep underestimating the Aryan race. Haven't you learned anything about us by now?"

"I've learned something."

"What's that, *mein freund?*"

"I learned that the Aryan race never existed. It's just a figment of your imagination, an obsolete theory that's been widely rejected and disproved."

"Spoken like a true Semite."

Gold was tempted to reach across the table and punch Kemmler in the face, but he'd promised to behave himself. He knew that Kemmler would become vicious when cornered, and he was determined not to take the bait. But it wasn't easy. His response was unnaturally calm. "We all have our peculiarities, don't we, Joseph?"

"If you say so."

"Well, take a look at yourself. You're a grown man who chews bubble gum like a six-year-old. What is that, some sort of oral gratification?"

"Just an old habit. Part of my uniqueness."

Gold raised his hand for silence. Quietly, he said, "Let me tell you something about your old habit. Something you might want to chew on. Bazooka Bubble Gum was the brainchild of Morris

Chigorinsky, a Russian Jew who emigrated to the United States in 1891. Morris and his four sons started Topps, the company that became famous by including small comic strips featuring Bazooka Joe, a swashbuckling kid who donned a black eyepatch. During the 60s, the gum was actually made in Tel Aviv, Israel. So you see, Kemmler, you've been a supporter of the Jewish state your whole life. All I can say is mazel tov."

Kemmler's jaw went slack. He leaned forward, then eased back. He opened his mouth to speak but found he had no words. Finally he shook his head and said, "Son of a bitch. There's hope for me after all."

Gold stood up and stretched his arms. "I wouldn't count on it."

"You leaving?"

"Just making room. Time for act two."

Sensing movement behind him, Kemmler turned. McVey walked past Gold and sat down in the booth. There was a dead silence. Kemmler shot McVey a look of disdain. "Who the hell are you?"

"My name's McVey. I'm the one with a badge."

"Uh-oh, did I forget to return a library book?"

"Do you know how to read?"

"I can read English, German, French, and a bit of Italian. What about you?"

"Only English."

"Figures."

"Too bad you stopped at four languages. If you knew how to read Spanish you would've understood the sign in the parking lot. The one warning customers to hide their possessions and lock their vehicles." He held up the keys to the Freightliner truck. "You left your keys on the front seat. Not very smart."

Kemmler grinned; then a sudden fear wiped the grin from his face; then it, too, was gone and he managed a nervous, almost embarrassed little chuckle. "Silly me. What was I thinking?"

"God only knows. You forgot to lock your vehicle, and you failed to adequately hide a valuable possession."

"What possession would that be?"

McVey leaned across the table and placed his mouth close to Kemmler's ear. "The late Marvin Katz."

Gold forced himself to smile, but it wasn't easy. "The man you have on ice."

Kemmler sat silently a few seconds, and Gold thought he looked pale and frightened. He cleared his throat several times, then looked directly at McVey. "Thank God you arrived when you did."

"Excuse me?"

"I had nothing to do with the death of Marvin Katz. He was murdered by the Mafia on the orders of Joe DeCarlo, a vicious mob boss. DeCarlo wanted a painting I had recently sold to Katz, and when Katz wouldn't turn it over, he was executed. The bastards killed my lawyer — and close personal friend — then hired some teamster thug to dispose of the body."

McVey paused, temporarily stunned. Then his face lit up in a smile, and he shook his head in wonderment. "So that's your story and you're sticking to it, huh?"

"Bingo."

Gold stepped forward. "Why did you come along for the ride? To see the countryside?"

"They forced me to go. They said my store would be torched if I refused." A twinge of regret seeped into his voice. "Do you know what I think? I think they wanted me to become an accomplice so I wouldn't be able to testify against them. God, those bastards think of everything."

"Nobody thinks of everything," McVey said. "It's always the small details that trip people up."

"Not in my case," Kemmler said. "As I told your lame associate, I'm always two steps ahead. In your case, maybe three steps."

McVey heard the sound of tires on the parking lot gravel and turned to see a black limousine coming toward the cantina. The vehicle had a Mexican license plate, and there were several passengers inside. When the vehicle stopped, the driver beeped the horn twice but kept the motor running. "Well, right on time."

Kemmler turned sideways and looked at Gold questioningly. "More fun and games?"

"Act three," Gold said. "When the curtain comes down."

Out of the corner of his eye, McVey saw a change in the expression on Kemmler's face. It was small and subtle. But he was almost certain it was there. "We've been outsmarted, Gold. Time to head home."

Kemmler let out a nasty laugh. "Better luck next time."

"If there is a next time."

"You can count on it."

Now it was McVey who felt like punching Kemmler in the face. Instead, he winked at Gold — a signal that he'd stick to the plan. "Before we go, we'd like to exchange gifts. We'll take the truck and return Katz's body to his family. You can have a photograph of the woman you burned to death in the dumpster." He placed the photograph of the de la Cruz family on the table. "Take a look at the young woman standing next to Miguel de la Cruz. She's identified as E. de la Cruz, but that was her maiden name. Her first name is Elena, and she married a man named Carlos Mendoza."

Once Kemmler's eyes had retracted back into his head, he murmured, "Elena Mendoza."

"Your former assistant."

"Oh my God."

McVey shook his head and made a sympathetic face. "Elena's brother and husband just pulled up, so I think we'll take our leave. I'm sure you'll think of something to say. You're always two steps ahead."

Kemmler tried to swallow, but his throat was too dry. "Wait a minute. We could be in big trouble."

Gold sputtered with laughter, stepped forward, and whispered into Kemmler's ear. "What do you mean *we*, Ke-mo sah-bee? You're on your own."

"You can't leave me here. Those Mexicans will kill me."

"Damn, you're insightful."

There was no hint of levity in McVey's voice when he leaned in and said to Kemmler, "We'd like to stay for the grand finale, but it's going to be a long and painful death scene, and we're pressed for time."

Gold looked uncomfortable. The skin around his eyes creased and he looked at McVey and then out of the window toward the parking lot. "We should go."

"I'm two steps behind."

Gold smiled wistfully. "Where have I heard that before?"

THE END.

ABOUT THE AUTHOR

Stephen G. Yanoff is a twenty-year veteran of the insurance industry and an acknowledged expert in the field of high risk insurance placement. He holds a bachelor's, master's, and doctoral degree from the Texas A&M University System.

In addition to DEAD ENDING, he is the author of six other award-winning mystery novels, including THE GRACELAND GANG, THE PIRATE PATH, DEVIL'S COVE, RANSOM ON THE RHONE, A RUN FOR THE MONEY, and CAPONE ISLAND.

Dr. Yanoff has also written several highly acclaimed history books, including THE SECOND MOURNING, TURBULENT TIMES, GONE BEFORE GLORY, and WONDER OF THE WEST. The author's non-fiction books have won numerous gold medals and over thirty national and international literary awards.

A native of Long Island, New York, he currently lives in Austin, Texas, with his wife, two daughters, and an ever-growing family.

For more information about the author or his books, readers can go to: www.stephengyanoff.com